**Praise for the Peggy Le**

**Pretty Poison:**

"A Fantastic amateur sleuth." ~ The Best Reviews
"Smartly penned and charming garden mystery." ~
Romantic Times

**Fruit of the Poisoned Tree:**
"I can't recommend this book highly enough."~ Midwest
Book Reviews
"I love the world of Peggy Lee!" ~ Fresh Fiction

**Poisoned Petals:**
"Joyce and Jim are a fabulous team who create poignant,
entertaining mysteries." ~ The Best Reviews
"An enjoyable and cozy read." The Muse Book Reviews

**Perfect Poison:**
"A fabulous whodunit!" ~ Fresh Fiction
"You will enjoy this to no end! Highly recommended!" ~
Mystery Scene Magazine

**A Corpse for Yew:**

"Awesome story with good and rational twists! Love that it
tells about places I know! And there is some great plant
info at the same time!" ~ Snows Acre
"Joyce and Jim Lavene prove once again they are an
excellent writing team as they provide a quality regional
whodunit." ~ Harriet Klausner
**A Thyme to Die:**

"Totally enjoy this character and the series. Not only are
these good stories, but I learn something about plants and
both their care and uses." ~ Gillian F. Brunner
"There are plenty of twists and turns to keep you guessing.
" ~ Cheryl Green

*Peggy Lee Garden Mysteries*

Pretty Poison
Fruit of the Poisoned Tree
Poisoned Petals
Perfect Poison
A Corpse For Yew
Buried by Buttercups—Novella
A Thyme to Die

*Renaissance Faire Mysteries*

Wicked Weaves
Ghastly Glass
Deadly Daggers
Harrowing Hats
Treacherous Toy
Perilous Pranks—Novella
Murderous Matrimony

*Missing Pieces Mysteries*

A Timely Vision
A Touch of Gold
A Spirited Gift
A Haunting Dream
A Finder's Fee

Taxi for the Dead Paranormal Mysteries

Broken Heart Ghoul
Undead by Morning – Short Story – Ebook only

# A Thyme to Die

## By

## Joyce and Jim Lavene

# Part I

# Buried by Buttercups

*Angel's Trumpet- **Brugmansia** - Angel's Trumpet is related to Datura or Jimson weed. It is an evergreen shrub that can be trained as a small tree. Produces large, drooping, trumpet-shaped flowers in white or pink shades. Wonderful fragrance. All parts of this plant are hallucinogenic and poisonous. Do not plant around children or pets. The basis for the drug Scopolamine.*

# Chapter One

"Excuse me, ma'am."

Peggy Lee realized a 30-something man was trying to get her attention. He looked a little scruffy—needed a shave and a change of clothes. When he flashed his badge, she knew he must be a police detective or undercover officer.

He was standing right beside her, but she'd been so interested in the investigation going on in the park that she hadn't noticed him until he spoke.

She glanced around herself. Had she strayed out of the boundaries set for the crowd? No. She was right where she should have been, even a little further back than those around her.

"Yes?"

"I'm Detective Tanner Edwards. Lieutenant McDonald would like to speak to you."

She sighed. *Now what?* She couldn't even show up at crime scenes without people getting their noses out of joint? The crime scene was right across the street from her house, for goodness sake. There were dozens of people watching what was going on.

Peggy followed the detective out of the crowd. She could feel questioning gazes burn her back as people around her wondered why she was being escorted toward the cordoned-off space.

She ducked under the tape. The fine fall weather had turned chilly during the night. A low fog had set in across the open ground. The branches of hundred-year-old pin oaks looked ghostly in it with their scarce, dangling leaves.

The majority of the leaves had turned yellow and spun to the damp ground, sliding under her feet. The dogwoods' leaves were red and green and had showy red berries that made a splash in the dim morning.

There was still grass underfoot that was lush and green thanks to the hard work and chemicals used by the Mecklenburg County Parks and Rec Department. There wouldn't be any worms living in that treated soil—a crime in itself. Most people didn't seem to care.

"Peggy!" Lieutenant Al McDonald greeted her with a cheerful smile. "Would you like some coffee? I'm sure there's an extra cup around here somewhere."

She raised one cinnamon-colored brow in his direction. "It hasn't been that long since we've seen each other, Al. You know I don't drink coffee. Thanks for offering."

Al McDonald had been her first husband's partner on

the Charlotte Police force for twenty years. The men had spent hours together, shared each other's lives. When Peggy's husband, John, had been killed in a domestic dispute, it was Al who'd brought her the bad news.

"That's right. Sorry." Al scratched the top of his head. His coarse, black, curly hair was graying now. His broad, dark face was aging but very dear to her. "I guess I was thrown off by this murder."

"Murder?" She tried to peek around the side of his much larger form. There was a body covered on the damp ground that she hadn't been able to see from her previous vantage point. "What happened?"

"I was hoping you could tell me. You live right across the road. Did you see anything unusual?"

Peggy knew Al had been recently promoted to lieutenant in the homicide division. She was sure he felt plenty of eyes on him too. Not only from the people who surrounded them, but his superiors as well.

"The only thing I saw was the police cars pulling up earlier this morning. When do you think it happened?"

"The ME says around midnight. You weren't out walking your dog that late, were you?"

Her green eyes narrowed. Of course he knew she wasn't out walking Shakespeare at midnight. The Meyer's Park area, with its hundred year old homes, was a quiet neighborhood. Not many people were out that late at night.

"What is it you really want from me?" she asked, a little sharply. "We both know I've been on the outs with the police department. Are you asking for my help?"

He laughed, sounding a little nervous. His dark brown

eyes shifted away from her. "You were on the outs with Lieutenant Rimer, not me. He didn't like your methods. I've known you most of my life. I could use your expertise on this one."

She smiled at him and squeezed his arm. "Why didn't you say so? I take it you think the murder involves botanical poison."

Al took her elbow and led her toward the victim on the ground. "This is for your ears only, Peggy. I think we might have a serial killer in Charlotte. And he picked my division to kill people. How lucky can one new lieutenant get?"

"How does Mary feel about your promotion?" Peggy stared at the form covered by a tarp. "Last time I talked to her, she wanted you to retire."

He shrugged his large shoulders. He'd once played football in college and still maintained that bulk that had made him a formidable fullback. "You know how it is. Mary wants me to retire. If I keep working for a few more years, I can retire with a better pension. She likes that idea. She always wanted to retire at the beach."

"That's what I thought."

Peggy knew she couldn't delay the inevitable any longer. They were standing by the victim. Drops of mist were falling on them from the pin oak branches. Peggy shivered, telling herself it was because of the chilly morning, not the fact that she was about to view a dead body.

"Are you okay with this?" Al knew better, but asked anyway.

"I'm fine."

Al had one of his officers flip back the gray tarp. There was a man in a suit and tie beneath it. His face was ghastly white and his eyes were closed. There didn't appear to be any bruises or signs of violence on his person, at least from the waist up.

Peggy's sharp eyes saw at once why Al had called her over. Tucked into the pocket of his suit coat was a bunch of buttercups. The bright yellow color made the red of the man's tie stand out even more against his white shirt.

"Buttercups," she said. "Not your usual boutonnière—and out of season. Do you think those have something to do with the murder?"

"You don't recognize him by any chance, do you? Maybe someone from the neighborhood?" His voice whispered like the leaves falling from the trees around them, as he drew her away from the body.

"No. I'm sorry." She tried to put the dead face from her mind.

When they were well away from the crowd, Al finally got down to business.

"I haven't specifically told anyone about my serial-killer theory yet. I think this is victim number two. The first victim was found in similar circumstances with some white flower pinned to his chest. The ME called it Jimson weed."

Peggy didn't like the sound of that. "Angel's trumpet. Deadly poison."

"That's what she said."

"Is it alphabetical?"

"I don't know yet." Al glanced around at the crowd. "I

hope this is it. I don't need something like this as my first case."

"No, I suppose you don't." She smiled at the frown on his dark face. "How did I miss a person killed by angel's trumpet in the paper?"

"We didn't release that information." He shrugged. "I was hoping it would help identify the killer later."

"But now you have what appears to be a second victim killed by poison."

"We can't tell for sure about this one yet. The ME says the poison appeared to be administered the same way."

"Was it ingested? Burned mouth and tongue?" she asked.

He looked surprised. "No. Should that have been there too?"

"Only if your victim ate the buttercups."

"The angel's trumpet poison was injected into the first victim. This man had a needle mark in the same place, right side, just below the ear."

Her brows knit together. "No wonder you think the same person is responsible. I suppose you haven't released *that* information yet either."

"No." He shook his head. "I'm trying to keep this as quiet as I can. I'd appreciate it if you don't say anything to anyone, especially the press."

"You know I won't," she promised. "What can I do to help?"

"You could assist on this case. You're trained to be a

forensic botanist. I could get you on the payroll, at least for the investigation. I really need your help here, Peggy. No one knows poisonous plants like you do."

"There are some." She grinned. "But they don't live around here. I'd be glad to help. I could use the paycheck to keep The Potting Shed up and running."

"Tough times," he agreed. "Thanks for helping me out. This is my first homicide case, as the lead officer, anyway. I need a big win to impress everyone if I'm going to retire on a lieutenant's pension. I've got nothing right now."

"All right." She put aside the fact that she'd been booted out of her forensic consultant's position by his predecessor. This was different anyway. This was for Al. "I'll come by the station later."

Al hugged her then looked around with a sheepish expression. Obviously he was worried how that would play with his superiors too.

Peggy made her way back through the crowd. She saw several familiar faces, her neighbors for the past thirty years. One of them was new. She tried to hurry past him. It didn't work.

"Mrs. Lee."

Mr. Bellows—she didn't know his first name—he'd introduced himself to her that way. He'd moved in next door to her last year. She'd only thought Clarice Weldon and her apricot-colored poodle, Poopsie, were annoying.

Mr. Bellows complained about everything. He was creepy to boot with his sallow face and cold blue eyes. He was always stepping out in front of her, seemingly from nowhere.

"Mr. Bellows." What else could she do but acknowledge him?

"I could hear your dog barking last night."

"I'm sorry. He was a little nervous. Steve isn't home and he—"

He raised one gloved hand. "I don't care. These concerns are your own. Keep him quiet."

"I do the best I can." She didn't go on to say that she felt safer with Shakespeare barking when he'd heard something unusual, especially when she was in the big house alone. Mr. Bellows had made it clear that it didn't matter to him.

"Have you thought about selling your home and moving into the country with your menagerie?"

Peggy's temper flared. "I don't think my one dog counts as a menagerie, Mr. Bellows. I'm sorry he bothered you. Maybe you should sleep with earplugs!"

She stormed off, not caring what he thought of her. He was always complaining about how the gardenia bushes grew between their houses and that her crape myrtles blew purple flower petals into his yard. It was exasperating!

It was still early enough that Queen's Road wasn't crowded with traffic headed for uptown Charlotte yet. She crossed the street to her house. She could hear Shakespeare barking loudly from outside. Bellows certainly wasn't going to like that.

Shakespeare was her one-hundred and forty-pound Great Dane. She'd rescued him from a man who'd been abusing him.

The dog was always excited to see her and worried when she was gone. She'd had him for a couple of years and they got along very well together—especially since he was her first pet.

She opened the side door to the kitchen. She hadn't closed it and set the alarm as she should have. She'd only been gone for a short time and was close by. Her son, Paul, also a police officer, would have thrown a fit. Doors were made to be locked and alarms to be set. Peggy loved him dearly but he could be a little paranoid at times.

Shakespeare greeted her by running toward her then pulling up short so that he slid across the hardwood floor in the large kitchen. She rubbed his head and gave him some breakfast as she put on the kettle for tea.

Peggy had lived in the big, turn-of-the-century house since John Lee had brought her here from Charleston South Carolina as a young bride. He'd frequently complained about the quirks and problems with living in the rambling house which had belonged to several generations of his family.

John had inherited the house, but Paul would not. At some point, John's nephew would inherit. Until then, Peggy was staying put.

Upkeep was ridiculous and sometimes improbable. It was difficult to replace items with duplicates when they were so old.

She didn't care. Peggy loved the old house as if it were a part of her family's history. She loved the feel of the cool marble stairs on her feet in the summer. She loved all the nooks and crannies. She kept a thirty-foot blue spruce growing in the entrance hall. Each room in the house had a fireplace. The ceilings were still the original plaster.

The basement was her passion. Here she dabbled and played with Mother Nature. In her botanical lab, she cross-pollinated and modified, looking for new varieties of plant life for pleasure as well as medicinal and other purposes.

The basement sprawled the length and width of the entire house but it still wasn't enough room for her 'experiments'. French doors opened into an acre garden that she cultivated by the season. Here she once produced a coveted black rose.

Under a two-hundred-year-old oak with branches thicker than her body, she grew purple mushrooms. She'd produced a small green melon that tasted exactly like a peach one summer. She'd also created a water lily that glowed in the dark.

Someday she'd be forced to move a lifetime's worth of work and memories somewhere else. Not today.

Today, it looked as though she was going to help Al find a killer. First tea and an English muffin. She needed to take a shower and get dressed. She'd have to call her partner at The Potting Shed, Sam Ollson, and let him know what was going on. She'd need him to open the shop.

She glanced at the laptop on the old wood kitchen table. There was a green light flashing. That meant Steve had called. With a little thrill, despite their old married status of one year, she went to answer it.

Paul and Steve had taught her how to use Skype for when one of them were out of town. Steve was at a veterinary conference in Tampa for a few days. He attended dozens of conferences and workshops during the year.

It was always good to hear his voice and see his face, even if sometimes he looked a little like a cartoon. That was only when they had a bad connection.

"I didn't know if you were going to answer," he said after she'd logged in.

"I was a little busy."

"Code words for getting caught up in your tomatoes or some other experiment in the basement." He smiled at her. "I'm at least as important as a purple tomato."

"At least. How's the conference?"

"Boring. I've learned a few things about treating terriers and a new billing system that I'll probably never use. How's Shakespeare doing?"

"He's fine. Are you still coming back tomorrow?"

"Yes. Is something up?"

She laughed. "Why do you ask?"

"Because you look particularly pleased with yourself. You've been worried for weeks about The Potting Shed. Now you look happy. New revenue source?"

"I had a little good news this morning—well, good for me—not really good for the two people who died recently due to poison."

"They want you to work with the police again?" He looked surprised. "I thought you weren't doing that anymore."

Peggy told him about Al asking her to help with the case. "I couldn't say no. He needs me."

He shook his head. "Someone always does. Just be careful. I can't rescue you from Tampa."

"Like you've ever had to rescue me."

"There was that time with the fire. And that time the man tried to shoot you." He counted off his rescues on his fingers. Some of them were true—not all.

"I'll be extra careful until you get home." She smiled at him, seeing his face that she'd once thought so ordinary, making her happier than anything else. "You be careful too. I'll pick you up at the airport tomorrow. I love you."

"I love you too. If there are any changes to the schedule, I'll let you know."

His face disappeared from the screen. Peggy touched the space where he'd been. This was better than not seeing him at all. Still, it left a lot to be desired. She'd be happy when he was home again.

Despite their age difference—Peggy was almost ten years older—they were very happy together. She had never believed she would ever love another man after John. Steve Newsome had been a gift from heaven. He'd changed her life again just as she'd thought it was settled and over.

She was about to close the laptop when she noticed an email had come in. She recognized the name. *Nightflyer*.

It surprised her to hear from her old, online chess buddy. It had been a long time since he'd contacted her.

Peggy opened her email, ignoring the hundreds of emails from fellow botanists and friends around the world.

She read Nightflyer's email. "More will come. What flower comes after buttercup?"

*Buttercup – Ranunculaciae - Known for their bright gold flowers that dot meadows and roadsides. All parts of the plant are poisonous to humans and pets. Toxic element is Protoanemonin. Can cause blistering to skin (external), vomiting and diarrhea (internal). May be fatal.*

# Chapter Two

Time hadn't changed her friend's cryptic nature. Nightflyer—that was the only name she knew him by—was always worried that someone would intercept his emails. He only wrote what he had to and then, in such a way that she had to guess what he was talking about.

One thing was for sure. He knew about the murders. Not surprising since he seemed to keep up with that kind of thing. He'd warned her before about events that had affected her. He'd always been right.

That meant there was another murder to come, unless Al stopped the killer. She thought about her long-time friend as she dressed in tan wool slacks and an autumn-hued tan and brown sweater.

The colors were good for her white-streaked red hair. Fall was all around her. Why not dress the part? She closely examined the fine lines beside her eyes and mouth, ignoring the scattering of freckles she'd always hated. Finally she put on some sun block and smiled at her refection. "You'll have to do. I don't have anymore time to primp."

Her partner, Sam, hadn't been happy about opening The Potting Shed that day. "I have a big order of mulch coming in. With Keeley gone and you out doing whatever you think is more important, that leaves Selena handling customers by herself while I unload the truck."

"I know it's difficult, but it's for a good reason. I'll be there by lunch," she'd assured him.

"That's fine. If you don't make money, I don't make money. I'm sure we won't miss a few customers Selena can't get to."

He'd certainly been in a bad mood. Her excitement over helping the police again was dampened by his attitude. She'd wanted to tell him about the murder case—and that the money she made from it would go to The Potting Shed. She was uncertain if she should mention it. It was possible it wouldn't work out.

"I'm sorry about this, Sam. Once I get there, you can take off for the day."

"I'm sorry too, Peggy." His voice cracked. "Hunter and I had a big fight last night."

Hunter was Sam's sister. She was also a fledgling attorney who was struggling to make a living.

"Anything I can help with?"

"Not really. She's in the same boat we are. Without joining a big firm, it's all she can do to pay the bills. She went out and tried to buy a new car. They wouldn't let her have it and she wanted me to co-sign. I wouldn't do it."

"I'd be happy to co-sign for her, Sam."

"See, that's the whole deal. She can't keep falling back on everyone else."

Peggy could tell this wasn't a good time to talk about it. "We'll talk when I get there. I promise not to take any longer than I have to."

Sam said that was fine and hung up.

With a sigh, Peggy sat back down at her computer and looked at Nightflyer's email again. She knew it wouldn't do any good to respond. He only used an email once and then changed it. She wasn't completely convinced that he wasn't making his problems sound worse than they were. What was he, after all, a spy or something?

She went down to the basement to check on her experiments after she let Shakespeare outside in the backyard for a while. She put on an apron to cover her clothes and slid on a pair of gloves.

Everything was progressing nicely. She was part of a group experiment with other botanists across the country. It involved independent studies of a new form of wheat that grew faster and used fewer resources. If the plants were successful, which they seemed to be, the wheat could be grown in smaller, drier fields in countries where people were desperate for it.

Another experiment was more for fun than to accomplish anything important. Peggy had received plants from a friend of hers at the University of South Carolina. They were a combination of every berry known. The fruit was delicious and very healthy. They were about the size of strawberries, but dark blue like blueberries, with large clusters like raspberries.

She ate one as she watched Shakespeare playing in the garden. He enjoyed chasing the falling leaves and scaring the squirrels.

Peggy couldn't stop thinking about the dead man in the park this morning. Why did people do such terrible things to others? It was something she'd never understand.

Obviously, the perpetrator was mentally ill. It was bad enough to use plant poisons to kill people. Doing it in alphabetical order was diabolical.

She wondered where the first murder had taken place. The park across the street was a very public spot. Mothers took their babies through it everyday and runners took advantage of its paths. What if one of them had found the body first?

If identifying plants and poisons would help bring this person to justice, she wanted to help. She let Shakespeare back in, grabbed her pocketbook, and made sure the door was locked and the alarm was set.

Shakespeare was barking again. She hated the idea, but she might have to muzzle him. Mr. Bellows was cranky— she didn't want her dog to be annoying. She hoped it would be better when Steve got back. Maybe Shakespeare missed him.

Peggy got on her bike and started pedaling down Queen's Road toward the police station in uptown Charlotte. Traffic was heavy now and drivers weren't particularly courteous. Horns blared at her and some people even made rude remarks from their car windows.

Honestly, weren't people ever going to get used to

sharing the road?

After the adventure getting to the police station, Peggy locked her bike into the stall for it. Right next to her bicycle and several others, was an azalea bush that was still blooming, despite the colder temperatures.

The pink flowers added a bright spot of color. No one else seemed to notice as they came and went. Peggy stroked the shiny leaves on the bush and marveled at the plant's ability to survive there.

"You know, it's going to be cold soon. This is a nice display, but you'd better get ready for winter. You're supposed to bloom in spring!" A slight breeze rustled through the trees and the leafy, green bush, making the flowers appear to agree with her.

The idea pleased her and she went toward the station with a smile on her face.

There were dozens of police officers and civilians walking in and out of the front door. Peggy had started up the stairs when she heard someone call her name—not her birth name, but one she'd known for most of her life.

"Mom!"

It was Paul, looking handsome and fit in his police uniform. He wore his penny-bright red hair cut short and spiky. His green eyes looked troubled, as usual. He was as tall and thin as his father, John, had been. It was too bad he'd also inherited his mother's temperament with that red hair. John had been very laid back and less prone to dramatic outbursts.

She turned and smiled at him, moved out of the way of the main traffic. "Hello. It's good to see you. How's Mai?"

Paul had married his long-time girlfriend, Mai Sato, shortly after Peggy and Steve had been married. Mai was an assistant medical examiner.

"She's fine. You already know that. You had lunch with her last week." His tone reflected the irritated look on his face.

Peggy took a deep breath. It was going to be *that* kind of morning. "All right. I was being polite. You remember being polite, don't you?" Her gaze met his. "You say nice things when you meet someone."

Her words fell on deaf ears. "I can't believe you're here! I heard you were going to work on those homicides with Al. I didn't believe it."

"Why not? It's not like I haven't done it before."

He took her arm and wedged them into a small corner of the cement landing at the top of the stairs. His back and shoulders sheltered their conversation from prying eyes and listening ears.

"You've done it before and it hasn't always been good. Remember almost getting killed? I thought we had an understanding about this."

She smiled at him in a way that only a mother smiles at her children—both pleased and infuriated.

"The only understanding I had about not continuing to consult with the police was that Jonas Rimer didn't want me here. Al does. Why does that bother you?"

"Because you're my *mother*. I think that says it all."

"Not really. Thanks for trying. I have to go inside now. Sam has a big shipment of mulch and he needs me at The

Potting Shed. Good to see you." She kissed his cheek.

"Mom—"

It was too late to say anything more on the subject. Peggy had put herself into the main stream of traffic going into the building.

She loved Paul, but he was seriously overprotective. It seemed as though he swung irrationally from completely ignoring her to checking on her every move. She had no doubt it wouldn't be his final word on the subject.

She'd worried about his reaction when she'd told him she was marrying Steve. It had only been a few years since John's death. Paul had been very close to his father. He'd changed his mind about becoming an architect to enter the police academy.

It wasn't something she or John had wanted for him. It was even worse when Peggy realized Paul wanted to become a police officer to help locate John's killer. The man had never been taken into custody.

She wasn't sure what was on his mind then, or now. She knew he worried about her. She worried about him too. He'd gone through with becoming a police officer despite her feelings on the subject.

She was doing the same, she realized. He had to understand that she had a job to do too.

Peggy went through the security scanner and emerged on the other side. She looked around for Paul. There was no sign of him. She grabbed her scanned pocketbook and smiled at the officer. At the front desk, another officer gave her a security badge and directed her to Al's office.

She passed by John's old office where a young

detective with egg on his tie sat talking on the phone. She knew she'd never forget the day she'd come here after John's death to collect his personal items.

Peggy had thought her life was over at that point. The only thing that had seen her through was opening The Potting Shed.

John had been an avid gardener, eagerly following her experiments in his time away from the job. They'd talked and dreamed for years of opening a garden shop when John retired. She'd wanted to fulfill that dream even though John had been gone.

"There you are," Al greeted her. He introduced her to his team of detectives that were investigating the two homicides.

"You taught me botany at Queen's." The grungy detective from the park said. "You probably don't even remember me."

Peggy tried to put the name—Tanner Edwards—to the face. It seemed she should remember something about him, but she'd taught hundreds of students in her time. His blond hair and blue eyes weren't familiar to her. She might recall his work in her class later.

"No, I'm sorry," she finally said. "But it's nice to meet you again."

"That's okay. I'm glad you're here to help with this, Professor," Tanner said. "If ever your knowledge was needed, this is it."

Al also introduced Detectives Molly Bryson and Dan Rodriguez.

They took her to a large room where pictures and other

information about the victims were displayed on a whiteboard.

"We found the first victim, John Spindler, near Park Road Books a few weeks ago. As far as we can tell there was nothing special about him. He was in his early sixties. Married. He has a son. He worked at a bank," Al explained.

She looked at the man's picture on the board. "And he was killed with poison from an angel's trumpet."

"That's right," Detective Rodriguez fingered his thin mustache as though it were a new addition. His thick black hair was trimmed close to his head, emphasizing his intense, dark eyes. "The medical examiner said he had a high concentration of it in his blood. She said death would have come very quickly. We figure whoever killed him did it right there."

Peggy looked at the next man on the board. She could barely recognize the face of the dead man she'd seen that morning. "And this is the man from this morning?"

"Yes. John Tucker." Al said.

"Anything up with the names being the same?" Peggy wondered.

"Probably not." Detective Molly Bryson wore her dark red hair combed back from her forehead. Her blue eyes reminded Peggy of the color of monkshood, another poison. "We think it's doubtful the victims were targeted. It was most probably a crime of convenience."

"They grabbed the first person they saw that was handy," Dan explained.

"Molly doesn't like the weird cases," Tanner said with a smile.

"Nobody likes the weird ones," Molly defended herself.

"Mr. Tucker was in his sixties," Al continued. "He had a wife and a son. He worked as a manager at a local trucking firm. The medical examiner just confirmed that he was killed by the poison in buttercups. He was also injected with the poison."

"Protoanemonin," Peggy supplied.

They all looked at her and she smiled.

"You can see they were staged with the plants on their bodies," Molly went on.

"So I think it's safe to call this a serial killer," Tanner added.

"No one wants to hear that," Al told him. "I'd better not hear that on the news tonight. We're holding back enough information that no one should be able to pick up on it—at least for right now."

Molly shrugged. "Unless they realize that two men around the same age and general description were murdered and left outside in the same area. Park Road Books isn't that far from the park on Queen's Road."

"Maybe that's another part of this," Tanner said. "Both have something to do with parks."

Peggy looked closely at the two men on the board again. They both had brown hair, and according to their description, brown eyes. They had similar builds. Both were wearing suits and ties.

"So what poisonous plant comes after B?" Molly asked.

"What did you say?" Peggy narrowed her eyes as she looked at her. Her words were so close to Nightflyer's.

"I'm just saying." Molly shrugged as they all stared at her. "If this is really alphabetical, the next one will be killed with a plant that starts with C, right?"

"There could be hundreds of choices," Peggy said. "I don't even want to speculate on that right now."

"What can you tell us about this?" Al asked. "As of this morning, you're officially my forensic botanist."

"Thanks." She organized her thoughts on the subject. "The poison would have to be extremely strong to produce these effects. I can't imagine this would be something you could buy, even on the black market. I'd guess that the killer distilled the poison himself. Once it was administered, the ME is right. Death would have come very quickly."

"So he'd need a lab or something to do this," Dan suggested.

"Yes," Peggy agreed. "But nothing special. The poison could be created in someone's home. I could do it in my basement. The knowledge of creating the poisons is more important. Not everyone would realize these plants were poisonous. Even fewer would know how to take advantage of that."

"Great." Al looked at his notes. "So the killer could be anyone. Anywhere. That doesn't make me feel any better."

"Have they found any other botanical evidence on either body?" Peggy asked.

"Nothing besides dog hair and grass stains," Tanner said. "And the dog belonged to the victim. That was a dead end."

"Maybe you could pay a visit to the ME's office and take a look at what they've got," Al suggested. "We have to find this killer before he strikes again. If that happens, everyone will be calling it a serial killing. No one wants that."

Peggy agreed, but she had to go to The Potting Shed. She wanted to help—God knew she didn't want another death. However, she had to work with Sam and keep her garden shop going too.

"I'll make arrangements to go later today," she promised. "That's the best I can do on the spur of the moment or Sam will have my head. Unless you want to send an officer to unload mulch from a truck?"

Al smiled. "I think this afternoon will be fine."

He instructed his detectives on what their next moves should be. There were witnesses to question, interviews with the victims' families. They could only hope something would turn up.

Peggy was about to leave and head to The Potting Shed when a call came in on her cell phone. It was her security company. Someone had attempted to break into her house.

*Cyclamen* - *Primrose family* - *A European perennial plant considered a good gift at Christmas. Seeds ripen under the protection of the leaves. Long used as a purgative by healers. Poison from the plant was used for centuries on arrowheads. Even small doses are poisonous to humans.*

# Chapter Three

The police had been called by the security company. Two uniformed officers were already at Peggy's house when she arrived.

Al had driven her home—after stashing her bike in the trunk of his car. He'd wanted to make sure everything was all right and save her some time getting there.

Peggy had assured him that her alarm sometimes went off and nothing was wrong. She didn't want him to waste his time driving her home when there was a killer to find. How would that look on his new lieutenant's record?

"Dr. Margaret Lee?" the older of the two officers asked when she got out of the car.

"Yes." Al answered for her and showed the officers his ID. "Dr. Lee is a consultant with the Charlotte PD. What happened here, Officer Kopacka?"

"Nothing so far as we know," the young officer answered. "We walked around the perimeter of the house. Everything looks fine. The doors are still locked. There are no broken windows. It must've been a glitch in the system."

Peggy wanted to hurry this along. The noise from the alarm was irritating. She would certainly hear about it from Mr. Bellows. She opened the kitchen door and turned the alarm off, heaving a sigh of relief when it was quiet.

It was good to know nothing was wrong. These false alarms happened occasionally. The city fined people if it happened too often. It was a waste of resources to bring officers out to check on it. It was one of the reasons she frequently didn't set the alarm.

Paul and Steve both called her since their names were on the contact list with the security company for emergencies. She had to take several minutes to explain to both of them, in front of Al and the officers, that nothing was wrong.

Al dismissed the two officers. "I'll walk through the house with you just to make sure everything is okay."

Peggy protested. She felt foolish enough about the event as it was. "You don't have to do that. I'm sure it's all fine."

Shakespeare was barking so hard, Peggy was afraid he was going to have a heart attack. His fangs were showing and the hackles on his neck and back were up. He was foaming at the mouth a little too. She wiped his mouth and hugged him, reassuring him. He was a little too high-strung to be such a big dog.

"There's nothing you can say that's going to prevent me from walking through the house," Al told her once Shakespeare was quiet. "It's probably nothing, but I want to make sure. So if you have any secret plant stuff going on in here, now's the time to tell me."

"What kind of secret plant stuff could I be doing?"

He shrugged. "I don't know. Some new, weird kind of marijuana or something. John used to tell me crazy stories about your experiments in the basement."

She laughed. "There's nothing you can't see. And if you insist on searching the house, that's fine. I'm grateful for your diligence."

"You're sure, huh?" He grinned. "Let's get going. I don't have all day."

Al and Peggy walked through the main part of the two-story house, through the dining room, parlor and living room. There was nothing unusual or out of place.

They walked up the wide, curved staircase to the bedrooms. It allowed a perfect view of the thirty-foot blue spruce growing up to the skylight.

"John never wanted this house, you know," Al said as they walked. "He said it was too old and drafty. He even called it creepy once. He didn't grow up here. It was his birthright. He loved it once he'd moved in with you. He was sorry Paul wouldn't be able to raise his family here."

Peggy smoothed her hand along the wood banister. "It might be old and drafty and in constant need of attention, but I can't imagine living anywhere else. It's a wonderful house. I've spent most of my life here. I'm glad John's nephew doesn't want to settle down yet. I hate the idea of leaving."

"How does Steve feel about living here?"

"He sold his house two doors down after we were married." She shrugged as they walked through three bedrooms that weren't being used, their antique furniture shrouded with white sheets. "I suppose he's all right with it."

Al smiled. "I think the man is just plain crazy about you and he wouldn't care if you lived in a shack. That's what I think."

"I hope that's it," she agreed. "We can always look for a new place when the time comes. It doesn't make John's family very happy that I'm still here even though John is gone. The house would be empty without me, waiting for John's nephew. That's never a good thing."

They went down to the basement and Peggy let Shakespeare outside for a few minutes. Al snooped through her experiments. Nothing seemed unusual or out of place there either.

"I don't know what half of this stuff is," he said.

"Mary does," she replied. "She was here a few months ago getting some cuttings from a new white azalea I'm growing."

He knew that was true. "Oh yeah. If there are plants involved, my wife is all over it."

His cell phone rang and he stepped away to take the call. Peggy let Shakespeare back in. The dog wasn't happy about being called away from the nice weather and the distractions he'd found in the backyard.

Al said he had to go. "We may have had a break in the case. It seems one of our victims wasn't as perfect as we thought. He was having an affair—with a woman who works at a florist. That could be our poison connection."

Peggy wished him well. She didn't think a woman who worked at a florist was likely to have the expertise needed to create these poisons, but she didn't say so. She knew from living with John that they had to investigate all possible angles of the crime. It was their duty and it was expected of them. The district attorney had to be able to say that all avenues had been explored when the case went to trial.

She stood in the driveway and waved to him as he pulled out into Queen's Road traffic.

Peggy went back inside for a moment to reassure Shakespeare again. A quick glance at her watch sent her back out on her bicycle, this time for The Potting Shed. It had already been more than two hours since she'd told Sam she would be there.

Mr. Bellows was waiting there for her, almost inside a large privet bush. "Mrs. Lee."

"I'm sorry. I know the alarm went off. I'll have the security company come and check it out."

"You're a terrible neighbor." He said it in a flat monotone, reminding her of Alfred Hitchcock.

"I try my best to be a good neighbor, Mr. Bellows. All of our lives can't be as well-planned as yours."

"I would be happy to buy your house to facilitate your moving away from here."

Her green eyes widened. "I don't own this house. You'd have to contact my former husband's family. I don't think they'd be interested. It's been passed down from generation to generation for more than a hundred years."

"Then I shall have to consider other options."

She looked at her watch again. "I'm sorry. I have to go."

Traffic had increased horrifically from Queen's Road to Brevard Court where the garden shop was located. She'd been cut off twice in traffic and one driver had tossed a partial cup of ice at her. Luckily she'd been able to maneuver around it.

Peggy went to the back of the shop where the loading dock was. Sam was still there unloading twenty-five pound bags of mulch. It was the time of year for gardeners to go out and mulch their plants, bushes and trees to protect them from the winter. They always tried to stay well-stocked.

"It's about time," Sam said when he saw her. "Selena has been driving me crazy. She says she needs time to study for a test. The shop has been super busy, of course. I finally started ignoring her. I can't keep running back and forth and get this truck and trailer back to the rental company today. Do you know how much they charge if you keep the equipment an extra day?"

Peggy left her bike at the base of the stairs next to the loading dock. "Good morning. I'm so sorry about this. There was a murder across the street from the house early this morning. They think the man was killed by glycosides from buttercups."

Sam Ollson put a bag of mulch on each of his broad shoulders with his gloved hands. The morning sun gleamed on his naturally blond hair. His face was tanned from hours working in the sun on whatever landscape projects he could find. Blue eyes were annoyed at the moment, but smile lines at the side of them gave away his usually sunny disposition.

"So it's Peggy Lee human poison detector to the rescue again, huh?"

"There's a paycheck. I'm putting it into the garden shop account since it involves gardening, to an extent."

He raised his almost invisible blond brows. "To a broad extent."

"I could have them make out the checks to The Potting Shed, if that would help."

Sam put the two bags of mulch into the storage area outside the shop. "I guess you should ask the accountant. I'm glad you're here anyway. If I had to be here alone with Selena much longer, there may have been another murder that wasn't as clever."

She grinned. "Well, at least you're wearing gloves. No fingerprints."

He smiled at that. Sam never stayed angry for long. "Thanks for the tip."

"Do you want to talk about Hunter's car problem?"

"No."

"All right then."

Brevard Court, where The Potting Shed was located, was built at the doorway to Latta Arcade—originally a cotton auction house.

Like a turn of the century mini-mall, the shops continued along inside the arcade of the restored 1915 office building. The antique light fixtures and parallel rows of shop fronts created the feeling of walking into the past.

The overhead skylight, which was part of the original architecture, kept shoppers dry. Its original purpose was to provide natural light for cotton buyers to inspect their goods.

Brevard Court was behind the arcade. Small shops and restaurants lined the cobblestone courtyard. It was a pleasant place to shop or sit and eat lunch. The shops depended on the forty-thousand workers who came to the uptown offices five days a week. It was mostly empty on the weekends.

The economy had been rough on some of the shops and restaurants that had been there when Peggy had first opened The Potting Shed. Several had closed. No new shops had opened in the area in the last two years.

The Kozy Kettle Coffee and Tea Emporium was still there with Emil and Sofia Balducci making coffee and Peggy's favorite, peach tea, along with breakfast and lunch foods. Anthony's Caribbean Café still made delicious, spicy lunches. The Carolina Expert Tailor Shop had survived too.

China King take-out was also still open. Peggy waved to Mr. Woo every morning when she opened the door that led to the courtyard.

The French restaurant that had been kitty-corner from The Potting Shed had closed. Peggy missed them because they'd been open for dinner. She and Steve had eaten there many times after a long day at the garden shop. A little travel agency beside it hadn't fared well either.

Every time a shop had closed, everyone there felt the blow. They were all hanging on, hoping for better times. Emil Balducci always insisted those better times were just around the corner. She'd never known a happier man in her life.

Peggy went inside where two customers were keeping Selena busy with their quest for garden bulbs. She smiled as she watched her long-time assistant. Selena wasn't always patient and pleasant, but she made up for it in her knowledge of plant lore and her willingness to work when she was needed.

A sigh of happiness, of being home, escaped from Peggy as it always did when she walked into The Potting Shed. The rent was a little steep, but she loved the look and feel of the place. The Potting Shed had real heart-of-pine floors that squeaked when she walked across them.

The shop wasn't huge, but it had a small warehouse space in the back to keep shovels, potting soil, and other essential items. She normally did a brisk business, even in the winter. Charlotteans were avid gardeners all year long.

Now she was scraping by. She hadn't hired another assistant after Keeley Prinz had left when she'd transferred schools. It had meant a little extra work for all of them. Peggy wasn't comfortable yet doing more than maintaining what she had.

Another customer came in from the courtyard, the little bell ringing as the door opened. Peggy put on her Potting Shed apron and went to help her.

"I'm looking for something to get rid of poison ivy," the well-dressed woman told her. "I don't know how it got into my yard, but I want it gone. I don't want to worry every time I go outside that I'll get a rash. I'm highly allergic."

Peggy smiled. "I know exactly what you mean. There's nothing like a poison rash to keep you inside. As for how it got there, birds actually spread it in their droppings."

"Really?" The woman's eyes grew round with amazement. "I blamed my landscaper. I guess I owe him an apology. So what can I do to get rid of it?"

"You can choose to poison it, which I wouldn't recommend as it poisons the soil too. The best way is to protect yourself—long sleeves, good gloves, long pants—and pull it out. It has to be pulled out by the roots. There's no other way."

The woman made an unpleasant face. "I don't want to poison the soil, but I don't know if I have time to pull it out. I wish I hadn't fired my landscaper. Maybe he could've taken it out for me. You don't know a good landscaper you could recommend, do you?"

"As a matter of fact, she does." Sam took off his gloves and offered the woman his large hand. "I'm Sam Ollson. I run the landscaping part of this business. I'll be glad to get the poison ivy out of your yard."

The woman looked impressed—Sam always impressed people. It was easy when you looked like the Norse God, Thor. "No poison, right?" Her gaze never left his handsome face.

"No, ma'am. If I used poison, Peggy would poison me. We can talk over here by the calendar and set up a date."

"Yes, please!" The woman was excited as she went to the counter with him. "Did I mention that I'm single?"

"He always makes it look so easy," Selena muttered standing next to Peggy. She'd already rung up her customers who'd left the shop with dozens of tulips, daffodils, and hyacinth bulbs for fall planting.

Peggy smiled at her. Selena Rogers had her long black hair tied back from her cocoa-colored face. Her golden, whiskey-colored eyes were focused on Sam who was busy charming his new landscaping conquest.

"It helps that so many of our customers are female," Peggy said.

"Do they have to look like they'd like to eat him up when they talk to him?" Selena asked in an annoyed whisper. She bent her head close to Peggy's. She was tall and thin, a long-distance runner at Queens University. After taking Peggy's botany class by mistake, she went to work for her a week later.

"If it makes you feel any better," Peggy said quietly, "the men who come in here look at you same way."

Selena grinned. "You're only saying that to make me feel better."

"Have you looked in the mirror lately?"

The young woman looked pleased with that response.

The new landscape customer left The Potting Shed with a last goodbye to Sam. As soon as the door had closed behind her, he raised a large fist into the air. "Yes! She wants full landscaping every week, even through the winter."

"Excellent!" Peggy applauded him. "You've become quite the salesman. I'm sure you'll be able to use that skill when you finish medical school."

Sam's triumphant expression turned sour. "Let's not get into that again. I'm not finishing school."

When he'd come to work for Peggy, Sam had been

planning a career in medicine. Later, he'd decided that it wasn't for him after all—much to the consternation of his family. There had been tears and some begging, even an accusation against Peggy from his parents. Nothing would change Sam's mind.

Every so often, since he'd made that decision, Peggy had tried to subtly remind him that he had other options besides working at The Potting Shed. More often than not, he'd thrown it back at her.

It didn't mean she wouldn't continue to try and convince him. Sam was enormously smart as well as good with his hands. She knew he liked working in the garden, but she also knew that could be a hobby rather than a career.

"I'm glad you finally got here." Selena heaved a sigh of relief. "Sam has been no help at all this morning. Give him some mulch to play with and he won't step foot into the shop. I guess that changed because you were here, Peggy."

"I just finished unloading a whole trailer full of mulch," he reminded Selena. "I told you we could change places and I'd watch the shop. You didn't want to do that either."

Selena started to speak. Peggy stopped her. She knew the two could go on bickering all day. They were like brother and sister when it came to that.

"I'm here now," Peggy said. "And I appreciate all the extra work the two of you have been putting in."

Sam muttered something unintelligible. "I have to get that rig back to the rental place. I'll be back as soon as I can."

"I need to study, Peggy." Selena had one last grimace for Sam. "Some people who dropped out of school don't realize how important it is to study."

"Especially if you're failing chemistry." Sam walked out the back after one last barb.

"Not a problem." Peggy patted Selena's shoulder to keep her from following Sam and continuing the disagreement. "You go on and study. I'll take care of the shop. Good luck with that test tomorrow."

Selena looked at the back door where Sam had disappeared. "You know, someday someone is going to kill him. It just might be me."

*Daffodil - Narcissus Family* - *Lovely yellow flowers bulbs, cousins to jonquils. Very popular flower for spring. Contains toxic alkaloids in all parts of plant. Rarely fatal. During World War II, starving cattle were fatally poisoned by daffodil bulbs.*

# Chapter Four

Peggy's purple water iris was about to bloom. It was planted in the pond that she'd put in the middle of The Potting Shed after a flood had caused significant damage to the hardwood floor. Since she'd had to take the damaged floor out anyway, it had seemed like the ideal time to put in the small pond and sell water plants and other supplies.

The shop was empty after the small flurry of customers. She sat in her rocking chair beside the pond and admired the small iris bud straining to open. Maybe she should have a small party for the event and invite all of her customers, past and present. She could have Emil from the Kozy Kettle serve some food and beverages. It might give both shops a little lift in sales.

She sighed as she looked at the well-stocked shelves and hoped the economy would pick up. She'd been hoping that for the last few years. Outside of the occasional uptick when the seasons changed, business was very slow. It didn't help that the owners of Brevard Court had raised her rent.

Feeling a little melancholy, she forced herself to get up and dust all the shelves. She rearranged everything and made sure her fall bulb display was eye catching. Winter and summer were usually slow. She depended on fall and spring sales to get her through.

The bell on the door jingled. She looked up and saw Mr. Bellows, her neighbor from Queen's Road. He was normally so reclusive. It was odd to see him more than once in a day. As far as she knew, he'd never visited The Potting Shed before.

"Mrs. Lee." He removed his ancient-looking tweed cap. Little tufts of gray hair stood up around his head. "I remembered when I saw you this morning that you had a flower shop. I wanted to see what it looked like."

Peggy didn't correct her name. She hadn't changed it after marrying Steve. She thought it might be too confusing for everyone. She'd been Peggy Lee for a very long time.

"Hello, Mr. Bellows. Yes, this is my garden shop. Are you interested in some bulbs for the fall? I have some nice daffodils."

He glanced around with a disinterested look on his sallow face. "No. Not really. I was interested in the shop itself. How much do you want for it?"

Now he wanted The Potting Shed? What was wrong with this man? "I've never thought of selling it, Mr. Bellows. I've had it for so long that it seems like my home away from home."

He waved aside her words with his long, thin hand.

"Yes, yes. No haggling, please. I'll pay fair market value for it. I won't cheat you and I expect you not to try and cheat me if we're going to do business."

Peggy smiled and held her temper in check. He was completely obnoxious.

"It's not for sale. I appreciate your offer. I wouldn't think of selling."

He gazed at her with his cold blue eyes, as though she were a thing to be purchased too. Was he weighing her merit to see if it matched the price he thought was fair for her?

"What do you want for it? I don't have time to stand here and wait all day, Mrs. Lee. I have more important things to do."

It was difficult, but Peggy managed to be polite. "Mr. Bellows, I'm not selling The Potting Shed. If you'd like to purchase something, I'll be happy to help you. If not, perhaps another shop owner in Brevard Court or Latta Arcade might be interested in your offer. Thanks for stopping by."

"You must be out of your mind. Anyone who was sane would take my offer on this place. Good day, Mrs. Lee." He tipped his cap to her then put it back on his head and left.

Peggy couldn't believe the nerve of the man. What had he expected her to say? What made him think she wanted to sell the shop, or the house, for that matter?

Still steaming, she dusted and rearranged a little more forcefully. At least one thing was good—she normally didn't see him at all. That had been a blessing she hadn't realized until today.

Emil Balducci brought Peggy lunch from the Kozy Kettle. His thick, gray mustache drooped a little on the right side when he frowned. That didn't happen often. He always seemed to be in a good mood.

With his broad Italian features, craggy brows, and shadowed dark eyes, he was quite a ladies' man. Especially when his wife, Sofia, wasn't at the shop.

"I made my special crusted eggplant on Ciabatta bread." He kissed his fingers on his big, callused hand. His voice was still heavily accented even after twenty years away from Sicily. "You're gonna love it!"

Peggy smiled. "I know I will. Thank you for bringing it over. I'm the only one here right now."

"Like the old days." He nodded as he handed her a cup of peach tea with a lid on it. "I remember when you were always here by yourself. I thought that would change once you married again. I think you married the wrong man. A husband should be around when a wife needs him."

"I suppose I could've put a note on the shop door and come over to get lunch."

"That's not it. You hire people. Where are they? You pay people money to help you, right? When you need them, they aren't here. That's what I'm talking about. That's why I don't pay no one. Sofia works with me now. Your husband should be here with you."

"He has a job, a career of his own," she reminded him. "He's a veterinarian, remember?"

Emil made a grimace that brought his big mustache almost up to cover his nose. "What's that? He could do that here. A woman needs a man, Peggy."

His swarthy face was very close to hers. Peggy had always thought Emil was joking around when he said such things, though she'd talked to other women who had insisted he wasn't. She'd felt sure he would never really go too far.

For a moment, she wasn't as certain.

"I have to go." He said with a sigh. "We're expecting a group this afternoon. Sofia is making those little sandwiches they like. You should come over."

"What kind of group is it?" she asked politely, knowing she didn't have time for a meeting.

"Sofia and I, we call it the lonely hearts club. The group, they call it singles." He shrugged. "Same difference. You should come over."

"I'll try. Thanks again for lunch."

He waved as he walked out of the shop.

Peggy was almost done with lunch when Sam got back. He ranted for a few minutes about the rental company refusing to give his deposit back.

"They said the trailer was dirty." He walked around through the narrow aisles, flailing his big arms in the air. "Can you believe it? I swept it out. They wanted me to wash it out. I'm never renting from them again."

"I'm sure it will be worth it to have the extra mulch in. We always sell a ton of mulch in the fall."

Sam stopped walking around and complaining. "Are we gonna make it, Peggy? I look at the numbers every day on my computer. I know we're holding our own right now, but there isn't much left over. Maybe we should think about moving to a cheaper place. The rent here is killing us."

"I know it's high," she agreed. "It's the location. I love it here, Sam. I'd hate to move."

He came close and hugged her. "I know. I like it here too. I guess we'll keep going, at least for now. Let me get cleaned up and grab some lunch and you can go investigate dead people. What's that? It smells good."

Peggy slapped at his hand as he grabbed a piece of her sandwich. "Eggplant."

"The bread is good anyway." He grimaced once it was in his mouth.

Sam was back in a few minutes with a burger and fries. They talked for a while about the shop and the murder investigation. Peggy and Sam were more than just partners in this business. Sam was nearly as dear to her as her own son, Paul.

"All right. Get out of here," Sam said when they were both done eating and their conversation began to wane. "Be careful. Don't dig up too many secrets."

Peggy hugged him. It was all she could do to put her arms around his wide chest. "I'll call you later and we can see how the rest of the day goes. Don't give up yet, Sam. I think we'll be okay."

He shrugged. "If not, we can always sell the shop."

Her green eyes narrowed suspiciously. "That's a peculiar thing for you to say." She told him about Mr. Bellows.

"Don't look at me." He held his hands up. "I don't

even know the man and you know I wouldn't do anything like that without talking to you first."

"I know." She frowned. "Just striking fear into your heart."

He went behind the cash register and put on a green Potting Shed apron. "Yeah. My hands are shaking. Get out of here before I start crying."

Peggy got her pocketbook and climbed on her bicycle. The weather had held—blue sky and puffy white clouds. It wasn't a long ride from Brevard Court to the medical examiner's office. Traffic wasn't even too bad.

She had to use her new police badge for identification at the entrance. There were many new faces since she'd worked here on a regular basis two years ago.

There was even a new medical examiner. Her name was Dorothy Beck. After Peggy had made it through the security check and let people look at her ID a dozen times, she met Dr. Beck.

"It's very nice to finally meet you." Dorothy Beck shook Peggy's hand. She was tall and thin. Her white lab coat hung badly on her. Peggy wondered why they didn't find the right size for her.

"It's nice to meet you too, Dr. Beck," Peggy said.

"Please, call me Dorothy. I'll call you Peggy. Let's start off on the right foot."

They walked together down the long, green-tiled hallway. Several doors led off of the hall including the main examination room, the cadaver cold storage, and the lunch room.

It had always bothered Peggy that the lunch room was so close to those other rooms. It seemed to her as though people should eat away from those areas. No one else seemed to mind. She'd eaten outside when she'd had to be there during a case in the past.

"Here's my office." Dorothy opened the door. "Please sit down."

"You've done a great job redecorating." Peggy took a seat in front of the glass desk. There were new, colorful curtains on the windows. A new, blue carpet was underfoot, and there were some delightful landscape paintings on the wall.

Dorothy smiled as she put on her glasses. She was about Peggy's age—mid-fifties. Her face was long and angular. Her brown eyes appraised Peggy at the same time that Peggy appraised her.

"It's been a while since you were here last." Dorothy picked up a file. "The former medical examiner ran this place like it was his own private theme park. I'm not like him. I like our work to be clean and accurate. I've read your record. I think we'll get along just fine."

"Thank you." Peggy didn't comment on the former ME. It was best not to speak ill of the man. "I'm hoping you have some information to bring me up to speed on these botanical murders."

"You mean The Poison Plant murders?" Dorothy looked at Peggy across the top of her glasses. "You haven't heard? Some enterprising reporter noticed there seemed to be a pattern and now it's all over the news."

"That's too bad," Peggy said. "It makes it so much harder."

"Don't I know it? I'm sure I don't have to caution you about sharing information with the press."

"No. I don't particularly like sharing with anyone." Peggy accepted the manila file from her.

"That's for the best. You'll find everything we know about the two homicides in that file, Peggy. There's a computer station for you and you'll be able to view the information and receive email there as well."

There was a knock at the door and Dorothy called for the person to come in.

It was Mai Sato-Lee, Paul's wife. Peggy restrained herself from hugging the young woman. She'd worked with Mai before and knew professionalism was important to her.

She also knew how unhappy Mai had been on being passed over for promotion when the former medical examiner had retired. She'd worked hard to take over that position. The board that had hired Dorothy turned down Mai's request for the position, saying that she was too inexperienced.

Peggy, Mai, Paul and Steve had talked about it for months over Sunday dinner.

"Mai." Peggy nodded to her. She couldn't hold back a smile.

"Dr. Lee." Mai nodded, without the smile.

"Oh please," Dorothy intervened. "I know you two are related by marriage. We don't need those formalities here, do we?"

"Of course not, Dr. Beck." Mai's voice was polite and cool.

Peggy recalled the first time she'd met Mai. It had been at a crime scene. The young Vietnamese woman wore a blue crime scene uniform. Her huge, almond-shaped, brown eyes and pretty face were half hidden by heavy, black glasses.

It hadn't been long after that meeting that Paul and Mai had started dating. They'd moved in together and finally were married. Peggy kept hoping for grandchildren. Mai was dedicated to her career and not really interested in that prospect.

"I'll be glad to show you your workstation, Dr. Lee," Mai said.

Dorothy sighed. "All right. I guess that's the best we're going to do today. Peggy, if you need anything, give me a call. I'd appreciate it if you come to me with any findings before you share them with the police."

"Of course, Dorothy. I look forward to working with you."

Mai and Peggy left Dorothy's office. The door was barely closed when Mai began to ask questions. "Did she bring you here? Isn't she happy with what I'm doing on the Poison Plant case?"

"I don't think that's it at all," Peggy answered. "Where did they get that information? How did the press find out it was plant poison that killed those men?"

"I don't know. But one minute, this is my case and the next you're coming in to work as a consultant." Mai made a growling sound. "I don't know what she wants from me. Sometimes I think she wants me to leave."

"I'm sure she doesn't want you to leave." Peggy tried to reassure her. "Why are you so stiff with her? Why not call her Dorothy?"

"It's awkward being friends with people at work—especially people who took my job."

Peggy knew Mai held herself to very high, sometimes impossibly high, standards. She'd truly felt her work was below those standards when the city had hired a new medical examiner from outside the office.

"You should try and loosen up a little with her," Peggy said. "I'm sure she's very friendly once you get to know her. I like her."

Mai rolled her attractive eyes. Paul had talked her into getting contact lenses. What a difference those had made! "That's easy for you to say. You're a consultant, not fighting for your job."

They stopped at a desk with an aging computer on it. "Here's your workstation. If I can assist, please let me know. I've done all the preliminaries on this case. I know something about it, even if no one appreciates it."

Peggy didn't even have a chance to say thank you before Mai left her there. She'd known her daughter-in-law was angry but hadn't realized how much she resented her new boss. She wondered if Mai would stay on with that attitude.

The thought made her cringe. Paul could get a job anywhere as a police officer. There was only one medical examiner's office in Charlotte. If she left her position, Mai might want to leave town.

Peggy spent the rest of the afternoon familiarizing herself with the case. There were a lot of facts, as Mai had said. It was clear, however, what the manner of death was. In both cases, poison had been injected into the victims.

Mai had made a note of the unusual types of poison. More often than not, poisoning came from arsenic, cyanide—something easy to get from commercial products.

These poisons were specially made, it appeared. As Peggy had told Al, a person with specific knowledge and the right equipment had to be responsible.

It seemed odd to her, as she looked at the files. Both men were named John and their middle names were Lee. One was spelled Leigh, but it was still the same name.

Maybe it was because she was married to John Lee that she found that fact unusual. Al and his three detectives hadn't thought both men being named John was strange at all.

It was starting to get dark when Peggy finally left for the day. She didn't feel as though she'd made any significant contribution toward finding the killer. She'd familiarized herself with the case. She'd have to work from there.

Traffic was heavy again going out of the uptown area. She stayed on the side of the road and avoided any trouble. Cars and trucks whizzed past her. They couldn't possibly be driving the lower speed limits that were posted.

The outside lights on the house were on a timer so they were on when she got there. Shakespeare began barking as soon as he heard her. She let him out for a few minutes before she went to the front door and checked her mail.

The house seemed empty without Steve. She wouldn't have thought she could attach herself to someone so quickly. She glanced at her watch. There was still an hour before their next Skype session. Time to change clothes and find something to eat.

It was then she noticed that the front door was slightly open. It surprised her. Had she forgotten to set the alarm again? She was going to have to be more careful about that. Someone had broken the lock on the door to shove a thick envelope between the door and the frame.

Peggy opened the door all the way and the envelope fell on the floor. It was addressed to her.

She opened it and read, *"Recognize me yet?"*

*Elder – Sambucus - Common wild shrub in backyards, roadsides and forests. Dark, hanging fruit that can be eaten or made into jelly or wine after ripened and seeds removed. Cyanide glycosides in leaves, twigs and seeds. Children have been poisoned by making whistles from the hollow twigs. Listed as a highly effective medicinal for many years.*

# Chapter Five

"It's probably your old buddy, Nightflyer, playing games with you."

Peggy had shown the note to Steve when she picked him up at the airport the next morning. It wasn't the romantic welcome home she'd hoped to give him. She'd been up most of the night thinking about the note.

"I don't think so."

"Why not? You said you'd heard from him again. This sounds like something he'd do. You should let the police handle it."

It was raining hard, crashes of thunder stalking the morning commute into Charlotte. Lightning stabbed across the dark sky. Cars moved slowly with their emergency lights flashing. The road was bumper-to-bumper when traffic moved at all.

"I plan on giving it to Mai this morning. I feel a little silly. It might not have anything to do with the case at all."

"I don't know. The murder happened across the street and you're involved. Why take chances?"

"I know you're right. I also know their budget is tight. I hate to waste it on something that doesn't matter."

"Just give it to her, Peggy. Mai will take care of it. Consider it the perks of having a daughter-in-law who happens to be an assistant medical examiner. We need one in the family."

"What's that supposed to mean?" She couldn't glare at him because she needed to concentrate on the drivers that obviously weren't nervous about the weather or bad traffic.

"You know what I mean. You said you weren't going to get involved with cases like this anymore. I'll bet Paul gave you a hard time."

"Not any more than you," she quipped. "I didn't know you felt so strongly about it."

"You were almost killed once or twice trying to solve a case the police couldn't. How did you expect me to feel?"

For starters, she'd expected him to back her up on all her decisions. She should've had that put into the marriage vows. Honor. Support. Never question.

Peggy didn't say anything else about it until they'd reached the house. She was relieved to have driven through the traffic from the airport without getting in an accident. They'd passed several bad wrecks on the way.

Steve seemed to agree with her silence. He hadn't said anything about it again either. He got out of the SUV with his bag and opened the kitchen door as Peggy parked the vehicle in the garage.

He and Shakespeare were enjoying their reunion when Peggy got inside. Steve was on the floor with the Great Dane standing over him, wagging his tail.

"At least *he* missed me," Steve said.

"Yes, well, he didn't take part in a murder investigation. He didn't have to listen to your lecture about his safety." Peggy closed the kitchen door with an extra push.

Steve got up and put his arms around her. "I'm sorry. I worry about you. Someone was killed right across the street and you received a mysterious message. That doesn't make me happy. Whoever left that message could've been inside waiting for you."

Peggy thought he looked tired. She ran her hand through his thick, brown hair. There were dark circles under his brown eyes and his face looked a little pale. He also had a small cut on one cheek. She got over her anger when she thought he might be getting sick.

"You have a vivid imagination and a suspicious mind. Didn't you sleep well at the conference? You look like you're coming down with something? How did you cut your cheek?"

He kissed her. "I'll be fine. I want you to be fine too."

"I am. Really. And I'm glad you're home." She hugged him tightly and he yelped, scaring Shakespeare who skidded across the hardwood in his effort to get away from the sound. For all of his size, the Great Dane was scared of everything.

Peggy let Steve go. She could see he was in pain.

"It's only my side," he told her. "I tripped going down some stairs and maybe bruised something."

"Maybe? Didn't you get an X-ray or something to find out?"

"It was right before the flight. I didn't want to stay an extra day. I'll be fine."

Peggy wouldn't hear of it. She wasn't happy until he'd taken his shirt off. There was a nasty bruise on his right side and some smaller bruises all over his chest and arms.

"Did you roll down the stairs?" she asked.

"No. The rest of it is from handling animals," he told her. "Don't worry about it. Things like this happen sometimes."

"I think you should go to the doctor. That one bruise may have cracked a rib. You're so worried about me. I don't have bruises all over my body like you do."

He grinned and grabbed her, despite the pain in his side. "Let's see."

* * *

Peggy had left Steve sleeping upstairs as she crept to the kitchen door. She cautioned Shakespeare to keep it down. "He needs his rest. No unnecessary barking. Not that I'm saying the barking you did yesterday wasn't necessary. Obviously you knew what you were talking about. Thanks for trying to protect me."

She called the locksmith to have the front door repaired and left Steve a note that the man was coming.

The rain had stopped even though the dark clouds still hovered. She didn't want to take Steve's SUV in case he needed to go out on a call. Sam had the Potting Shed pickup. His car had broken down last week and she'd told him not to worry about it. He probably wasn't making enough money from the shop to have his car repaired.

She'd put on her poncho and rain pants to ride her bicycle back to the medical examiner's office. Sam and Selena had texted her earlier to let her know they would be at the shop that morning. That meant she could put some time into the murder investigation.

As Peggy got her bicycle out of the garage, Mr. Bellows suddenly popped out again, this time from behind a large, red maple.

"Mrs. Lee."

He'd managed to startle her again. This was getting ridiculous! She wasn't a nervous person and didn't scare easily. It was probably because of the note at the door and Steve's warning.

*You're also working on a double murder and you've been looking at dead bodies,* she reminded herself. *It's different than pollinating plants. Get a grip.*

"Good morning, Mr. Bellows."

"I'm here to talk with you again about your garden shop."

"I'm really not interested in selling. Please take that as my final answer." She got on the bike so he'd get the idea that she was in a hurry.

"I have a considerable knowledge of plants myself," he continued. "I know you're a botanist. Perhaps we could share thoughts at some point. I'll show you mine if you show me yours."

Peggy didn't want to know what he was talking about. There was something a little repulsive about him. She knew she shouldn't be so judgmental. He probably was lacking in social skills. Many men who lived alone seemed to have that problem.

It wasn't her job to teach him either.

"I'm sorry, Mr. Bellows. I'm late for work. Maybe we can talk later."

Peggy started peddling for all she was worth. She was in Queen's Road traffic before she noticed that Mr. Bellows was walking down the driveway toward her. She didn't look back. Whatever he was trying to say would have to wait for another time.

Because the roads were wet, puddles had formed everywhere. Cars splashed her several times. That's why she'd taken to wearing the unattractive rain pants. She had to carry dry shoes with her, but at least her pants would stay dry.

Getting into the medical examiner's office was much easier this time. She showed the officers her ID and passed through the security checkpoint in less than two minutes. It took longer to find Mai and convince her to check the note Peggy had received.

"You think someone is trying to harm you?" Mai asked. "You should take it to the police."

"I'm not sure what's going on," Peggy said. "If you could check it for fingerprints, I'd appreciate it."

Mai looked up at her. "How much?"

"How much what?"

"How much would you appreciate it?"

Peggy was a little confused by the question. "If you and Paul need money—"

"Not money. I was thinking about acorn squash for dinner on Sunday."

"Is that all?" Peggy laughed. "Of course."

"Plenty of brown sugar." Mai took the note from her with gloved hands. "No skimping. I've had this raging sweet tooth for a few weeks. Maybe we can have candied yams with it. And ham with pineapple and brown sugar on it too."

Peggy had never known of Mai to be so intense about food. She agreed to the dinner and watched curiously as Mai walked away with the note.

There was an email from Al. The investigation into the girlfriend who worked at the florist hadn't produced anything. He asked how her work was going. She answered that she was looking over all the information again this morning.

Rain and storms came back across the city as Peggy spent hours poring over the information from the files. There didn't appear to be any connection to the two men—except the way they had died. They lived similar lives but nothing close enough that could be considered a clue to what had happened to them.

And there was the thing about their names. Every time she saw their names, it bothered her again. John Lee. John Leigh.

She started to call Al and ask him about it. She put the phone down. They already knew the men's names and didn't think anything of it.

She had lunch with Steve. He'd come to get her during the worst part of the storm. They'd gone to check in at The Potting Shed and had lunch from the Kozy Kettle.

Peggy knew she'd promised not to share any of the official information about the investigation outside of the medical examiner's office. She felt like her family was different. After all, she was only a consultant. She hoped in talking about the case she might gain some insight.

Over tea and croissant sandwiches, Peggy explained everything to Selena, Sam and Steve.

Steve told them all about the note that had been left at the house. "It may not have anything to do with this case, but Peggy has been talking to Nightflyer again. The lock was broken on the door. I think he may be involved."

"I thought he went into hiding because things got too hot for him," Selena said.

"He didn't mention that again," Peggy explained. "I think he does know something about the murders."

"You think he left the note in your door?" Sam asked.

"No. Not really." Peggy poured herself more peach tea. "I don't agree with Steve. It's not really Nightflyer's MO to leave notes on my door. And he'd never break in that way!"

Sam laughed. "MO? There she is—all into cop speak. Sorry, Steve. You'll be seeing a lot less of her."

"So will we," Selena mourned.

"This is it for Peggy," Steve said. "She's not going to

keep doing this."

Peggy arched a questioning brow in his direction. "I don't remember that conversation."

Selena and Sam exchanged glances.

"I have something to straighten up in the storage area," Sam said.

"Yeah. And I'm going to help him." Selena dusted croissant crumbs from her Potting Shed T-shirt. "Or something."

When the two of them had left the shop area, Peggy sighed. "I hope we're not going to fight over this. I have specific knowledge that can be used to help the police."

"You already use that knowledge at the university."

"I want to help, Steve. I'm not good at backing away from challenges."

He frowned. "This is dangerous work. People get hurt and killed every day working for the police. I don't want that to happen to you."

"People get hurt and killed every day going back and forth from the airport. That's not a reasonable argument. Look at *you*. You got hurt at a veterinarian's conference. That should tell you something."

He studied her freckled face and stubborn green eyes. "I'm not going to talk you out of this, am I?"

"Probably not. At least not with that lame argument."

"Lame, huh?"

"Totally." She drank the last of her tea. "I have to get

back. Do you have plans for this afternoon?"

"No. I cleared my schedule to get over my conference. Was there something you had in mind?"

"Dinner. Maybe around six?"

"Sounds good." He stood up and held her in his arms for a few minutes. "Please be careful. Call me if anything doesn't seem right."

She smiled at him. "You'll come and shoot them with a tranquilizer?"

"Yes. Or whatever else it takes." He kissed her.

"Oh God!" Selena covered her eyes when she walked into the shop. "You know this is like seeing my mom and dad making out, right? I'll be scarred for life."

Peggy laughed at her. "You should've knocked first. Something worse could've been going on."

The bell at the door jingled as a customer came in, shaking the rain from her umbrella. Selena grimaced. "She might have seen you two. You should go home if you're going to do that kind of thing."

Sam had told Peggy that business had been brisk that morning, despite the rain. They'd sold twenty bags of mulch. That was a good sign. She went back to work feeling happier. She enjoyed working with the police, but The Potting Shed was even more important.

She'd kissed Steve goodbye in the parking lot of the medical examiner's office. Paul was waiting under the overhang from the roof. The look on his face didn't bode well for their coming conversation.

"Want me to referee?" Steve asked. "I know Paul feels

the same way I do, except stronger."

"No. I can handle it. I'll see you tonight. If you aren't busy and it's still raining, will you come and get me?"

"I can buy you a car," he offered. "You don't have to ride your bicycle."

"I like my bicycle. A car ride now and then is fine. I'll see you later."

Peggy had assured Steve that she could deal with whatever Paul had to say. When she saw his sweet face—and all that anxiety written there—she wasn't so sure. Being someone's mother was very different than being someone's wife.

"Hello," she greeted him first. "It's good to see you. Having lunch with Mai?"

"I was. I got a call. Al wants me to bring you to Dilworth. There's been another murder."

"Oh." She hadn't been prepared for that.

They got into the police car together. Paul was tight-lipped as he started the car and pulled out into traffic.

"I know you aren't happy about me doing this," Peggy ventured.

"Not happy doesn't really express it." He glanced at her as they stopped for a red light. "I'm sure Steve isn't happy either."

"No. But he understands that he's going to have to live with it."

"Good for him. I don't get it, Mom. You're an intelligent, remarkable woman. People in the academic community worship you. You have a thriving business. Why do you need to mess around with this too?"

"As I told Steve, I have a talent. It's very specific. I'm surprised you don't understand. I can help stop whoever is doing this from killing again."

"Can you stop him from killing you if he finds out you're part of this?"

The light changed and Paul pulled forward. Though Peggy had this conversation with Steve, she didn't have an answer from a mother to a concerned child. She knew he wanted to protect her. She loved him for it, but she couldn't live her life being protected from anything that might hurt her.

They arrived at the crime scene in the Dilworth area of Charlotte, also close to Peggy's home and the other murder scene, without coming to an understanding on the matter.

The heavy rain and storms had knocked down yet another old oak tree. Slowly but surely, these giants that had made Charlotte green for a hundred years, were being lost. Too many building projects had uprooted them or damaged their root systems. Too much smog and not enough rain during the hot, dry summers were taking their toll.

Paul jumped out of the car as soon as he'd stopped. Peggy wished she could find the right words to reassure him, even though they might not be true. How could she guarantee that nothing would ever happen to her?

At the same time, hadn't that been the biggest reason she hadn't wanted him to become a police officer? She didn't want to lose him as she'd lost John.

It was a problem for them both.

Al met her before she could get close to the scene. She saw a form covered by a tarp that was protecting it from the suddenly heavy downfall.

"I wanted to hit you with this before you find out for yourself," he said as he drew her into the shelter of his big, black umbrella.

She didn't like the concerned look on his face. "What is it?"

"The victim's name. It's Paul Lee."

*Foxglove – Digitalis - Prized for their tall stalks of beautifully colored, bell-shaped flowers. Native to Europe. Plants are the original source for the heart drug, digitalis. When planted with root vegetables, they will stimulate the growth of the crop. Dried, this plant is harmless. Fresh stalks can be deadly. Digitoxin is the poison. Should not be planted in a garden where children and pets play.*

# Chapter Six

Peggy had to sit in the police car for a few minutes. The rain slammed into the roof and across the windshield. The old oaks moved with the wind, as much as they could. Yellow and red leaves plummeted to the street with the force of the rain.

"I'm sorry," Al said. "I knew it would have an effect on you. I didn't realize how much. It's not really Paul under there, you know. Not your Paul anyway. He's right out there." He pointed to the group of policemen taking shelter from the rain under the eaves of an old building.

"I know that isn't Paul," Peggy replied. "I'm not upset about that part of it. I think there's more to this than meets the eye."

She told him again about both previous victims being named John—this time including the fact that their middle names were also Lee. She also told him about the note she'd found in her front door.

"Mai is looking it over for me. I really think this somehow involves me and my family. Does that sound crazy?" she asked.

Al considered it. "Not when you put it that way. Especially since we have a new victim with your son's name. Was the note what made the alarm go off yesterday?"

"No. I don't think so." Peggy bit her lip. "The front door was locked when I checked it after the alarm went off. It's almost like someone worked around the alarm system and put the note there later. If that's even possible."

"There haven't been any threats against you, have there?" he questioned.

"No. I don't understand it. It feels like the killer is baiting me, daring me to find him. I don't think it's an accident that these murders have happened close to my house and the victims were killed with plant poison."

"I'm beginning to agree with you."

A news van pulled up next to them. Two reporters with a video camera scrambled out into the rain. They headed for the crime scene. Officers stepped out of the makeshift shelter to keep them away from the body under the tarp.

"What was the flower this time?"

Al took out his cell phone. "I don't know what it is. I took a picture of it for you."

Peggy looked at the wilted pink flower on the dead man's chest. "Cyclamen. Very poisonous. I suppose the delivery of the poison was the same?"

"Yes, as far as I can tell. We're still waiting on the ME."

The black van marked Medical Examiner pulled up behind the news truck. A young man Peggy recognized from the office got out with his jacket over his head. He came back after an officer pointed to the news van. It was obvious from the sign language that the reporters were going to have to move.

Peggy saw Dorothy sitting in the passenger side of the black van. Dorothy had a puzzled look on her face, as though she was trying to figure out how Peggy had arrived before her.

The news van pulled out to allow the medical examiner access to the crime scene, but afterward, the driver pulled right back into the alley between buildings. The reporters weren't backing down from their story.

As the rain slacked off, Peggy and Al got out of his car. Dorothy and her driver met them.

"I see the news traveled quickly on this," Dorothy remarked with a less than pleasant look at Al. "Lieutenant McDonald—my office is priority on homicides. Everyone else comes after me."

Al didn't try to explain why he'd called Peggy. He nodded and walked down with Dorothy to the victim. Two of the four police officers kept the reporters from following them. They couldn't stop their camera lenses from filming the scene.

"Are you okay?" Paul asked Peggy.

"I'm fine." She glanced up at him. He was soaked. She

bit her tongue to keep herself from telling him that he needed to dry off and change clothes. "How about you?"

He shrugged. "I looked it up once when I was in high school. There were one hundred and eighty five men named Paul Lee living in Charlotte. I'm sure that number has grown since then."

"There maybe more to it than that," she said.

Dorothy turned around and called her name. Telling Paul the whole story would have to wait.

The young man from the medical examiner's office that Peggy had recognized put down a mat on the wet concrete for Peggy to kneel. It was right next to the one he'd put down for Dorothy. It seemed to be his job doing whatever she needed him to do.

"Looks like another poisoning," Dorothy commented when Peggy was beside her. She moved the victim's head so that the right side of his neck was exposed. "Same place to inject the toxin. Get pictures of this, Morgan. Also get the flowers."

"Cyclamen," Peggy added.

Dorothy looked at her. "Why were you here before me?"

"It's a long story."

"Give me the Cliff's Notes."

Peggy explained briefly about the man's name and the other aspects of the case that were beginning to make sense.

"So the first two victims may have been stand-ins for your already deceased husband and this one is for your still living son. Is that the theory?"

"I can only speak for myself," Peggy said. "It's beginning to look that way to me."

"There's a random kind of logic in that, I suppose." Dorothy nodded at Al who was speaking to Detectives Dan Rodriguez, Tanner Edwards, and Molly Bryson who'd just arrived at the scene. "You and Lieutenant McDonald go back a'ways, I take it?"

"He was my husband's partner. They went to college and the police academy together."

"I see."

Peggy looked carefully at the victim. This man was younger—probably in his late twenties or early thirties. His coloring was the same as Paul's, except that his eyes were blue, not green.

She watched as Morgan bagged the cyclamen flowers, taking them carefully from the dead man's fingers. She noticed the digits were still pliable. The man probably hadn't been dead very long. She'd know after she read Dorothy's report.

"What do you think?" Dorothy asked her. "Do you see anything unusual?"

"It looks very similar to the man in the park," Peggy told her. "And he's disturbingly like my son."

"If you are being targeted in some way, we have to assume that the person doing this knows you well. He knows where you live. He knows about your family. He's sending you a message."

"I think he's daring me to catch him."

Dorothy nodded, her eyes still on the victim. It had started raining again. Morgan held a large umbrella over her. "What are you going to do?"

"I'm going to keep working. He's not killing my family, but he's destroying other people's lives. We have to catch him."

"I was hoping you'd say that." Dorothy smiled at her. "Would you like to ride back with us to the office?"

"Yes. Thanks."

Al thought this was a bad idea when she told him. "Peggy, maybe you should consider going home until we figure out what's happening. I'm thinking about telling Paul he should do the same."

"The killer could've made Paul his victim," Peggy reminded him. "He's choosing effigies instead. I don't think either one of us is in any immediate danger."

"You're as stubborn as a mule, you know that?" Al shook his head. "All right. Do it your way. You always do. Let me know if you come up with anything."

"Thanks. I'll talk to you later."

Peggy called Steve when she was in the van heading back to the office. She didn't want him to hear the news and not understand what had happened. Sam called her because Selena had already seen the incident on the Internet. Peggy assured him that everything was all right.

When Peggy and Dorothy got back to the medical examiner's office, Mai greeted them at the door. Her pretty face was set in a worried frown. She grabbed Peggy's arm and drew her away from her boss.

"You didn't tell me this could involve Paul," Mai accused her.

"I didn't know until today." Peggy was getting concerned about Mai's irrational behavior and pale face. She didn't look well.

"Paul called me and told me everything. I can't believe you'd endanger his life this way."

Peggy wasn't sure what to say to that accusation. She wanted to hug Mai but that seemed out of place for what was happening between them.

"Anyway," Mai continued. "I checked your note for fingerprints. There were none, except for yours. There was a dog hair on it. It belonged to a Great Dane so I think that must be Shakespeare."

Dorothy approached them. "Anything I should know?"

Mai glared at her. "No." She walked away without another word.

"I don't know what to say about her," Dorothy confided to Peggy. "She's brilliant. I would hate to lose her."

Peggy watched her go back to her office. She knew a warning when she heard one. She wasn't sure how to convey that message to Mai when she had become the enemy as well.

With a sigh, she went to her workstation.

She looked at the note again. Clearly, this had been written by the killer. He was taunting her. She wished she could get in touch with Nightflyer. He'd probably have some ideas on how to end this. She seemed to be fresh out of that commodity.

Peggy went back over all the notes and histories of the men who had died. There wasn't much compiled on the latest victim, as yet.

She closed her eyes. It sent a shaft of fear through her spine when she saw that name again. The killer was close to her. It could've been Paul, her Paul, who'd been lying there dead.

She made some phone calls to people she knew in the area who might know botanists besides herself who were involved in creating toxins. No one had heard of anyone working locally in that field. They promised to keep her updated if there was any news.

Peggy and Mai went back over all the victims' clothing to search for any leads that might have been missed earlier.

"The killer was very thorough," Mai said. "I'm betting on someone with medical knowledge as well as an understanding of forensics. Besides being a psychopath, of course."

"A psychopath who wants to play games with me," Peggy added.

"True. I tried to talk Paul into taking time off until this is over." Mai sat down wearily at a table in the examiner's room. "He won't. I don't know what it is with your family. Isn't anyone afraid of dying?"

"I think everyone is afraid of dying, to one degree or another," Peggy said. "Why do you say that?"

"Maybe it's just stubbornness then. You're still working. Paul won't go home. He told me his father could've stayed home the night he was killed. He could've let someone else handle it. He didn't. Obviously a family trait."

"You're probably right about that." Peggy smiled. "Mai, I don't know how else to ask this question—are you well? You look so pale. And you don't seem yourself."

"It's Dr. Beck and the whole thing with being passed over," Mai answered. "I can't shake it. I'm angry and I'm not sleeping or eating right. All I want to do is eat jelly donuts. I think I'm obsessed with them."

"Everyone handles stress differently." Peggy carefully scrutinized her face. "Maybe you should consider going to the doctor. There might be something else that's causing more stress than you realize over Dr. Beck's hiring."

"Thanks but I'm going to hang tough like the rest of the Lee family. I'll keep eating jelly donuts until I feel better."

"Well, there doesn't appear to be anything else I can do here for now and I have a lecture to give in about an hour. I'll be back after that."

Mai unexpectedly stood up and hugged her. Peggy couldn't remember another time that she had done so. "Be careful," Mai said. "Don't take any unnecessary chances."

"I won't. Please reconsider what I said about that doctor visit. I'll see you later."

Peggy went to her workstation, took off her white lab coat and picked up her pocketbook. Steve had texted her that he'd had a call from a farmer friend of his outside the county. One of the farmer's cows was having a hard time with delivering a calf. Steve told her to expect him to be gone most of the day.

She checked in with Dorothy before she left. "I wish I had something useful to report. It's got me flummoxed for now."

"Sometimes it helps to get away from it for a while. Clears the brain," Dorothy replied. "No matter how much we want to make progress in this case, we can't until the evidence comes together."

"I don't know if giving a lecture to my first year botany students will clear my brain or wipe it." Peggy grinned. "Sometimes when I talk to them, I can feel brain cells dying."

Dorothy laughed. "It wouldn't be my first choice for de-stressing either. I close my eyes, put on my headphones, and zone out to Bach when I get stumped."

"Sounds like a good idea."

"This case has everyone baffled right now," Dorothy confided. "They might decide to call in the FBI. Whoever the killer is, he seems to know what he's doing. Now with the media following every move and coming up with some ideas of their own, there's no telling where this will end."

"I hope it ends soon," Peggy said. "I don't like thinking that someone else might die for this person to get my attention."

Dorothy agreed and the two of them parted company.

Peggy planned to grab lunch on her way to Queen's University. There was a very good yogurt shop close to the campus.

Outside, the weather had cleared somewhat. The heavy rain had stopped, leaving mist and a watery sunshine. Cooler breezes blew threw the trees.

Her bicycle was wet but it dried quickly with a paper towel. She was taking off the lock when a police car pulled up to the front of the office beside her.

"Professor Lee." Detective Tanner Edwards leaned out of the window. "Can I give you a lift somewhere? Lieutenant McDonald sent me over when he heard you were leaving."

"Is he spying on me?"

"No, ma'am. Keeping tabs. He's worried about you. Dr. Beck told him you were on your way to Queen's. It's my job to take you there."

"That's silly." She took the bike from the stall.

"Maybe," Tanner agreed as he got out of the police car and opened the trunk. "He wants to make sure you're safe. That's my job today. Please don't make me look bad. I only passed the detective's exam right before these murders started. I don't need any black marks on my record."

"I guess if that's what you're supposed to do." Peggy shrugged. "Have you had lunch yet?"

Tanner told her he hadn't eaten yet. She explained her plan to eat at the yogurt shop. He was happy to oblige.

"I feel terrible taking you away from the investigation." The yogurt shop was deserted when they arrived. It only took a few minutes before both of them were eating strawberry yogurt with protein powder. "You shouldn't have to babysit me."

"You're at the center of all this. Maybe the killer will change his tactics and come after you. Taking down a serial killer would look good on my record."

He explained to Peggy that Molly and Dan were looking up stores and manufacturers that could have the equipment the killer would need to create the poisons he was using.

"Those things are available on the Internet too," she reminded him. "It probably won't be enough to look around Charlotte. The Internet is more anonymous too. That's what I'd do if I were trying to avoid being caught."

He nodded. "The Internet has definitely changed things. I'll be sure to suggest that to Lieutenant McDonald. Thanks."

Peggy looked up—directly into a pair of hostile eyes in an unhappy face.

"Excuse me a moment, Tanner. I see someone I know."

"Not the killer, right?" He grinned and looked around the yogurt shop.

"No. Just someone annoying."

She walked right up to Mr. Bellows who was seated at one of the white and red tables. "Are you looking for me?"

"Not exactly. This is a public place. I didn't know you'd be here."

"I teach at Queen's," she explained. His popping up at strange times was beginning to unnerve her. Maybe it was because of the killer. Maybe it was something more.

"And I'm here for a lecture." He took out a piece of paper and showed her. "The ABCs of Botanical Poison. Are you giving that lecture?"

***Goldenseal – Hydrastis** – Used popularly as a healing herb in teas for generations. Diminishing stands grown in the wild due to demand and over collection. Identified by dark yellow root. Contains alkaloids which can be poisonous in large quantities.*

# Chapter Seven

Peggy's name was clearly listed on the free lecture. She'd done this particular subject so many times, she thought she could do it in her sleep. It was why she'd almost forgotten the lecture in the first place. She hadn't prepared for this topic in years. She could speak on it almost without thought.

The title—ABCs of Botanical Poisons—hit her suddenly. Wasn't that exactly what was going on?

This was the format the killer was using. Her mind raced with the knowledge. The plants in the lecture were different but the idea was the same.

She had no doubt the killer was mocking her. He'd probably heard the lecture before.

Peggy stared at Mr. Bellows. Surely it wasn't him.

Yes, he was irritating and seemed to want to get rid of her. That was quite a leap from pretending to kill members of her family.

On the other hand, he was at the park and it would've been easy for him to put the note into her front door after setting off the alarm.

She realized she knew nothing about Mr. Bellows besides him being her neighbor. He liked peace and quiet. He probably had some money since he'd offered to buy her house and garden shop to try and convince her to move away.

That didn't make him a killer, she reminded herself.

"I think you know the answer to that question," she finally replied. "I didn't realize you were interested in botany."

"Oh yes. I have a degree in botany from UCLA. I have studied poisonous plants for many years. I didn't know you were interested in the same field."

All right. That might change things. That information, added to the other facts, could make him a killer.

Peggy glanced back at Tanner who was still eating his strawberry-protein added yogurt. Should she say something to him? Was this the career-enhancing event he was looking for—his opportunity to save her life and nab a killer?

She needed more evidence. It might be risky, but if Al arrested Mr. Bellows too soon, he wouldn't be able to make his case.

"Well, I hope you enjoy the lecture," Peggy said, forcing herself to smile.

"I'm sure I will."

A possible way of catching him occurred to her. "Afterward, you should stop by my house. I'd love to show you my experiments. We could have tea and talk about our careers."

His expression brightened. "I would enjoy that very much, Mrs. Lee. Thank you."

To make her case clearer, she added, "It's actually Dr. Lee. I would enjoy that as well."

He looked even more pleased. "Dr. Lee it is then. And I am Dr. Walter Bellows."

Peggy left him there. She knew scientists almost too well. There was nothing they liked better than to talk about themselves and their careers.

She was glad now that Tanner had been assigned to protect her. Al was much smarter about these things than she was. She might need his help at the house if Dr. Bellows decided to make his move.

On the way across the rain-drenched campus, Peggy explained to Tanner about her next door neighbor.

Tanner took it all in. "It might be better not to try this, Professor. I'm supposed to keep you safe, not further endanger your life."

"I realize that. Maybe you could call for backup but keep them at a distance until we need them. I believe I'm on to something here. At least I'd like to think so."

"I know what you mean. I'm tired of this man making

fools of all of us too. Let's be smart and careful about taking him to your house. I'll call for backup in case we need it. Get information from him but don't provoke him. Okay?"

She agreed. "I have to run up to my office for my laptop if I want to use my visual aids. You can't have a lecture without pictures or everyone falls asleep."

He laughed. "I never found your lectures boring. It amazed me the stuff people don't know about plants. We take them for granted, don't we? They can kill or heal. I've been fascinated by them since I took your class."

"Thank you, Tanner. I'm glad that I helped inspire your love of plants. Do you garden at home?"

"No. Not really. I don't have a big yard like yours. I play around with some indoor plants. I wish I had a farm to work with. That would be great."

"Maybe someday you will."

He accompanied her to her office for her laptop. Peggy enjoyed talking to a kindred spirit even if they'd chosen different paths in life. There wasn't much use for plant lore in police work.

"I remember now that you were an exceptional student," she told him as she packed up her laptop. "I could tell you stayed awake through my lectures."

"My parents thought I was crazy taking botany. I told them one day it would make a difference, even though I always wanted to be a cop."

Peggy and Tanner went into the lecture hall together. He set up her laptop so that the information from her program would be on the big screen behind her.

A large crowd had already gathered. Free lectures were popular for both students and interested visitors from the community. Poison plants were something people never seemed to get enough of.

She'd sometimes wondered if her lectures on this subject were inspiring people to take another look at poison plants or using them for the wrong purposes.

Seeing Dr. Bellows face in the crowd made that all the more apparent. Of course, he probably already had all the expertise he'd needed to kill those three people. He'd used her as a focus for his crimes, but she would be wrong to believe she'd provoked him.

The lights went dark and her first slide came up on the screen.

"Good afternoon. I'm Dr. Margaret Lee. I teach botany here at Queen's. My specialty field is botanical poisons. Today I'll be showing you some familiar plants, some of which are deadly poisonous. I'll be taking questions at the end of the lecture. Please bear in mind that this information is to acquaint yourselves with plants that you might not want to have around children or pets. It is not intended for any other purpose. Thank you for coming."

The first plant was anemone. The bulb was deadly poison. "Anemone is a common bulb. You see plenty of the white flowers here in the spring. There are many bulbs that are poisonous including hyacinth and daffodil. Tulips aren't poisonous, and in fact, the Dutch survived a famine many years ago by eating tulip bulbs."

The next plant was the bleeding heart. "This is another common plant. I'm sure many of you recognize the delicate, heart-shaped flowers. They are a gardener's delight."

She saw heads nodding in the audience. The light from the screen illuminated the people closest to her.

"The leaves and roots of this plant have been known to be fatal to animals and humans when eaten in large quantities. How much is that? It all depends on the size of the animal or person who eats it. It would take far less to poison a small child or animal than one with more weight."

The next plant was chrysanthemum. "Gardeners call these mums for short but this is their correct name. They were brought here from Asia where they are considered the queen of flowering plants."

She pointed to the plant on the screen. "The stalks and leaves are poisonous. They are a frequent problem for those who work in the floral industry as they cause contact dermatitis. They are also poisonous to ingest, although probably not deadly. Again, the amount would determine that. The Chinese drink a tea made from the flowers."

There were some whispers that rippled through the group in the audience. Some people were scribbling down the information. She could always tell when people were engaged by what she was saying.

Peggy made it through the entire alphabet, pointing out various types of poisons and the plants that contained them.

"And I conclude with Z." She smiled at her audience. "I also admit to cheating a little when it comes to this last plant—zantedeschia aethiopica. It was the only way I could find a plant that started with Z."

Her audience laughed, as they always did.

"Really, this is another plant you'll recognize, calla lily. They're very beautiful and very deadly. Their beauty inspires people to get careless with them, placing them in vases on the dining room table and even using them to adorn plates of food as a garnish. You would be better off taking photos from a distance, believe me."

When her lecture was over, there was spontaneous applause, followed by dozens of questions. Most of these questions never bothered her.

It was the inevitable question—how to use plants to kill people—that sometimes worried her.

Normally, she tried not to let it bother her. She'd never known anyone from a lecture or class she'd given that had tried to kill a person with a poisonous plant.

That day, she was a little more on edge.

A man came up and identified himself as a mystery writer and told her he was interested in learning about how the poisons worked. "How quickly does someone die from this type of poison? How much does it take?"

It wasn't that she was worried that he might be the killer. Knowing this basic information had killed three people made her more sensitive to the subject.

"I'm afraid I can't discuss specifics," she told the man. "Some things should be learned after years of study. Perhaps you should consider that before you kill someone in a book with a poisonous plant!"

Tanner was putting away her laptop. He smiled at her when the man frowned and left the lecture hall. "You never used to say things like that to people who asked those questions."

"It seems different now," she confessed.

"Don't let the killer get you down, Professor. I'm sure

you're his equal on this subject. He's only trying to play mind games with you. Are you gonna let him beat you?"

For now, at least, she admitted that the killer was showing her an ugly way of looking at her profession. She didn't want to talk about poison plants or discuss how they worked. She wanted to go home with Dr. Bellows and find out if he could be the killer. She wanted all of it to end.

"That was a very interesting lecture, Dr. Lee." Walter Bellows was at the end of the group of excited audience members who'd wanted to speak to Peggy. "I knew all of that already, but you did it with such finesse. Are you still game to show me your experiments?"

"I am if you are." Peggy thought this would be the best way to expose him as the killer. As soon as she saw what he was working on, she'd be able to tell Tanner to arrest him. "Let's start with your experiments."

He raised one dark brow in question. "No, Madame. We should begin with your work."

Peggy wasn't sure what to say about that. She wanted to get this over with. Taking him to her house wasn't going to do that.

On the other hand, what were a few more minutes? She could walk him through the basement then they could go to his house. Tanner would be there—with police backup somewhere behind them. What could it hurt?

*Horsenettle – Nightshade* - *The genus of horsenettle includes black nightshade and potatoes. Grows wild along roadsides and in yards. Small purple flowers on plant that resemble flowers on potatoes. Glycoalkaloid poison, solanine. Berries are more toxic than leaves. Poison content higher in fall. Ingestion can be followed by death in a few days. Lab detection: not routinely available.*

# Chapter Eight

Queen's University was only a few minutes from Peggy's home. She and Tanner drove back together. He helped her take her bicycle out of the trunk.

She looked around her quiet yard where a few red and yellow mums were still blooming. Squirrels and birds played along the moss-lined pathways between the oak trees and the large azalea bushes.

"The police backup is very well hidden," she whispered to Tanner.

He glanced over his shoulder. "Not to worry. They're out there. They train us to be able to blend in."

Peggy knew that was true—to a certain extent. Being the wife of a police detective made her acutely aware of such things. She could usually pick out unmarked cars in traffic. She'd expected to see some sign of Tanner's backup in her yard or the yard next door.

She could hear Shakespeare barking. That was a good sign. She went to the kitchen door, turned off the alarm, and went inside. He was very happy to see her. She patted his head and gave him a treat.

"I'm going to have to put you outside. I don't want you unsettling Dr. Bellows before he has a chance to confess."

That was fine with Shakespeare. He lived to play outside on fine autumn days.

"Is it okay to come in now?" Tanner looked inside the kitchen door. "That's a big dog you've got there, Professor."

"I know. There are many times I wished I'd found a nice cat to rescue instead of Shakespeare." She smiled to lighten her words. "But he's mine now and I love him. I wouldn't have it any other way."

"Dr. Bellows isn't here yet. Maybe we should take a look in the basement and make sure we're set up in case he has something else in mind besides looking at your plants."

"Good idea, Tanner. It's a little dark and maze-like down there. It would probably be good for you to have the lay of the land, so to speak, before he gets here."

Peggy took him into the basement. She switched on all the lights available. Even with those, it was still dark. On sunny days, she got a lot of natural light through the French doors going into the backyard. Not today.

"Wow!" Tanner looked around at her work. "You really have a lot going on down here, Professor. I can't believe Dr. Bellows has as much."

"Thanks. And you know, I've been thinking all afternoon about you, Tanner." She switched on the lamp in her small office area that was in the original spot for a washer and dryer. "I think I might have your last essay from my class. It was so good that I kept it all these years. I'd forgotten until now."

"Really?" He looked surprised, even embarrassed. "I did okay in your class. I wouldn't call my work exceptional."

Peggy rummaged through her file cabinet and located the file she'd kept with some of her students' work. At the time, he'd seemed to be very talented and she'd thought he would advance in the field.

"I was really surprised when you chose to become a police officer." She pulled out the essay and looked at it. "I wouldn't even have known except John was still alive when you graduated from the police academy. We always attended those graduations."

As she looked at the essay—it was handwritten—not done on a computer as essays were today—she realized that she recognized the handwriting. It was the same as the handwriting on the note that had been left in her door.

Her heart skipped a beat. For a moment, it was hard to breathe.

Dr. Bellows was the wrong person.

She was in her basement, alone, with a killer.

That had been why she hadn't seen any backup outside. There was none. Tanner obviously had something planned for her. Maybe for Dr. Bellows too.

"Professor?" Tanner looked around the corner into her office area. "You were saying?"

Peggy collected herself. She had to think what to do. She had to play along with Tanner until she could get help. She couldn't let him know what she had seen.

"I was saying that you were a very good student." She smiled at him and handed him his essay. "I was so sure you'd go on to become a great botanist."

He shrugged as he looked at the essay. "I really had bad handwriting back then, didn't I?"

"I think that's why they invented word processing," she said. "Everyone has bad handwriting. Take it from someone who has graded thousands of papers in her lifetime."

"I guess."

"What made you become a police officer, Tanner?"

She had to keep him talking.

"I wanted more action, I guess. I still enjoy working with plants. You'd be surprised by what I've learned since I graduated from Queen's."

*I'm sure I would.* "Well, you can see what it looks like down here. I wonder what's keeping Dr. Bellows? Maybe I'll go upstairs and make some tea."

If she could get upstairs without him getting suspicious, she could excuse herself, go to the bathroom, and use her cell phone. She could call Al or Paul and help would be there quickly. She had to keep Tanner calm.

She had to keep herself calm too.

"You know, don't you?" Tanner asked in the same tone of voice he always used.

"Know what?" she asked, heart pounding in her chest.

"You saw this." He held out the essay. "You recognized my handwriting, didn't you? I guess it hasn't gotten any better since I took your classes."

"I'm not sure what you're talking about. What's wrong?"

He frowned and balled up the essay, shoving it into his jacket pocket. "I didn't want this to be over so soon. I've enjoyed our game, Professor."

The door upstairs opened. Dr. Bellows called down to them. "Hello? Dr. Lee? Are you down there?"

"Perfect timing." Tanner smiled and pulled a syringe from his pocket. He quickly grabbed Peggy and held her against him with his hand over her mouth. "I was going to use this on him. Believe me, I don't want to hurt you. I've always admired you. I guess this works just as well though. Everyone will think your new friend killed you and those other people."

Peggy went very still. It was something John had told her to do if she was ever in this kind of situation. At the time, it had seemed laughable to even talk about it. Why would she be in a life or death struggle?

She had to wait for the right moment.

She couldn't panic because she knew he was holding that syringe very near to her throat, even though she knew it was full of poison. She had to be ready to move quickly when the time was right.

Tanner was very strong. She could feel it in the way he easily held her in place. She wanted to scream and run for help. She had to fight her instincts.

Peggy closed her eyes and prayed for the strength to save herself. She couldn't die this way. Paul and Steve would be furious.

She heard Dr. Bellows' footsteps on the stairs. Was Tanner waiting until the other man was in the basement too?

She knew he was right—the police would blame her neighbor. Tanner would see to that. He might even kill Dr. Bellows and say he'd been trying to save her.

"Dr. Lee?" Dr. Bellows called out again as he cautiously came down the stairs. "Are you down here? Is this some game you're playing?"

Peggy realized she and Tanner were standing very close to the large pond filled with miniature cattails, a new strain of rice, and water lilies. It was deep, four feet, with rocks on the bottom, and ten feet wide. She'd had it put in years ago when she'd begun working with water plants.

She remembered John joking with her about it one sunny summer afternoon. He'd smiled at her and suggested they could swim naked in the pond. Peggy could still see his face as clearly in her mind at that moment as if it had happened hours ago.

As she remembered how much she'd loved his smile, she forced herself to do what John had told her—go completely limp.

"Professor?" Tanner whispered. "Did you faint on me? I thought you were tougher."

He moved, sliding his hand from her mouth, as he tried to peer into her face. His foot had moved one step closer to the edge of the pond.

With all her strength, Peggy brought her head up hard into his jaw. Surprise put him even more off balance. She used that opportunity to push him into the pond.

She didn't wait to see what came next. By the time she'd heard the splash, she was already opening the French doors. Shakespeare ran past her, back into the house. Peggy ignored him and ran into the backyard.

*You need a place to hide. You need to press speed dial and call Paul or Al.*

A thousand thoughts flew through her mind.

Shakespeare ran back out of the basement and started jumping at her, thinking this was a new type of game. He was always ready to play whatever Peggy wanted to play.

Peggy heard Tanner's shout of rage as she was trying to make it to a stand of red tip bushes near the end of her property line. They were thick and would make good cover.

The grass underfoot was wet from the rain, the ground muddy and slippery. Shakespeare jumping at her made her lose her balance.

Tanner was on her in an instant.

"You can't get away that easy." He ground the words out hoarsely as he tipped her head to the right. "You and I have unfinished business. Let's get this over with."

Shakespeare, thinking he had encountered another playmate, bounded against both of them. Tanner dropped the syringe and lost his hold on Peggy.

Peggy crawled away from him, trying to get to her feet, when a shot rang out in the backyard behind them.

"This isn't what I had in mind, Dr. Lee." Walter Bellows was holding a nine millimeter pistol, staring at her and Tanner. He'd followed them out of the basement. "I heard the splash in the pool. Are you in need of assistance?"

"Dr. Bellows," Peggy yelled. "This man is trying to kill me."

"Oh! Well, why didn't you say so, my dear? I always carry my weapon with me. Can't be too careful in the city. Hold still, you ruffian. My pistol is trained on your head and I'm quite a good shot with it. Cease and desist."

Peggy managed to press Al's number on speed dial. She scrambled to her feet, breathing hard, covered in mud.

Tanner had turned around to face Dr. Bellows. "Take it easy." His hands were in the air. "There's no reason to get crazy. Dr. Lee and I were having a disagreement. That's all."

Shakespeare was disappointed. No one was moving. He lunged back and forth between Peggy and Tanner. Finally, he gave up and ran back into the basement.

It wasn't more than a few minutes before Al arrived. He hadn't brought backup since he had no idea what was going on. The look on his dark face was comical when he took in the situation.

"Peggy, what the hell is going on?"

* * *

Long before Sunday dinner at Peggy's house, Tanner had confessed to poisoning the three men and trying to kill Peggy. He'd been smugly unrepentant—until the police had found his lab where he'd made the poison extracts.

He told Al that he'd wanted Peggy to start working with the police again so they could talk about poison plants. It was the best way to have the police put her back on staff. In the basement, he hadn't planned for what had happened. Tanner asked Al to tell Peggy that he was sorry.

Sunday dinner went on as planned. Peggy had invited Al and his wife, Mary, along with Sam and his sister, Hunter, and Selena. She'd also invited Walter Bellows. He'd saved her life after all. She wanted him to know that there were no hard feelings.

Dr. Bellows also apologized for trying so hard to get Peggy to move. "I'm sorry we got off on the wrong foot. I'm sure we'll be fine now."

Peggy made sure Steve and Paul knew that she would've ended up being involved in the investigation no matter what. Tanner had manipulated the situation so it would end up that way.

"I get what you're saying, Mom," Paul said as he cut the ham he'd made for his wife. It was dripping with brown sugar and pineapple. "I still think this was aggravated by your participation."

"In other words," Sam said, "he still thinks it's all your fault."

Peggy had already talked to Hunter about her car. They'd reached an agreement—Peggy was going to loan Hunter some money—Sam would never need to know.

"I think the important thing is that it all worked out,"

Steve said as he brought in the baked acorn squash from the kitchen. "If the case hadn't involved Peggy, Tanner could have gone on killing and never been caught."

"Amen to that!" Al raised his glass of iced tea.

"So, what else is new?" Mary asked with a broad grin.

Mai stood up abruptly. "Why not go ahead and say it? You all know the truth. I hope you have a good laugh while you're at it."

Peggy put her hand on Mai's shoulder. "Mai, what's wrong? What are you talking about?"

"I'm pregnant." Mai burst out crying and ran out of the room.

Paul stopped slicing the ham. "What? What did she just say?"

"You heard her, son." Al nodded in the direction Mai had fled. "Best go talk to her right away. Whatever you do, don't admit you didn't know. They hate that."

Peggy was surprised for an instant then put all of the data together. *Of course.* It was obvious. That's what had been going on. She smiled, excited about being a grandmother.

The front doorbell rang. "I'll get it. Will you take over the ham slicing duties, Steve?"

He agreed and she went to answer the door. Two men in dark suits were standing on her doorstep. They looked at her then looked past her into the foyer.

"Excuse us, ma'am. We're looking for Agent Newsome."

"Who? Do you mean Steve Newsome? Is this a veterinary emergency?"

The two men exchanged glances then looked back at her.

The taller man on the right took out a badge. "I'm Agent Tim Johnson with the FBI. This is Agent Pat Anders. We're new in Charlotte. We need to speak to Agent Steve Newsome about an operation. Is he around?"

"I'll take it from here, Peggy." Steve came up behind her.

Peggy moved back into the foyer. She listened to what the two agents told Steve. When they were gone, he shut the door and faced her.

"You're an FBI agent?"

He took a deep breath. "They didn't know not to come here."

"What are you saying?"

By this time, everyone except for Mai and Paul, were in the foyer.

"We need to talk about this, Peggy," Steve said. "I want you to know the truth."

# Part Two

# A Thyme to Die

*Sweet Potato*

*The sweet potato belongs to the family Convolvulaceae. Its tuberous roots are a vegetable. The young leaves are also eaten. The sweet potato is barely related to the white potato, Solanum tuberosum. They are known by other names around the world: camote, kamote, goguma, man thet, ubi jalar, ubi keledek, shakarkand, satsuma imo, batata or el boniato. The U.S. Dept. of Agriculture requires sweet potatoes to be labeled as such, instead of as 'yams', which many people call them. Yams are a different species.*

# Chapter One

Peggy Lee woke up and smacked her hand hard against the 'off' button on her alarm clock. It was early, barely five a.m. Her bedroom was still dark. She groaned as she rolled over, remembering as she did, why she was up.

She'd had a late night getting ready for the International Flower Show. She'd worked hard to have the show brought to Charlotte, being part of the process from the beginning. It was exciting, but it was also exhausting.

A large, wet tongue licked her face from chin to forehead. Before she could wake up enough to move away, a cold, wet nose with whiskers snuffled her cheek.

"Shakespeare! What are you doing on the bed?"

The one-hundred-forty-pound Great Dane thumped his tail hard. He was ready for a walk outside and breakfast.

"Where's Steve?" Peggy opened both her eyes. The only thing she could see on the pillow next to her was a large head with a black muzzle, a goofy grin, and floppy, unclipped ears. "I guess that means he's not here, right? If you're on the bed, there's not enough room for anyone else."

She threw back the sheet and comforter, awake now. It was just as well. If she was going to have time to shower, dress and check on her plants before she left for the flower show, she was going to have to get up.

Taking Shakespeare outside seemed to be the most important task at hand. He was racing around the bedroom like a dog tornado, as he always did when he needed to go out. That might be fine with a terrier, but with a Great Dane, it was a prelude to broken furniture and glass.

Peggy put on her slippers and robe and went downstairs, making sure Shakespeare went first so he didn't knock her down the wide, spiral stairs.

Before she'd reached the ground floor, she heard Steve's voice calling the dog. He was already outside with him before she could reach the kitchen door.

"I guess this is going to be that kind of day." She yawned and put some water in the kettle to boil. "Breakfast first, it seems."

Peggy usually had peach tea for breakfast. In this case, she opted for Earl Grey. There was no doubt in her mind that she needed the pick-me-up.

She glanced over at the old wood kitchen table and saw Steve's laptop on it. That was probably why he was up earlier than her. She sneaked a peek—there were no secret FBI files she could look at. *Rats!* She was curious about what he did.

Since Steve had accepted the FBI's director's job for the Charlotte, North Carolina area, he'd been keeping odd hours getting the office set up.

He'd told her he was a veterinarian when she'd first met him, which was true. It wasn't until recently that she'd found out that he was also an FBI agent who'd been sent to keep an eye on her after her first husband, John, a homicide detective with the Charlotte PD, was killed.

John and Steve had been working together on a case that might have caused John's death. Steve had been worried that someone might also try to kill her.

Peggy had thought her meeting with Steve was an accident. Now she knew he'd gone out of his way to be her friend. Later, he said, he'd fallen in love with her. By that time, she had loved him too.

He'd explained all of it, including the need for secrecy. She understood that he couldn't tell her the truth at the time. She trusted him.

She probably wouldn't have married another man in law enforcement after John's death, but Steve was exceptional. She had no regrets. It was hard, though, worrying about him, and her son, Paul, who'd decided to follow in her husband's footsteps and become a police officer.

It had also made her ask uncomfortable questions about John's death. Steve had told her that the investigation was still 'ongoing'. Peggy was determined to find out exactly what that meant.

Steve seemed the same since she'd found out about his real career. He was gone more, but had told her that would change when the transition was over. He'd be in Charlotte more often. The director's job was mostly a desk position, with agents reporting to him.

She toasted and buttered an English muffin. John had often spoken to her about his cases. Steve was secretive and didn't seem to like talking about what he did. She didn't like being shut out of that part of his life.

"Good morning." Steve removed Shakespeare's leash before the big dog could barrel through the rest of the house. He put down a bowl of food and stood back as Shakespeare raced toward it.

She smiled back at him. "It looks like you've been busy."

He kissed her, closed the laptop, and sat down. "Just going over some information."

"Always important to double check your facts."

It seemed as though their conversations were like this recently. Back and forth with no discernible information exchanged. They'd managed to have a long talk when Peggy had first found out that he wasn't just a veterinarian. Everything had seemed like it was out on the table. She wished he'd share as much now.

"So you have that flower show today, right?" he asked.

He kept trying. *Bless his heart.* Peggy stirred a little milk into her tea.

"That's right. And you?"

"Still going through the transition. I'm not sure how long it'll take. Maybe we can go away for a while when it's over."

"That would be nice." She chewed and swallowed a bite of her muffin. "So what exactly will you do when you've transitioned? I know agents answer to you. Will you be in the field at all?"

"I could be supervising in the field on some cases." He stood and poured another cup of coffee. "It shouldn't be dangerous, if that's what you're worried about."

"Just curious. I've never really known an FBI agent before. At least not that I *knew* of."

He put down his coffee cup and took her in his arms. "I think we know each other pretty well. I'm the same man you married."

"I guess I mean what they do, as part of their job."

Steve kissed her and smiled. "You're asking me for a detailed list of duties, right?"

"Something like that."

"We'll work on that," he promised. "I have to go."

"I like that blue suit on you with the lighter blue shirt." She smiled at him and picked up her tea. "I'm going upstairs to get dressed. I'll see you later."

He held her in his arms for another minute. "I love you, Peggy."

"I love you too, Steve. Think about that list."

He laughed. "I will."

Peggy didn't go upstairs to get dressed right away. Her projects in the basement needed her attention.

The basement sprawled the entire length and width of the turn-of-the-century house on Queen's Road in Charlotte. It was filled with her botanical experiments and plants she loved. She bred and modified plants for pleasure as well as for food and medicinal purposes.

Peggy had worked recently on projects to increase the rice yield without using any genetic modifications and had created a strain of wheat that grew faster and in poorer soil. Her work as a botanist had received many awards down through the years.

The basement wasn't quite big enough for everything she wanted to do. In the heart of the rapidly growing city, it opened into an acre garden that she cultivated by the season.

She wasn't much of a lawn person. Countless corporations had asked her to help them work on creating ornamental grass that only grew to an eighth of an inch tall, and even some that glowed in the dark. That type of work didn't interest her, though the money was good.

Peggy had created a large grassy area that was home to a new variety of tall grass that was edible. It contained all the essential vitamins a human needed and tasted a little like lemon. The only problem was that it couldn't withstand drought or cold temperatures. She was still working on that.

"Hello. Good morning." Dr. Walter Bellows, her next door neighbor, opened the sliding glass door that separated the garden from the basement. He was a short man with an ancient-looking tweed cap and matching jacket that he wore year round. Little tufts of his gray hair stuck out all over his head from under his cap. "What are we working on today?"

Bellows had been an annoying neighbor at first, but they'd slowly discovered that they had similar interests in plants. He was also a botanist. They'd become good friends.

"Not much. I'm on my way to the flower show. I wanted to check in on the sweet potatoes before I leave." She walked over to the huge basket where a new variety of sweet potatoes were growing. "I think these are going to be ready next week. The university will be surprised. They weren't expecting them until next month."

Walter stuck his fingers into the warm rich soil. "They're huge! I wouldn't have believed it except that I was here when you planted them. Imagine—sweet potatoes in two weeks!"

"We have to find ways to grow food faster if we want to keep on feeding everyone."

He nodded, his pale blue eyes, showing his fascination with the project. "If you need me to water them, or anything else, I'll be glad to."

"Are you sure you don't want to go to the flower show?"

"No, thank you! I'm not interested in daisies and roses. What you're doing here is amazing work, Peggy. You go on. Get dressed. I'll rummage around here for a while."

Peggy trusted Walter now. He knew what he was doing. She would rather have stayed in the basement all day with her projects, but she had to go to the convention center and make sure everything was set up.

"Thanks. I'll talk to you later."

She went back upstairs, past all the nooks and crannies she loved so much in the old house. Upkeep was expensive for the rambling dwelling filled with dozens of rooms. She paid her part to live there but the house would never belong to her. Someday her husband's nephew would take possession. Her son would never live here with his family.

The house was set in a trust that followed the family line. Her husband, John Lee, had brought her here as a young bride. Their son, Paul, was born and raised here but wouldn't inherit.

The Lee family wasn't happy that Peggy still lived there after John's death. They were especially unhappy after she'd remarried two years ago, but really, what was the use in the house sitting empty?

John's nephew was a journalist who was always in interesting parts of the world. He didn't have time for the place.

Peggy planned to stay there as long as she could, until she died and they carried her out, if that was possible. Steve had sold his house a few doors down and come to live with her after the wedding.

Shakespeare was asleep and snoring on the bed again when she got upstairs. She didn't disturb him. She took a shower and put on a wonderful forest green suit she'd found especially for the flower show. The color was perfect, shimmering with highlights when she was in the sun. The low-heeled sandals had been a little problem, but she'd finally had a pair dyed to match.

She'd wanted to look her best to step into her role as local chairperson for the International Flower Show. It had taken two years to convince the show's owners to come to Charlotte. Normally they set up in Atlanta, but a coalition of city and state had enticed the owners to take a chance.

Peggy was excited about the show. She never missed one. There were vendors and growers from around the world with exhibits that couldn't be found anywhere else.

Just watching all the setup it had taken for the event had been fascinating. There were houses and animals completely made out of flowers. Some growers had actually brought full-sized trees to create their exhibit. The exhibits were living art as growers found new ways to set their plants apart and entice buyers and investors.

Many of the vendors were dedicated to growing larger flowers, smaller trees, or hemp plants that could be spun into materials that would be used for clothing and other necessities. There were some, like her friend Dr. Aris Abutto from South Africa, who'd dedicated themselves to preserving and improving orchids.

Peggy had only met Aris in person for the first time since he'd arrived in Charlotte for the show. They'd only talked online before in the years they'd known each other. He was a delightful man.

In short, it was her world, housed in the Charlotte Convention Center for one week. It was a perfect week for her. She felt like a sponge soaking up all the new ideas from so many gardeners, biologists and botanists.

The taxi she'd taken from her house (she couldn't ride her bike as she normally would have in these circumstances) dropped her off at the front gate of the center.

"Hello, Peggy." The guard at the gate waved her through without looking at her pass. He'd seen it almost every day for a month. "Looks like you're gonna have fine weather for the opening day. Good luck to you."

"Thank you, Reggie. It's very exciting. I don't know if I've ever been so tired."

He laughed. "I know what you mean. Hey! I tried that salve you suggested for my dry skin. It's great stuff. Thanks."

The salve was a personal favorite of hers made from oatmeal and seeds from the cotton plant.

"Glad it helped! I'll see you later."

There were no vendors there that early. Peggy opened the doors to what amounted to a cave of botanical wonders. Everyone had worked so hard to bring the show to life. Despite the time, and sometimes ridiculous problems, she was thrilled to have been a part of it.

Her own garden shop, The Potting Shed, had a nice-sized exhibit. She'd gotten the space at a discount because of her participation. She was very proud of the work her partner, Sam Ollson, had done. It was comparable to even the biggest, most expensive exhibits in the show.

One thing was out of place, though, as she walked into the main area of the building. She could have sworn it wasn't there the day before.

The exhibit beside The Potting Shed was supposed to be an older-looking farmhouse with flowers and vegetables planted everywhere. There were chickens made of carnations and cows made of wood chips.

What there wasn't supposed to be was a large mound of black dirt in the center of the make-believe field. She shivered, thinking it almost looked like a grave.

*Just being fanciful after thinking about what Steve does for the FBI.*

Peggy walked through the area, mindful of her new shoes in the dirt and mulch. She walked right up to the side of the high mound. There was a cross, *or at least it looked like a cross,* fashioned out of dogwood branches at the head of it. The dirt was covered in pink thyme flowers and leaves.

Her heart pumped a little faster as she looked at it. Something was wrong. This shouldn't have been there. In the language of flowers, thyme was associated with the grave and with death. The plants were used on graves long ago as a memorial to the dead.

She hoped her sick feeling of dread was misplaced as she dialed 911 on her cell phone.

### *Thyme*

*Thymus vulgaris is native to Europe. The word comes from the Greek thymus, meaning courage. Known usage dates back to 3,000 BC. It was used as an antiseptic by the Sumerians and an ingredient in the Egyptian mummification process. Wearing a sprig of thyme in the hair was believed to be an attractant to men. It was the home of fairies and a potent snakebite remedy. Its association with the grave may have started in Egypt but it continues to this day when thyme is still thrown into a grave for protection and purification.*

# Chapter Two

The Charlotte police responded quickly. Within five minutes, officers in uniform were looking at the unusual mound of dirt with her. There was a discussion of whether or not someone should dig up the dirt to find out if anything was inside.

Peggy had tried calling the exhibit owner but there was no answer.

Her son, Paul, had been sent as part of the group of responding officers. Paul had his father's tall, lanky body and her green eyes. He wore his bright red hair short and spiky.

Peggy hadn't been happy when Paul had joined the police department after John had been killed. It had been hard for him and Peggy to get through those dark days. She hadn't wanted him to give up his dream of being an architect, and she suspected that Paul was looking for revenge. John's killer had never been found.

As the years had passed, Paul had proven to be dedicated to the job and serious about his task of upholding the laws of the city. He wasn't reckless, despite having her red hair and fiery temper. She'd relaxed, especially after his marriage to assistant medical examiner, Mai Sato. They had a pretty little house and Mai was pregnant with their first child. It seemed her initial fears had been unfounded.

Still there was that tightness in her chest when she knew he was on duty.

"What happened here?" Paul asked her. "Any idea if something might be in there? I guess it's not supposed to look that way."

She shuddered. "All I can tell you is that the Egyptians buried their dead with thyme. Maybe that doesn't mean anything—I hope it doesn't. Are they going to dig it up?"

"I'm not sure yet. We're waiting for whoever is going to take jurisdiction on this." He shrugged. "Could be the FBI. It is the *International* Flower Show."

She knew he was teasing her. Friends had joked about them working together since they'd learned of Steve taking the job in Charlotte. Peggy infrequently worked with the Charlotte PD on cases requiring forensic botanical expertise.

"Surely the FBI has better things to do than dig up dirt mounds, even if they might be graves." She took a quick look at her watch. "I wish they'd do whatever they're going to do. The show opens in an hour. Where is everyone?"

"Probably being held outside until we figure out what to do. If there's a dead body in there, like you think, you know what that means."

Having been married to a cop for thirty years *and* consulted with the police on occasion, Peggy knew exactly what that meant.

It probably also meant the committee that chose sites for the flower show would never choose Charlotte again.

"Who's making the decision? Should we give them a call? I could be completely wrong about this and opening day would be ruined for nothing." Peggy was beginning to regret that she'd called the police.

"Actually, I think Al is making the decision. Calm down, Mom. He'll be here." Paul patted his mother on the shoulder in a perfunctory manner.

"That's right. I guess as head of homicide, that would be his job."

Peggy thought about all the years that Detective Al McDonald was her husband's partner. He was notorious for being late. She loved him dearly, but the man couldn't make it to his own wedding on time when he'd married his wife, Mary.

There was a disturbance at the door. Al, along with Charlotte's new medical examiner, Dorothy Beck, walked into the convention center. They had a technician with them in a gray coverall who was holding a shovel. Peggy hoped this would be the person who could dig up the mound and figure out what was going on.

*Please don't let there be a dead person in that grave. I want to be wrong.*

There was someone else with Al and Doctor Beck. Peggy would have known his handsome face anywhere. It was Steve, no doubt there in his capacity as area director for the FBI.

She watched him walk toward her, talking on the phone and conversing with another man in a suit and tie, probably an associate.

She felt so lucky to have found love twice in her lifetime.

Steve was ten years younger than her. They'd literally run into each other one morning at a coffee shop. He'd apologized and offered to repair her bike, even though it was her own fault for daydreaming while she was in city traffic.

She wondered, but hadn't asked, if he'd facilitated that accident to get to know her. Or was it exactly as it had seemed? Not that it mattered, but—

"Peggy." Al smiled and acknowledged her. "I might have known you'd be here. Plants and murder. They always call to you."

Al's heavy-set black face sat low on his thick, muscular neck. He was a large, strong man even so many years after he was the high school and college star quarterback. He and John had grown up together before both going to the police academy, and later, becoming partners.

"Believe me, I don't want this to be anything but a poor joke." Peggy's green eyes flashed under her white-streaked red hair. "Can we do something to speed this up before the opening?"

"I understand you're in charge of this whole shebang." Dr. Beck stepped forward and shook Peggy's hand. They'd worked together on a case last year.

"You could say that." Peggy's gaze flickered toward Steve. She couldn't help it. She forced herself to focus on Dr. Beck's brown eyes. "I'm the chairman of the committee that brought the flower show to Charlotte."

In the meantime, Al had been walking leisurely around the dirt mound on the concrete floor.

"And you think this might really be a grave?" he asked.

"It's the thyme." She showed him the flowers and explained about the plant's meaning as it was used in Egyptian burial practice. "I can't believe anyone here at the show would have anything to do with it."

"Wouldn't it be out of the ordinary for anyone else to have that information?" Steve asked.

It felt to Peggy as though the large convention center grew totally silent after he'd spoken. Al glanced away and Dr. Beck put on her glasses.

"Millions of people know about the language of flowers and about plant meanings. It wouldn't only be the people here that have that information." Peggy responded as though she wasn't talking to her husband. He was just another person working for law enforcement.

"Anyone else here using this plant for their exhibit?" he asked.

She consulted her tablet PC that had all of the information about the growers and vendors. "No. No one has it listed."

Al took a deep breath and nodded at the technician standing next to Steve. "Watcha got for us, Director Newsome?"

Steve stepped up to the mound. "I have a portable scanner that should tell us if anything is buried in there. That way we'll know if we need to dig it up."

"Nice toy." Al grinned, shaking Steve's hand. "Congratulations on the promotion."

"Thanks." Steve cast a doubtful look in Peggy's direction. "Let's see if anything is in there."

He and Al stepped back from the grave. The technician set up the scanner. Dr. Beck slid her tall, angular form close enough so that she could see the images relayed back.

Peggy stayed where she was, beside Paul. She wondered if Al had known about Steve working with the FBI before she did but also wasn't able to say anything. They hadn't talked about it.

"I see something in there," the technician said. "Not sure what it is."

Dr. Beck carefully surveyed the image. "I'm afraid what we're seeing is a foot. I think Peggy may be right about a dead body in this mound of dirt. I'll send for a team to excavate it properly."

Peggy took a deep, calming breath. "I guess that means the opening will be delayed."

"I'm afraid so." Al took out his worn notebook and a pen. "When were you here last, Peggy?"

"Last night at ten-thirty. Everything seemed to be ready. The mound wasn't there. I got home at about eleven."

She glanced up at Steve again. Their gazes clashed and skittered uncomfortably away.

"Any idea who might be in there?" Steve asked her.

"Absolutely none, *Director Newsome*." She answered with a cheeky smile.

"I guess we'll know when we get rid of that dirt." Dr. Beck got on her cell phone with her team who were in the parking lot.

"I'll go and tell the vendors the bad news." Peggy walked away, the only thing holding her back straight, a refusal to let everyone see how disappointed she was.

She felt their gaze on her.

Her new shoes pinched her toes, the sound of the heels echoing in the huge room. She kept herself from falling apart after all the hard work by reminding herself that all of the vendors and growers deserved to know what was going on.

Hundreds of flower show participants were waiting at the gate with several police officers stationed between them and the chain link fence. When they saw Peggy, they rushed to the gate asking dozens of questions.

Peggy held up her hands and called for quiet so they could hear her.

"I'm very sorry to tell you all that the flower show won't open this morning." She knew better than to tell them that she'd found a dead body inside. That would have to be for later, after the police had released their information. "The police are checking out an irregularity that could make it dangerous for any of you to be inside."

"The police?" A grower she recognized from Florida pushed forward. "What kind of irregularity? I've got twenty thousand dollars' worth of plants in there that aren't getting any fresher."

"I know. And I'm sorry. That's all I can say right now. I have all of your contact information. Someone will get in touch with you as soon as we're able to open."

There was a lot of grumbling and complaining until the crowd of participants finally started moving away from the gate. That left a smaller group of visitors who had paid for tickets on opening day.

"There will be a full refund," Peggy assured those unhappy people. "You'll also be able to come to the flower show on another day. We're trying to work out this problem as quickly as possible."

That group of people complained before heading back to their cars. There was even a bus from Huntersville, North Carolina with at least fifty people on it that had to turn around and go back home.

In the midst of all the disgruntled people leaving the parking lot, Peggy caught sight of Sam and Selena from The Potting Shed. She told the police to let them through the gate.

"You two are a welcome sight." Peggy hurried them away from the officers.

"What gives?" Sam Ollson had been working for Peggy since his first year of college. His blond hair and year-round tan from working outside made him look like a large, muscular surfer. He'd given up attending med school to become her partner in The Potting Shed.

"I think someone may have been murdered in there last night after I left," Peggy whispered.

"Murdered?" Selena Rogers's voice went higher and

louder than Peggy would've wished. "How is that possible? It's a bunch of flower growers."

"Hey! I'm a flower grower." Sam spread his large hands that he frequently used to express himself when he wasn't shoveling dirt or planting flowers. "I think I could get rid of someone giving me a hard time. Maybe you."

"You wish." Selena glared at him, her cocoa-skin emphasizing her whisky-colored eyes. Long, black hair blew across her shoulders in the morning breeze. She was very thin but muscular, a long distance runner at Queen's University.

Peggy was used to the two of them bickering back and forth, but now wasn't a good time.

"Don't make this any worse." Peggy said.

"I don't see how it could be much worse." Sam nodded toward the rapidly emptying parking lot. "There were hundreds of people at the gate already. We can't get inside for no telling how long. We have a sizeable investment in our exhibit that might be ruined. What could be worse than that?"

"FBI Director Steve Newsome is here." Peggy rolled her eyes as she dramatically pronounced the name.

"Great." Sam knew all about what had been going on in Peggy's life. He shoved his hands into the pockets of his tight jeans. "Just when I thought everything bad had already happened."

"Newsome?" Selena wrinkled her nose as she tried to make her brain work without caffeine. "Wait. You mean Steve, right? I mean, he probably should be here, right? The FBI is good. Maybe the job will get done faster. And you have an 'in' with someone who can tell you what's going on."

Peggy looked into her assistant's pretty, hopeful face. "It's not exactly the 'in' I was looking for."

Sam shook his head and frowned at Selena. Their non-verbal communication was sometimes better than when they spoke. Selena scuffed the toe of her shoe on the gravel parking lot and didn't reply.

"What can we do?" Sam asked.

"I don't know yet. We'll have to wait until they uncover the body and secure the scene. Nothing is going to happen until then. We might be able to open the show tomorrow. I guess you two should go back and open The Potting Shed so the day won't be a complete waste."

"But we're officially closed for the day," Selena said. "There's a big sign on the door, and I posted it on our website."

"I know, but when our customers realize what's happened, they might show up there."

Sam shrugged. "With this fiasco, we can't afford not to make some money. Come on, Selena. Let's go. Call us if you need anything."

Peggy agreed she would call them. She watched them leave before she turned back to go inside.

Steve met her outside the door to the convention center. He was alone, and his expression was troubled. "I'm sorry this happened. You've worked hard on this for a long time."

"Did they find anyone?"

"Not yet." He looked past her as a white crime scene

van was allowed through the gate. "It shouldn't be too much longer."

"Why are you here?" She got to the heart of the matter. "Since when does the FBI come in on a local case?"

"You have more than eighty vendors and growers from all over the country, some from outside the country. This event has been on our radar for a while. I'm sorry I couldn't tell you."

"Let's stop saying that, okay?" She opened the door and went inside without him.

Steve took a deep breath and followed her.

It wasn't long before Dr. Beck's crime scene team had carefully dug up the mound. All the dirt would be taken back from the area along with the dogwood cross and other items close to the grave.

"Whose exhibit is this, Peggy?" Al asked her.

Peggy again took her tablet out of her enormous flowered bag. She pulled up her file of vendors and growers, in case he needed the address. "This area was set up by Bandy's Flowers of Distinction from Richmond, Virginia. Rebecca Bandy is the proprietor and vendor."

"Everything okay?" Paul whispered as he gravitated to her side again.

"Everything is fine."

"I thought you always told me it was bad to lie."

"Thanks, Peggy. We'll speak with Ms. Bandy." Al flipped over to a clean sheet of paper in his tiny notebook.

"You should get one of these," Peggy said. "It's easy

to carry and you won't need a pen. Besides, you and I both know you can't read your writing."

The police officers, including Paul, snickered a little.

"No, thanks. I've been doing it this way since I started walking a beat." Al flipped over another sheet of paper. "Anything unusual happen here yesterday? Any fights or disagreements?"

"Not as far as I know. I didn't see anything."

"Okay," Dr. Beck called out from the area they were clearing. "We have something."

Peggy and Al went closer into the exhibit. The whole space was torn apart, and in the center of the area where the pile of dirt had been, was a body.

It was a black man, dirt smudging his features. He was wearing a colorful robe that reached down to his ankles. His shoes were gone. Other than being covered in dirt, he looked as though he was asleep.

Peggy sucked in a sudden breath and held her hand to her chest.

"Do you recognize him?" Al took her arm. "Peggy? Do you know him?"

"Yes. His name is Aris Abutto. He's from South Africa. He's here to exhibit his new orchids." Her voice broke. "I've known him for a long time."

### *Orchid*

*Historically the meaning of orchids is wealth, love, and beauty. The ancient Greeks believed orchids improved virility. Orchids have also been credited with healing properties. The Aztecs were said to drink a mixture of the vanilla orchid and chocolate to give them power and strength.*

# Chapter Three

Dr. Beck and her team prepared to move the body to the morgue. Al asked Peggy to walk him to Dr. Abutto's exhibit. It was a long way down the concourse and up to the second floor.

Peggy lamented each wilting flower she saw as they passed dozens of exhibits. She hoped the police could clear up enough of the investigation that the show could open tomorrow.

"I'm sorry I couldn't give you a heads up about Steve." Al huffed as he walked slowly beside her. "You didn't know he was going to be here, did you?"

"He didn't tell me before I left the house, but he probably didn't know until I called it in." She stopped walking. "Did you know about Steve—before I did? Have you worked with him before?"

Al took her hand. "It was a surprise to me when the FBI sent me his information. I guess he's worked in our area, but not with me. I didn't know about him and John either. I've asked around. They still won't talk about it. I don't like it."

She closed her eyes, and opened them to look into his bloodshot brown ones. "I know what you mean. It's bad enough John is dead. Now that I know his death was more involved. Honestly, this whole thing with him has had me up in the air a little."

"Steve is a good man. I don't care if he's a vet or an agent. Or both. He'll explain when he can. John didn't tell you everything about every case he was involved on either. You didn't know he was working with the FBI, did you? I know I didn't."

"No." She smiled at her old friend. "You're right. I guess I've been silly about it. It was such a shock. I would never have guessed the truth. It scares me a little."

"That Steve was watching out for you after John was killed? Or that he fell in love with you?" He squeezed her hand. "I know it's not easy being married to someone who might not come home again after shift. Mary tells me all the time."

"Thanks, Al." She kissed his cheek. "I talked to Mary the other day. She says you broke your promise to her when you became head of homicide. You were supposed to retire."

"I put a down payment on a house at the beach last week." He laughed, his bulbous nose shaking a little. "I don't think she wants me to retire yet."

"You haven't told her?"

"It's a surprise. I'm taking her there for our anniversary next month. See? Steve isn't the only one who keeps secrets." Al looked back the way they'd come from Dr. Abutto's crime scene. "Looks like your hubby wants to know what's taking us so long."

Peggy glanced covertly back that way. Steve was walking quickly toward them.

"I guess we should wait for him."

"It's probably a good idea," Al agreed. "This way you don't have to say everything twice."

"Dr. Beck just left with the body." Steve reached them and searched both of their faces. "Is something wrong?"

"No." Al started walking again. "Except that this place is too darn big."

Steve's eyes went quickly to Peggy's face. "I thought I'd join you taking a look at Abutto's exhibit, if that's okay?"

"That's fine." Peggy gave him a small smile. "I haven't said anything important yet anyway, if there's something important to say. Al reminded me to wait so I don't have to say it again."

"Sure. I understand."

They finished walking to the end of the building then took the elevator upstairs. The sun was beginning to warm the morning, shining through the huge skylight above them. It made the scents from the flowers and other plant life stronger.

"This place smells good." Al took a deep breath, first off the elevator. "I think Mary has some air freshener that smells like this."

Peggy laughed. "They wish they could manufacture something that smells this good."

"It smells a lot like dirt to me." Steve held the elevator until she was off.

"Some of the plants are in soil or mulch," she explained. "Others are in water or a planting solution. Many of them need spritzing with water every few hours to combat the effects of the dry air in here."

"We'll get those people back in here as soon as we can," Steve promised. "Dr. Beck's team was very efficient. If we can handle everything else that quickly, the show might be able to open tomorrow."

"Really?" Peggy's eyes were filled with the hope in her heart. "That would be great."

She walked ahead of Steve and Al as she consulted her tablet to find Dr. Abutto's exhibit.

"That was a mighty ambitious proposal," Al muttered to Steve.

"You would've done the same thing if it was Mary. She's worked so hard for this." Steve stared lovingly at Peggy's back. "Maybe it can happen."

Al shrugged. "You better hope so. You think she's unhappy now. . ."

"Yeah. I hear you."

Peggy stopped and looked back at them. "This is it. Aris's grasp on understanding orchid species is remarkable. Look at this—a blue orchid. Can you believe the size, and depth of the color?"

Al glanced at it and then took in the state of the rest of the exhibit. "Looks like a tornado came through here. Wasn't he finished setting up like everyone else?"

Peggy had been so enthralled with the orchid in the glass case that she had completely missed the mess that had been created behind it. The blue orchid was the only one left.

"No. It wasn't like this." She started to go behind the table.

Steve put his hand on her arm. "We should wait and let forensics go over it. I'm sorry."

She took a step back. Al was already on his phone getting someone to come up and look for any evidence left behind.

"Why would someone go to all the trouble of smashing his whole exhibit this way?"

Peggy mourned the loss of her friend's work.

"Probably looking for something," Al said. "What was the exhibit? It looks like a bunch of poster board and papers."

"That's all it was," she said. "He was a grower. He felt as though his orchids showed themselves off. He didn't do anything elaborate, like some of the other participants."

"It looks like a rage thing to me," Steve said. "Whatever someone was looking for wasn't here. I think they took it out on his exhibit and the orchids he loved."

"Unless, of course, they were trying to throw us off." Peggy stifled the urge to go into the exhibit and clean up, holding her tablet tightly with both hands.

"We've got a few teams headed up here." Al got off the phone. "I think it's a good guess that the killer was looking for something. Are there any pictures of the way his exhibit was supposed to look?"

"Yes." Peggy pulled it up on her tablet. "I went around before I left yesterday and took pictures of everything."

"Do you have a picture of the area where we found Dr. Abutto's body?" Steve asked.

"Of course. There was nothing there."

"Send that to me, Peggy." Al handed her a card. "They're always screwing around with the email. This is my new one, second one this month."

She took it from him and read the large, plain black text and then looked at Steve. "Do you want me to send the information to you too?"

He took a card out of his wallet and gave it to her. "Thanks."

Peggy read it and put it away. Steve turned back to Al and she saw the gun hidden in a holster beneath his jacket. *A reminder that, no matter what he says, his job is dangerous.*

"If there's nothing else I can do here," she smiled at both of them, "I'm going to The Potting Shed. If you have any questions for me, you both have my cell phone number."

"That's fine, Peggy. Thanks." Al nudged Steve with his elbow. "Good with you too, Director Newsome?"

"That's fine." Steve grimaced at the title. "You can still call me Steve."

Al winked at Peggy. "Yeah. We're good here."

The four-person crime scene team bolted up the stairs with their satchels and cases.

Peggy waited until they had passed and then headed for the elevator.

Steve stopped her at the door. "I know this is weird. It's weird for me too. I wish there would've been more time to get adjusted to the idea before this happened."

"Me too." She lowered her voice.

"I didn't even know you carried a gun." She said.

"I know. We haven't talked about the particulars, I guess."

She smiled and he took her hand in his.

"Peggy, don't do anything with this, huh? No side investigations. No well-meaning looking into ideas as they hit you. If you think of anything we should know about, call me. Or text me. Or tell me tonight in bed. Okay?"

Peggy was calm and collected. "Don't worry. I'm not involved in this investigation."

"I *know* you. I've participated in some of your 'adventures', looking for justice. Keep me in the loop. I haven't suddenly become the enemy."

"Of course not." She moved her cold hand out of his grasp. "I'll see you later." She got in the elevator and the doors slid closed in front of her.

"You know that's never worked for me, right?" Al asked Steve.

"It's different—"

Al *humphed.* "Yeah. Keep believing that."

### *Chrysanthemum*

*Chrysanthemums (mums) were first cultivated in China in the 15th century. It was brought to Japan in the eighth century, and the Emperor adopted the flower as his official seal. The Festival of Happiness in Japan celebrates the flower. It was brought to Europe in the 17th century and named for the Greek word for 'golden' which was the original color of the flowers. Colonel John Stevens imported a variety in 1798 from England. Today, mums are one of the most popular flowers in the US.*

# **Chapter Four**

Peggy tapped her foot impatiently in the elevator on the way downstairs. Whether she liked it or not—whether Steve liked it or not—things were a little different between them. It felt odd. Not impossible. Strange, maybe.

He was right. There were many times in her duties as a forensic botanist, working on contract for the Charlotte Police Department, that she had followed some hunches that had led her to answers she later shared with the police. Steve had participated in a few of those occurrences.

That could never happen again.

Now he was Director Steve Newsome, not veterinarian Steve Newsome. He'd be in direct contact with Al and the rest of the police department. He'd get all preachy and stiff about working outside the normal chains of command.

John would've been the same way, she admitted to

herself. Paul was pretty much like that too. They were all entrenched in their professions and believed it was better for trained individuals to handle investigations.

She was trained too, even if it was only six weeks to get her forensic certification. She knew how to handle evidence and how to store it. She had enough common sense not to step in front of a moving car, or a criminal with a gun.

Peggy was walking down the long concourse again, this time going back to the entrance and the parking lot. Dr. Beck was still there, working with her team on the area that had surrounded Dr. Abutto's corpse.

She could hear Dr. Beck talking into her tape recorder as she walked by. The team was taking samples of all the botanical evidence—flower petals from chrysanthemums, geraniums, and magnolia leaves. It made her smile because she had no doubt that she'd be called in to work with the evidence.

She was the only forensic botanist in the area. Who else would they call?

Dr. Beck was cataloguing what she'd seen on the body and around it. She was talking about the pink flowers that had been buried with Dr. Abutto and thrown on the grave.

Peggy tapped her on the shoulder. "They're thyme, not oregano."

Dorothy Beck turned off her tape recorder. "Thanks. I thought they smelled like something that went into spaghetti sauce. I'm sure I'll have my forensic botanist check it out before filing my report."

"I'm sure you will. Was he killed here?"

"You sure you want to hear what I think about your friend's death?"

Peggy nodded, swallowing hard on a lump in her throat. "He came because I invited him, Dorothy. I want to know."

"Then, yes. I think he was killed here. He was shot. I think the dirt absorbed the blood, which is why we aren't seeing more of it."

"I'm guessing that he wasn't dead very long. The flowers on the grave were fresh. It couldn't have been more than a few hours."

"You should've applied for my job when the post was vacant."

"No. If it doesn't involve plants, I'm not interested. You know Mai wanted the position."

"I've heard that. Her attitude toward me has improved. I don't worry so much that there might be poison in my coffee or a knife in my back when I lean over. Maybe it's the pregnancy."

They both laughed. Peggy knew her daughter-in-law, Mai, had really believed she'd be the next medical examiner. She was very good at what she did and had worked hard for that position. The board had decided she didn't have enough experience and had hired Dorothy.

Mai hadn't been happy with the situation, although she did seem to be coming around in the last few months. Dorothy was right about the pregnancy. Mai wasn't as angry about the job now. She was more interested in her baby.

"I'm sure I'll hear from you later. I'm headed to The

Potting Shed where my talents are appreciated."

Dorothy nodded. "I know what you mean. The boys always like to play with other boys. Don't worry. I appreciate you. See you around."

Peggy stepped outside into the brilliant sunshine, the deep Carolina blue sky smiling down on her despite everything that had happened. She called a taxi and waited at the outside of the gate with Reggie, the security guard.

"Too bad about that whole mess in there." He jerked his head toward the convention center. "You were gonna have a good first day too. I've turned back hundreds of people who haven't heard about the murder yet."

"Let's hope for a better second day." Peggy had seen hundreds of emails, texts and voicemails from vendors, growers, the local group that had helped bring the flower show to Charlotte, and the International Flower Show committee. She didn't plan to answer any of them yet.

"I knew I shouldn't have let Dr. Abutto into the building last night all by himself." Reggie took off his gray cap and wiped the top of his bald head with a clean handkerchief. "Don't ask me why. Lots of people come in after hours at this type of thing. Everyone can't get stuff done during the day. It's like I knew something was wrong, especially when he didn't come back out."

"Did you see anyone else go in or out?"

"No, not for hours. As far as I know, the old guy was alone in there. Bad way to die, huh?"

"Did he say anything? Did he look agitated?"

"No. Nothing like that. He brought in a duffel bag. I thought it must be some kind of flower stuff, you know."

Peggy thought back quickly to what she had seen when she'd first arrived, and then later when Al, Steve, and everyone else were there. She couldn't remember seeing a duffel bag around the grave. She supposed there could've been one upstairs in the mess someone had made of his things.

"Do you remember what color it was?"

"It was plain and black. Nothing unusual." Reggie answered his phone in the guard shack. He turned back to her after hanging up. "It's already starting. TV and newspapers want to know what I saw. I already told the police everything. I don't know why those people don't mind their own business."

Peggy's taxi pulled up. "I have to go. I'm sure it will blow over quickly. You know Charlotte—something is always happening."

"That's sure enough true. Have a good day, Peggy."

She thought about what Reggie had said after giving the driver the address to The Potting Shed.

If Reggie saw Dr. Abutto go in alone and not come out, someone could have been hiding in there, waiting for him. She couldn't imagine who would want to hurt Aris. She wished she could see it as an accident, but it looked more like murder.

The convention center wasn't impenetrable. It was surrounded by the high chain link fence, but the doors were frequently left open. The vendors and growers going in and out the last few weeks with their exhibits didn't have keys.

She had a key, and the security guard on duty had keys, probably along with the maintenance staff. Literally, anyone could have been in there at any time.

Was the missing duffel bag significant?

There was no way to know yet. Aris's orchids were all in place before she'd left yesterday. She'd thought the rest of his work was there too, but he could have had other items he had to bring in.

"Here we are," the driver said.

"Thanks." Peggy paid him and got out.

The Potting Shed was in one of the few historic areas left in Charlotte. Brevard Court was built at the doorway to Latta Arcade, a two-story brick building that was a restored 1915 cotton exchange with an overhead skylight. The purpose was to provide natural light for cotton buyers to inspect their goods.

The arcade, with its antique light fixtures and parallel rows of shop fronts, was now a shopping mall that welcomed buyers with dozens of colorful storefronts.

Brevard Court was an open-air extension where shoppers could sit down at umbrella-topped tables and enjoy lunch or a latte. There were shops in the courtyard too, including The Potting Shed.

Peggy waved to Sofia Balducci at The Kozy Kettle Tea and Coffee Emporium across the cobblestones from her garden shop. Sofia, rings on every finger, waved back as she swept the stoop in front of her shop.

The rent in the courtyard was a little steep, but Peggy loved the spot. She'd had the shop here since John had passed. It had taken his insurance and all the money she could muster to open what she hoped would be an urban dweller's garden paradise.

She pushed open the heavy wood door. Sam and

Selena looked up.

"Any customers?" she asked.

"Customers?" Sam was immediately at her side. "Never mind that, tell us what happened? Do they know who killed Dr. Abutto? Will the flower show open tomorrow?"

"I don't know anything yet." Peggy put down her bag and sat in her rocking chair next to the large indoor pond. The shop sold a lot of pond supplies. "I think I need some tea."

"I'll make you some," Selena volunteered. "It's been quiet here. We had a few regulars call and ask if we were open since the flower show was closed. None of them came in. Maybe they were just checking."

Sam sat on a stool near Peggy's rocking chair. "Claire Drummond wants me to plant a few willow trees in her front yard. That's a good contract for next week—unless you think the flower show will stay closed. I could do it tomorrow while the weather is still nice."

"No. Let's plan on being at the flower show tomorrow. We have too much invested in our exhibit to forget about it. I need you there."

"Okay." He shrugged his broad shoulders. "You think Steve will give you a heads-up tonight? Or is discussing police/FBI business going to be a no-no between you?"

Selena scoffed as she gave Peggy a cup of her favorite peach tea, fresh from the mini microwave. "You don't know anything. There are no holds barred between a man and woman when they're in bed together. That's why they call it pillow talk. How do you think Mata Hari got all those secrets out of men? Men can't keep anything secret from a woman. Right, Peggy?"

Peggy looked up from her tea. "I don't think I'm the right person to ask about that, at least not right now."

### *Willow*

*Hippocrates wrote of the medicinal properties of willow and its ingredient, salicin, in the fifth century BC. It had already been used for generations by ancient peoples for headache, fevers and body pain. In present day, we use a synthetic form of salicin as aspirin. The name aspirin was patented by Bayer in 1897. Willow was also the beginning of some of mankind's earliest tools. Willow fishing nets, baskets, and other items were used as early as 8000 BC. The wood has been used for boxes, toys, paper and fiber. People ate the catkins from the willow. Today we admire its form and aesthetics, but in the past, humans relied on it for so much more.*

# Chapter Five

Sam made faces at Selena who frowned and went into the back of the shop to look for something.

"Don't worry about it," Sam recommended. "This is a transition for you and Steve. You're finding your way in a new relationship."

Peggy sipped her tea. "Thanks for the advice. I'd like to know your source. Was it the last three week relationship you had, or was it the ten-day relationship?"

"*Ouch*." He frowned. "I think you need some chamomile tea in that cup. You know Steve didn't want to keep all of this a secret from you. Anyone with eyes can see how much he loves you. He had to do this for his job."

"What about Mata Hari?"

"That was different. She never loved anyone she seduced. She only did it for information. I don't think even your amazing knowledge of botanical poisons would be enough to keep Steve around all this time if he didn't care about you."

She smiled at the thought. "I know you're right. I'm a little afraid of history repeating itself. It's not a normal life, Sam. It's scary not knowing if there will be another knock on my door late one night."

"I know. At least you two love each other. Most people don't even have that, and there can still be scary knocks on the door late at night. Cops aren't the only ones who don't make it home."

"Thanks for the pep talk. And good news about the willow trees."

He grinned. "While I'm on a roll, I could really use another hand in the landscape part of the business. Things have picked up, and with Keeley gone, I don't think I can keep up with it by myself."

"I trust your judgment. You know where we are financially. If we can afford it, do it." She put down her cup of tea and picked up the phone. "I have a ton of phone calls to make to angry and frightened people about the flower show. Steve and I will be fine. I hope the flower show will be too."

Peggy sat outside in the pleasant courtyard returning phone calls and other messages. She noticed some of the large pots of plants The Potting Shed maintained were in need of work.

While she talked to vendors who were worried about losing the money they'd invested in the flower show, she got out a small pair of pruning shears and took care of the yellow leaves on tulips and hyacinths. The plants couldn't be cut back yet because it would ruin them. Later, she'd remove the bulbs and plant them somewhere else.

The shop's name was on each planter. It didn't look very good if they couldn't keep up with their own work. She'd have to mention it to Sam.

A few waitresses from Anthony's Caribbean Café came out to sit in the sun for their break. A few other shop owners were outside in the fresh air, too, during lulls in their day. Dozens of customers wandered through the arcade to reach the courtyard. They carried bags from various shops which had always meant to Peggy that they were in a buying mood.

Phone calls complete, Peggy went back inside The Potting Shed. Selena was half asleep in the rocking chair by the water pond. Peggy roused her and had her take a few samples outside.

"We don't usually do that," Selena protested as Peggy loaded her up with a few daisies and hostas.

"When things are slow, it's best to take it to the customer. I'll bring out one of those pretty rolling flower carts and we'll set the scene. Who can resist them?"

"Who indeed?" Selena was less than enthusiastic. "Shouldn't Sam have to take some potting soil out there too? And what about some of those new, hand-painted flower pots?"

"Good idea." Peggy called for Sam as she was pushing Selena out the front door.

She asked Sam to take out two bags of potting soil while she took out a few of the flower pots. Peggy really liked the artist who'd created them, Mandy Burke. Her designs were very original and she was a wonderful person.

The problem was that the pots were priced too high. Yes, they were hand-painted, original designs, but they were from an unknown artist. She had yet to sell a single pot in the six months they'd been at the shop. Even Peggy's deep-pocket customers had waved them away.

They set everything in front of the shop and went back inside. It was only a minute before a customer came in.

"Hello!" Selena greeted the young woman. "Can I help you find something?"

The woman, who was probably a few years younger than Selena's early twenties, looked around the shop without moving. Her clothes were very nice, expensive, and her black hair was piled on her head, the style emphasizing her high cheek bones and dark eyes.

"I am looking for Dr. Margaret Lee. Is she here?"

Selena shrugged. "Sure. Peggy, it's for you."

Peggy had been washing her hands. She dried them quickly on a towel when she heard her name and bustled to the front of the shop.

"Yes?"

"I am Tanya Abutto. My father was Dr. Aris Abutto. He was found dead this morning at your flower show. I want to know how this happened." Her accent was a mixture of French and something else.

Peggy scanned the pretty young face before her. There was not a sign of tears or even anger. Her eyes were dark, placid pools. She didn't look like someone who'd recently lost her father.

Besides, Peggy knew Tanya. This wasn't her. What

was going on?

"I am so sorry for you loss. Come right outside and we can talk. Would you like some tea?" Peggy ushered her out of the door, frowning as Selena made horrified faces at her over the top of 'Tanya's' head.

They sat at the same table in the courtyard that Peggy had recently vacated. 'Tanya' stared at Peggy as though her life depended on it. The only other sign that she was upset was the stranglehold she had on her large brown leather bag.

"Have you spoken with the police?" Peggy was going to try hard not to step on anyone's toes, but curiosity kept her from telling the girl to go away while she called Al.

"No. You were my father's contact here. I came to you for assistance."

"I'm not sure what help I can be as far as your father's death is concerned. I was there when they found him. I'm sure the police would like to talk to you about hwne you saw him last. Would you like me to go with you to talk to them?"

"Perhaps later." The girl seemed to be mulling something over. "My father carried with him a large, black bag. A satchel, I believe you call them. I would very much like to find it."

Peggy thought about it. The duffel bag Reggie had mentioned, no doubt. It seemed a strange thing to be concerned about, especially if the girl was trying to pass herself off as Tanya. What could she be looking for?

"I talked with your father while he was setting up his exhibit. He never mentioned a bag of that sort and I didn't see him with one. Are there important documents you need in the bag?"

"That is a personal matter," she snapped. "I need the bag as soon as possible. Bring it to this hotel where I am staying."

'Tanya' got up quickly from the bench and handed Peggy a card from the Hilton. She stalked toward the sidewalk and got into a new, black Mercedes that had been parked at the curb.

Peggy watched her drive away. There was a sticker on the back that proclaimed the car a Friendly Rental vehicle. It was a local rental agency with one office at the airport.

Still wondering what was going on, Peggy went back inside The Potting Shed. It had been a curious conversation, not at all what she'd been expecting.

"Well?" Selena was waiting for her. "Does she want to sue you because her father died or is she planning a vendetta?"

"Neither, as far as I can tell. That wasn't even Tanya."

"What? Did you ask her who she really was?"

"No. I thought it would be better to let her talk. She left before I could learn anything useful."

"Oh, Peggy. This doesn't sound good." Selena wrung her hands.

"She said she wanted her father's bag, the same one Reggie was talking about this morning, I think. She didn't ask anything about him personally, not the normal questions you'd expect from a grieving daughter, even a fake grieving daughter."

"Selena shrugged. "You should call the police. Or call

Steve. He's like the police."

A real customer came in the door next and asked about the painted pots outside. To Peggy's surprise, she bought two of them. Maybe Mandy knew what she was doing after all.

After that, several other customers came in looking for mulch and blackberry bushes. Peggy routed the customers to Sam for him to take care of. He might even be able to convince her to let him plant a berry garden for her. Sam was very good at persuading customers to become landscape devotees. It always helped when it was a woman. They found him, and his Norse God good looks, irresistible.

While Peggy was walking the new customer to the back of the shop where Sam was working, another woman came in and asked about water plants for her pond.

"I only have a small pond I keep on my balcony. I'd have a much bigger one if I didn't live in an apartment." Starr Richards laughed as she introduced herself. "I work over at the bank and I've almost stopped in here several times. If I'd known you had this huge pond in here, I would've stopped sooner."

*And that's the problem*, Peggy thought. How was she supposed to tell people about everything she had in the shop if they didn't come inside? She couldn't have a sign outside that was large enough for her whole inventory. She was at the mercy of drop-ins to discover her, become great friends, and loyal customers.

"How deep is your pond and what do you have in it now?" Peggy asked her.

"It's not very big. Maybe a foot deep. I put some water lilies in it last year. They filled the whole thing up, but it's only leaves now, no flowers. Any ideas?"

As Starr and Peggy talked, they realized that Starr's pond wasn't getting enough afternoon sun to make the flowers bloom.

"You probably get enough sun for water irises," Peggy told her. "Mine aren't blooming in the pond right now, but they're sensational. I have a couple of white ones and a few purple irises. They aren't hard to grow at all."

Sam had joined them while they were talking. "You'll have to pull out the water lilies. Sorry. The lilies will choke out the irises if you don't."

Starr's eyes lit up when she saw Sam. They shook hands as they introduced themselves. "Maybe you could come home with me and show me what I'm doing wrong."

Selena rolled her eyes at the typical female reaction to Sam. She got behind the counter to ring up Starr's water iris purchase.

"I'd be glad to." Sam took out his phone and looked at his calendar. "I can be there at three, if that works for you."

Starr was still holding his left hand. "That totally works for me. Whatever you want to charge is fine. I have some house plants you could look at too."

They exchanged phone numbers and Starr gave him her address. Peggy recognized it as being in one of the new, expensive apartment residences downtown.

"See you then," Starr said.

"I'll be there."

Starr almost left without her irises. Selena reminded her.

When the door had closed behind Starr, Selena took a deep breath. "Seriously? Why do all women act like Sam's the gift of God?"

"Don't be jealous," Peggy counseled. "Women like Sam, and it's not only the way he looks. He's very respectful and has a sweet way of talking."

Selena *humphed*. "All I can say is—her mistake."

"Don't worry," Sam said with a grin. "Someday a man will walk through that door looking for a woman like you. And even though I try to warn him off, he's going to ask you out. I'm sure it will happen. Don't give up."

"You'd better go throw some mulch around in back before I throw a flower pot at you," Selena threatened.

"Not one of the expensive ones, please," Peggy said. "Will you take two more of those hand-painted pots outside to replace the ones that were purchased? Maybe they look better out there."

"And maybe that way the perfect man won't have to come into the shop and find you," Sam razzed. "If you're out there on display, who knows what might happen?"

"Okay. That's enough." Peggy's cell phone rang and she stepped outside to answer it.

It was Al. "I have some good news and some bad news."

"I'll take the good first, please."

"Looks like we can have the investigation wrapped up sometime tonight, at least the crime scene part. The medical examiner gave you the all clear to open tomorrow."

*Thank you, Dorothy!* "And the bad news?"

"Because of the nature of the crime and the victim being from out of town, the FBI will continue to assist the Charlotte PD on the case. Don't blame me. I'm just the messenger."

"That's fine. Except as the head of the flower show committee, I'm not really personally involved."

"Uh-huh. Did you get a phone call from Dr. Beck yet? I believe she mentioned using you on the case. It seems she wasn't a fan of botany in school."

Peggy understood what he meant. "Don't worry about it. It'll be fine. I can handle working with Steve on this." *If he can . . .*

"If you need a liaison, give me a call."

"Thanks. I'll talk to you later."

Peggy put her phone away and thought about the visit from the fake Tanya Abutto. She should've mentioned that to Al.

She started to call him back when her phone started ringing with vendors and growers. The shop was surprisingly busy too. Peggy kept thinking she should call Al back, but by the time she noticed, it was four-thirty and she still hadn't called him.

Sam was excited about the flower show opening again and upset that no one could go in to check on their exhibits until the doors opened tomorrow.

He wasn't the only one. Peggy called and texted participants who called and texted her back again, expressing their frustration that their living exhibits might be damaged without proper care that night.

She repeated dozens of times that she had no control over what the police had determined to do during their investigation. At least the flower show would go on.

A few more customers came in and made small purchases. Some regulars stopped in to gossip about what had happened at the convention center. They wanted to know all the juicy details.

So did Sofia and Emil Balducci from the Kozy Kettle across the courtyard. Emil loved to gossip. With his broad Italian features, craggy brows, and shadowed dark eyes, he fancied himself quite a ladies man, unless Sofia was around.

"Did you see the body?" Sofia asked as she crossed herself. "God forbid you're cursed by it like my Uncle Francesco. He saw them dig up a murdered man once and he was dead the next day."

Peggy carefully smiled. Sofia could get a little upset when she openly laughed at some of her crazy curses and weird stories. The woman had one for everything that happened.

"I'll be careful," she promised Sofia.

"Why kill this man?" Emil asked. "He should've been carrying a Taser. I have one. Sofia does too. Show Peggy your Taser."

Sofia ran back to the shop and brought her Taser. It was more like a cattle prod, almost two feet long.

"You could stun an elephant with that," Selena said.

"You never know," Sofia said darkly, waving the

Taser in the air. "Did I ever tell you about my cousin Rafe, who was killed by a rogue elephant?"

Emil crossed himself. "It sat on him."

Selena turned away to hide her laughter. Sam hurried to the back of the shop with a muttered excuse.

"So what are the police doing about this?" Emil asked Peggy. "When will they know who killed this poor man?"

"I don't know yet. They're doing the best they can. I'll let you know if there's an arrest."

Sofia handed Peggy her Taser. "You should take this with you. There's the curse, and my papa always said, where there's one murder, there could be two."

### *Oregano*

*The first recorded usage of oregano was in ancient Greece. The plant's use continued through the Middle Ages, and was considered a common spice to make bland foods more appetizing and disguise the taste of slightly spoiled meat. The plant was also used as a cure for rheumatism, toothache, and indigestion.*

# Chapter Six

Peggy insisted she couldn't accept the Taser. "I'd feel terrible if you were mugged leaving your place tonight."

"She has me." Emil pushed his fist against his wide chest. "You have a husband, but he's never around. Would you like me to talk to him for you? A man should be there to protect his wife. It's no good being a person who takes care of animals if you can't take care of your family."

Peggy didn't plan to tell Emil about Steve's FBI job. It was bad enough that he had managed to figure out so much about her life on his own. He might have more respect for Steve being a federal agent than he did thinking Steve was a veterinarian. She didn't care. She certainly didn't want to have that conversation with Emil and Sofia.

Tired but happy that the day was finally over, Peggy locked the front door to the garden shop as she left at five. Most of their business came in during the day when employees from banks and other offices around them went out for lunch. The Potting Shed was open banker hours, and the occasional Saturday morning.

Sam had come back with good news about Starr's pond. She wanted him to replace the entire thing and start over. It would be an expensive, short-term project for him.

"I'll lock up the back before I leave," he said. "I want to go ahead and order everything for the pond today. See you tomorrow at the convention center."

"Okay."

"And Peggy?" Sam stopped her. "If you see anything out of the ordinary, look the other way. The flower show has to happen tomorrow, or it's over."

"Right. I won't look at anything. Goodnight, Sam."

Peggy walked out of The Potting Shed, dialing the taxi company for a ride home. She looked up and saw Steve leaning against the side of the car he'd received from the FBI. She smiled at him as she reached the wrought iron and brick gate that separated the courtyard from the street.

Looking at him made her realize that worrying about what could happen to him could ruin their relationship. She had to find a way to make peace with it.

"Excuse me." A young woman wearing a blue scarf on her head approached Peggy. She was short, barely five feet. The scarf masked a great deal of her face.

"Can I help you?" Peggy asked.

"I am Tanya Abutto. You knew my father." She sniffled a little as though she'd been crying. "I am desperate to talk to you regarding the return of his property."

Peggy glanced at Steve who'd approached from the car. "In particular, a leather satchel, right?"

"Yes! Exactly. Are you in possession of it?"

"As I told another woman with your name earlier today, the police have everything that was found with your father. You'll have to contact them."

"There must be some mistake. I have never spoken to you."

"I agree. But the other woman told me she was Tanya Abutto too. I know Tanya. Neither of you are her. My answer stays the same. All of Aris Abutto's possessions are with the police. I'm sorry. You'll have to talk to them."

The young woman grew agitated. "You don't realize how important the bag is. I must have it."

"Is there a problem?" Steve interrupted.

With a muffled screech, the girl fled back through Latta Arcade, probably running down Tryon Street from there.

"I guess so." Peggy turned from watching the girl to looking up at her husband. "I think I might need to speak with a law enforcement official."

He put his arm around her. "I'm listening."

Peggy told him about the strange appearance of the two women who both claimed to be Tanya Abutto. "They both thought I had his duffel bag—I'm guessing the one Reggie told me he took into the convention center with him."

Steve opened the car door for her and closed it after she was inside. He got in on the driver's side and started the engine. "Who's Reggie?"

"The security guard at the gate. I wonder if Al talked to him."

"Was there something special about the duffel bag?"

"Not besides the fact that it should have been with Aris. I think it's possible that whoever killed him took the bag. He may even have been killed for what was in the bag."

Steve laughed. "I like the way you take those broad leaps without any facts to back them up."

"That's not my job. Are you taking me out for dinner to make up for the shabby way you treated me today?"

"Shabby way I treated you?" He raised his eyebrows. "I was hoping you were taking *me* out to dinner for that reason."

"I thought I acted professionally as a liaison figure between the flower show and the police. Besides, you didn't tell me you were going to be there."

"I didn't know until you found the body of a dead orchid grower from South Africa and I got the call from Charlotte PD."

"You could've texted me."

Steve pulled the late model Ford over to the side of Providence Road. "You know that's not possible, right? I'm sure John didn't update you when he went out on a call. You know what to expect from this. You can handle it, Peggy, if you want to."

Her head felt wooden. She stared at him, trying to find that peace she'd promised herself. He was the same man she had loved before she knew that his life could be in jeopardy. Nothing had changed.

Except that now she was afraid—wondering who would come and tell her when something happened to him.

"I want to," she assured him. "I have to get past remembering the night John didn't come home. Please don't try and placate me that your job is safe, Steve. We both know better."

He sighed and took her in his arms. "And you're doing it again on this case, Peggy. Trying to figure it out without telling anyone else what you really know."

"I don't know anything that I haven't told someone."

"Except this thing about Tanya Abutto and the duffel bag? Does Al know about it? Maybe it would be best if we go and see him."

Peggy touched his hand on the steering wheel. "I'm sorry. I'm trying to work it out. I wish I understood your job more. I'm sure you're a very good FBI agent."

"Thanks." He headed back into traffic. "Peggy, there's no way to assure you that nothing will happen to me, like it did to John. I can only promise to be careful and not to take any unnecessary risks."

"I know."

He laughed. "I wish you'd promise me the same thing. You don't give a thought to putting yourself in harm's way."

"I don't mean to."

"That's part of the not thinking aspect, I'm afraid."

They were quiet for a few minutes while Steve maneuvered the car through heavy evening traffic. When they'd reached the police station where Al's office was located, Steve parked and turned off the engine.

"I wasn't trying to hold anything back," she assured him.

"I know. You seem to be inspired by events around you." He lightly touched her face. "People trust you and say things to you that they forget to say to the police. I've seen you at work."

"Thanks, I think." She smiled. "I help where I can."

"That's what scares me." Steve took her hands. "My point is that I'm sorry you're afraid. I wouldn't have put this on you—except that I fell in love with this beautiful woman with the greenest eyes. I couldn't go back after that."

"Flattery will get you somewhere."

"You know all my secrets now. I wish I'd been free to tell you sooner, but you were very involved with your Internet friend, *Nightflyer*. We suspected him of killing John. It was important for you to put on an innocent face. Your life could've been in danger if he'd guessed what was going on."

Peggy wasn't surprised by his words about *Nightflyer*. He'd partially explained about that right after she'd found out about him being with the FBI.

She'd met *Nightflyer* in an Internet chat room and they'd proceeded to spend a lot of time on the Internet, playing chess and sharing information. She still didn't believe *Nightflyer* had killed John. He'd saved her life with his information more than once.

Steve kissed her quickly and got out of the car. "Let's see what Al makes of the many Tanyas that have come into your life today."

Peggy got out of the car and followed him to the building. "I really meant to call Al, but with the shop getting busy and talking to the flower show people, I forgot."

Before Steve could answer, Al walked out of the building, almost bumping into them.

"Steve! Peggy! What brings you here? And please don't tell me it has anything to do with what happened at the convention center. Unless you're here to take me out to dinner, I don't want to know about it."

Steve shrugged. "We were headed that way."

"Good deal. I haven't eaten since breakfast, and that was one of Mary's homemade granola bars. This healthy eating is about to kill me."

"I know some place that doesn't have any healthy food at all," Peggy said.

"Lead on then." Al laughed. "Don't say a blessed other thing to me about work until I have either a biscuit, some fried chicken, or a big glob of buttery mashed potatoes in my mouth."

Peggy directed Steve to Bob's Chicken Coop Restaurant on Tryon Street. It was tucked away from the usual places people went in the downtown area, but it was always crowded. People who'd lived in Charlotte a long time knew the best food was found here, as long as you didn't mind fat and calories.

Pictures of state senators, N.C. governors, and even a president or two, were up on the walls but that was the only pretention the old place had, except for serving a good meal. The chairs were wooden ladder backs and the tables were worn smooth. There was always a single flower in the middle of the table. It was a daisy tonight.

"What kind of flower is that?" Al asked after he'd ordered his chicken and biscuits.

"Even I know that," Steve said. "It's a daisy. It has pyrethrum in it. That's what they use to make insecticide. Right?"

"Close." Peggy smiled. "That's what they use to make mosquito repellant."

Al laughed at him. "That's what you get for showing off. Speaking of which, are the two of you couples who talk about cases or not? Mary doesn't want to hear it."

Steve and Peggy exchanged glances as the waitress brought them all sweet iced tea.

"We're deciding that." Peggy unwrapped her silverware. "I'm good with talking about it. Not sure about Steve."

Al rolled his eyes. "Don't make me have Mary talk to you all. You know she'll do it."

"I don't want to have any more secrets between us," Steve echoed Peggy. "I'd like everything out in the open."

"I know you both pretty well. I'd say you'll be the talking couples, all up in each other's business. That's fine."

Steve changed the subject and told Al about what had happened to Peggy. "Do you know anything about a missing duffel bag?"

"The security guard said something about Abutto coming in with one. We've gone through his things, at his hotel and at the convention center, and couldn't find it. He could've hidden it or dropped it somewhere. Did you feel threatened by the daughter?"

Peggy shrugged. "No. Neither girl was actually Tanya. Both girls wanted the duffel bag badly. Maybe you should look a little harder for it."

"Is there surveillance at the convention center or the hotel?" Steve asked. "Maybe we could get a picture of Abutto coming or going with it and at least have an idea of what the bag looks like."

Al slapped him on the back. "Good idea. Why didn't I think of that?"

"No security footage?" Steve guessed.

"Inside, not outside. So far, we haven't seen hide nor hair of Abutto carrying a bag inside. Maybe he checked it at the door." Al frowned. "I guess we'll have to take the bag a little more seriously if Peggy is being harassed about it."

"Thanks, Al," she said. "If there are any more Tanyas, I'll give them your cell phone number."

Al made a note in the book he always carried. "Anything you want to share from the FBI?"

Steve shrugged. "Nothing unusual about his travel arrangements or anything at his home. We're still looking into his background."

"I never met Aris Abutto in person until the day he started setting up at the convention center," Peggy said as their food arrived. "But I've known him through years of correspondence and talking on the phone and the Internet. I've seen pictures of Tanya."

"Maybe he was growing something he shouldn't have been growing." Al mimicked smoking. "He might've had drugs in that bag. With his background, he could've cleared customs without anyone batting an eye."

"Or knowing what they were looking for," Steve agreed, making a note in his cell phone.

Bob Richmond, the owner of the restaurant, came out of the kitchen. His frantic eyes scanned the busy eating area until he found Peggy's face.

"There you are!" He pointed and yelled across the room. "I need your help. Come into the kitchen quick."

*Azalea*

*Azaleas are members of the Ericaceae family which are ancient plants dating back 70 million years. They are related to rhododendrons and blueberries. Most azalea types we know today were cultivated by monks in Buddhist monasteries. Seeds of the rhododendron, sent to England, became the azalea hybrids of today. The early spring bright pinks, reds, and whites brighten even the gloomiest of days. They are also deadly poisonous.*

# Chapter Seven

Bob's real surname name was Christou. He'd changed it for the restaurant, not wanting anyone to know he was Greek when he'd first come to Charlotte.

Peggy had met him for the first time the day after his restaurant had opened more than twenty-five years ago. He'd become fast friends with her and John. They'd shared many meals here.

"What is it?" Peggy scooted back her chair to follow him. "What's wrong?"

Bob led her, Al, and Steve back into the bustling kitchen area. There were cooks and servers everywhere, no spare inch to waste. Everyone was moving at the same time but in different directions. They dipped and weaved to avoid running into stock pots, plates of vegetables, and huge trays of fried chicken and biscuits.

They finally reached a large window which overlooked the alley behind the restaurant. It was dark now but Peggy knew it would be sunny during the day. There were a dozen herb plants sitting on the recently painted window sill.

One of them appeared to have fallen. There was potting soil on the floor and the oregano plant was half out of its red ceramic pot.

"I think it's going to die," Bob said dramatically, his dark eyes moistening and lips trembling. "You remember this plant? You gave it to me all those years ago when you and John first came here."

Peggy smiled. "I remember. It certainly has grown."

"Can you save it? Some stupid nephew of mine knocked it down. I owe everything to this plant. It brings me luck. If it dies, I think I'll lose my business."

She handed Steve her bag. "Let me take a look. Are these others cuttings from this plant?"

"A few of them. Of course, I have some thyme and some marjoram. I try to keep a little of everything. People like the fresh herbs." Bob held up the other plants as he spoke.

"I think this one needs to be repotted." Peggy diagnosed the oregano. "The soil is depleted. Every so often you should give it fresh dirt, even if you fertilize. And it's too wet. Water it a little less often. It should be moist or even a little dry."

"And I cut off the flowers as soon as I see them, like you told me." Bob grinned. "It's been a long time, but I don't forget."

"And remember to cut the whole stem before you strip

away the leaves, even though you don't want the stem."

"What not wanting the stem?" Bob showed her several large bundles of stems tied together. "I give them for gifts. I read on Goggle that it's good for you to add to the bath."

"That should be it." Peggy tucked the roots of the old oregano plant back into the soil. "I think it will be fine. You've done a good job taking care of it."

The plant reminded her of how young and carefree she and John had been when she'd given it to Bob. They were just starting their lives together with wonderful plans for the future.

Not that their life together hadn't been glorious, she reflected as she wiped her hands on a towel and took back her bag. John's life had been cut short, too short. It wasn't fair.

She'd started The Potting Shed on her own after his death. He should've been there to enjoy it. It was his dream too.

"Thank you so much, Plant Lady!" Bob kissed her hand. "I don't see you here often enough."

Peggy patted her stomach. "I can't eat those sweet potato fries all the time!"

They all laughed, agreeing that none of them could eat the things they could when they were younger.

"I saw you on TV yesterday with that bad business at the convention center," Bob said. "That poor man who was killed. It's a terrible thing for a man to be shot tending to his own business. He was here for lunch the day before. I didn't know him then but I knew the man he was with."

Al perked up as much as any plant in the right environment. "You saw Mr. Abutto here at lunch time? Who was he with?"

"He was with that man who runs the convention center." Bob thumped his gray head. "I can't remember his name. Where has my brain gone?"

"Dabney Wilder," Al supplied. "Mr. Wilder failed to tell us that in his interview. He said he'd never met Abutto."

"Did he have a large bag with him?" Steve asked.

"I don't know." Bob shrugged. "I wouldn't even remember him except I saw his picture on the TV after he died. A bad way to remember, huh?"

They all agreed and had another good laugh at old age before Peggy and her companions went back out to the dining room to eat dinner.

"I'd like to know how Dabney came to have lunch with Abutto but completely forgot about it." Al tucked his napkin into his shirt collar and started on his huge plate of fried chicken. "Maybe he can tell us a little more about him."

"What about taking a drug dog into the convention center?" Steve suggested. "If the duffel bag is still there and had drugs in it, the dog could find it."

Peggy smiled as she ate her sweet potato fries. "The only problem with that are all the plants in there right now. Even the best-trained dog would get lost in the scent of all those flowers."

"That makes sense," he agreed. "I don't like the idea that people are sending a fake 'daughter' of Mr. Abutto's to visit you. They were friendly today, but tomorrow, they might get pushier."

"I think they'll get the idea that the police have the bag. It makes more sense than me having it. I didn't see Aris before he was killed."

"Steve's right, Peggy." Al looked up at her across the table. "I'll assign someone to keep an eye on you for the next day or so until we see how the investigation progresses."

"I'll take the night shift on that." Steve grinned.

"No offense, Mr. Director, but an officer outside the house would be better." Al's tone said that the matter was resolved. "Hey, it's almost eight-thirty. I have to get going. Mary is gonna have my head. I'll see you two tomorrow."

When Al was gone, Peggy and Steve finished up quickly and drove home. Their conversation was sporadic and less personal. When they got out of the car, Peggy noticed the patrol car across the street in the shadow of a hundred-year-old oak tree.

"He didn't waste any time," Steve remarked. "He cares a lot about you."

"We've known each other most of our lives." Peggy unlocked the side door to the house. "John would laugh at the idea of Al and me working together."

"So you weren't into forensic botany when John was alive?"

"Maybe a little, but it was unapplied theory. I was working full-time at Queen's University."

She opened the door and Shakespeare ran out into the

yard. His enthusiasm was humorous even though Steve felt like the Great Dane should have been better trained than to run out because the door was open.

"I'll stay out here with him and get the mail," Steve told her.

"All right. I'll have to check on my plants. It shouldn't take too long."

"Good. I think we have some talking to catch up on."

Peggy sighed as she left him outside. She wished she had better answers for him. She was afraid it was going to be a matter of time and learning to adapt to this new version of Steve. There was no magic pill or herb tea she could think of that would make a difference.

She kicked off her shoes and went downstairs to the basement. Switching on the lights, she could see Walter had done an excellent job tending to her plants. He was an eager, talented gardener, as well as an enthusiastic botanist. He wanted to know about everything she was working on. It was nice to have someone to talk to who was as interested in her experiments as she was.

John had loved gardening. He'd called working in the yard his getaway. He'd come home and put his hands in the dirt to forget all the ugly, sordid things he'd seen and heard on the streets of Charlotte. He was amazing with trees and shrubs and had grown azalea flowers the size of grapefruit. All of their neighbors had been envious.

She missed that close kinship in their interests. She and Steve talked about the things they were interested in, but they were very different things.

Her phone rang. It was Dorothy Beck, wanting her to come and work at the morgue tomorrow.

"I can't do that," Peggy said. "The police are letting the flower show open again tomorrow. I have to be there."

"All right. We'll just keep piling things up on your table." Dorothy paused for humorous effect. " Seriously, I really need you here to cover the botanical findings. If you can delegate some time to someone else, come on over. It's possible those plant things we're missing could help solve the case."

"I'll come if I can. If not tomorrow, since it will be opening day for the show, I'll come the next day."

Dorothy sighed dramatically into the phone. "We'll do the best we can without you. The cause of death was easy enough. Dr. Abutto died from the gunshot wound. Whoever killed him was in a hurry to bury him. He had some dirt in his lungs."

*Aris was still alive when he was buried.*

Peggy took a deep breath to calm herself. She didn't mind helping the forensic lab at the morgue with information about botanical evidence, but she wasn't very good with the other parts. She was still as squeamish now as she had been the first time she'd been involved in a murder investigation. She hoped she was better at hiding it.

"In other words, not a very nice person," she said to Dorothy.

"Not many murderers are, my friend. Goodnight. I hope to see you tomorrow."

*Cedar*

*Cedar trees (Cupressaceae) have been very important to humans for hundreds of years. They have been used to make canoes, weapons, bowls and baskets. The pleasant smell humans enjoy is deadly to insects and fungus. They can reach 100 feet in height and can live a long time.*

# Chapter Eight

Peggy and Steve stayed up late that night, talking about everything from the time they'd met to the present day. It was early spring in Charlotte so Steve had started a dry cedar fire in the hearth where they sat. The smell was wonderful. At about ten p.m., they made hot chocolate and drank it as the words drained from them.

"Paul called me while I was outside with Shakespeare," Steve told her. "He has the morning shift watching the house—and you. He's not happy that you're involved in the investigation."

"He never is. You know Paul wants to protect me from everything." She stared into the flames. "I'm sure he's talked to you about it before."

"He has," Steve agreed. "I feel the same way. I'm not your son, so I know you're going to do whatever you think you should do. It's different."

She smiled and put her empty cup on the side table. "I suppose it is. I know you worry too. That's one good thing about finding out that you're with the FBI. I can worry about you too."

"Is that the best thing you can think of about it?"

"John was killed doing his job. I wouldn't have chosen to marry another man who could die the same way."

Steve's eyes were steady on hers. "So you wouldn't have married me if you'd known?"

Peggy leaned over and kissed him. "I don't think I could've stopped myself. Even if I'd known, we'd still be sitting here by the fire, ready to go upstairs."

"Well, that's a good thing. I know this has been crazy for you. It was hard keeping it from you too."

"You're better at keeping secrets than I am." She put her arms around him. "You didn't give me my new bicycle until the day *before* my birthday party."

He laughed. "Okay. I'm better with keeping big secrets. Maybe I'm not so good at keeping the small ones."

"I don't care. I love you, Steve. I want to be with you. I need a little time to get used to all of this. I'm sure we'll work it out. Just don't shut me out when something is going on, okay?"

Steve got to his feet and held out his hand to her. "Let's finish this upstairs, huh? I'd rather talk to you in bed."

How could she say no?

* * *

Peggy came downstairs with Shakespeare the next morning to find her son invading her kitchen.

"Good morning. I didn't know surveillance meant eating all my food."

"I'm starving." Paul pulled out some hard boiled eggs and cheese from the refrigerator. "I had to leave before breakfast, not that Mai eats breakfast anymore. I'll be glad when her morning sickness is over. I like the food situation here better since Steve moved in. At least there's always something to eat."

Peggy put the kettle on the stove to boil. "It seems odd that Al would assign you to keep an eye on me."

"I volunteered." Paul sat down and poured some orange juice. "I thought it might as well be me. I know you. I know how sneaky you can be."

"Sneaky?" Steve joined them. "Your mother? Only when she isn't sure if she'll get to do something no one else wants her to do."

"You two can stop talking about me like I'm not here anytime." Peggy got down a cup and a peach tea bag. "I'm not sneaky, and adults get to do whatever they want, as long as it's legal."

Paul laughed. "Funny you don't feel that way about me."

"Me either." Steve took Shakespeare outside for his morning walk.

"Do you have any English muffins?" Paul asked as he peeled an egg.

"You're so like your father," she remarked. "Always

hungry. It used to make me so mad that he stayed skinny no matter what he ate."

"Maybe you don't eat enough." Paul rummaged around until he found two slices of bread that he slid into the toaster. "Mai is always telling me the same thing. That's why we never have anything good to eat at our house. Of course now we only have food that's good for the baby."

"Dr. Beck called me in to work on the botanical finds on the murder case. It will be nice to spend some time with Mai at the lab. Otherwise, I only get to see her when we have dinner once a month."

Paul groaned. "I'm looking forward to that. After she spends 'quality' time with you, she picks up a lot of your opinions. Quit trying to brainwash my wife."

She smiled at her son who looked more like his father every year, except for the red hair and green eyes. That was all from her and her family.

"I'll be sure to tell her you said that."

He grabbed his toast when it popped up. "That's exactly what I mean."

Steve brought Shakespeare back in and fed him. "What did I miss?"

"Nothing." Paul buttered his toast. "Same old mom."

"If you're watching out for your mother today, why aren't you in uniform?" Steve asked.

"The captain thought it would be better for me to blend in." Paul looked down at his jeans and T-shirt. "All I need is some dirt on my hands and no one will know that I'm not an excited gardener."

"Good call." Steve reached above Peggy's head to grab a bag of donuts. "Breakfast of champions."

"That's what I'm looking for!" Paul's hand made a quick snatch and grab when the bag of donuts was close enough. "So do we like anyone for the murder yet?"

"Not that I've heard." Steve sat down with a cup of coffee. "Did they fill you in on why Al wanted to keep an eye on your mother?"

"Something about her being harassed by people who might be involved. Nothing definite."

Peggy and Steve filled him in on the women who'd approached her about Dr. Abutto's bag.

"Nice. So I'm there to protect you from some cute, young thing?" Paul smiled.

"I'm *definitely* going to tell Mai you said that." Peggy stirred honey into her tea.

"By the way, while we're on the subject, I got an email this morning. Dr. Abutto's daughter is in London at the university. Scotland Yard will keep an eye on her while we work the investigation." Steve popped a donut into his mouth.

"Well, maybe they'll approach me again today and Paul can grab whichever version of Tanya comes to ask for the bag again. She might have some information. I'd like to get this over with."

Paul *tsked.* "You always wanted me to be more interested in your plants. I have all day to stand around listening to you amaze everyone with what you know about seeds and weeds. How can you want that to be over?"

"No one you meet at the flower show today will be amazed at anything I know," she corrected him. "These are experts, like Aris. If anything, I'll be the one that's amazed."

Steve and Paul exchanged looks across the table and burst out laughing.

"We're not buying it, Mom. It won't matter how much they know, you'll know more."

"I'm with him," Steve agreed. "And I have to get out of here. I'm meeting some agents at the airport to go over the private plane Dr. Abutto flew in on. Maybe it will give us some other clues as to what he brought into the country."

Steve and Peggy kissed briefly before he left. When he was gone, Paul went down to the basement with his mother to check on her plants. Shakespeare ran loose in the walled garden outside, chasing birds and squirrels.

"How's it going with you and Steve?" Paul poked around in her plants until Peggy told him to leave them alone.

"It's going fine. Everyone is more worried about us than we are."

"I talked to Steve, Mom. He's worried."

"I won't say that it's not difficult." She adjusted the temperature on one of her experiments. "But I'm sure we'll work it out."

"Maybe you should tell him that."

"I have. We talked about it for a long time last night."

"Okay. I'm just saying—"

Walter poked his head into the open doorway. "I'm not intruding, am I?"

"Not at all." Peggy was glad for the subject change. "Would you like to check the rotations on the plants for me? I want to make sure the sunlight is even."

"I'd be happy to." He bowed a little formally. "I'm going to change my mind about coming to the flower show, however, if that offer of a free ticket still stands. I watched the news last night. Who knew there'd be such drama?"

Peggy shook her head. "I think you'll find the flowers and trees more interesting than the drama of someone's death, especially since you enjoy the field so much."

"I wouldn't mind a ride there—you know how I hate to drive. I can have these calculations done by the time you're ready to go." He looked at her fuzzy lady bug slippers and robe.

"I took a taxi yesterday. It's too far to ride my bike." Peggy glanced at her son. "But since I'm going to be in protective custody today, maybe Paul can give both of us a ride."

"You know I'm not supposed to do that," Paul reminded her.

"In normal cases, yes," she agreed. "But since you're supposed to keep me safe, I think a ride for me and Walter would be in order."

"Okay. If the captain comes down on me, I'm sending him to Al."

"I'll be ready in a few minutes."

Because Peggy had been so careful with her new green suit and heels yesterday, only to have the flower show close down, today she wore something a little less formal. The black slacks and shell-knit pink sweater were lightweight and very durable. She wore black flats instead of heels and added a little makeup to cover some of the fine lines that ran from her eyes and the heavy number of freckles on her face.

She thought again about dyeing the white streaks out of her bright red hair but it hardly seemed worth the effort. She wasn't a glamorous figure. She was more worried about her plants than what she looked like. Steve seemed to be all right with that. Who else mattered?

Her computer on the desk in her bedroom chimed, telling her there was a new email. She sat down and brought up the hundreds of emails from universities and botanists around the world. She was looking for a particular email that she'd been expecting since yesterday.

There it was. She knew *Nightflyer* would send her something. He always seemed to know what was going on, especially if there was trouble.

*Dear Peggy,*

*I see you've managed to get in the way of trouble once again. There is more than meets the eye on Dr. Abutto's death, and many involved who will stop at nothing to complete the task he began when he left South Africa. Be very careful. Here is the number of a burner phone where you can reach me only for today. Don't hesitate to call if you need help. ~ Nightflyer*

Peggy copied the number into her cell phone but didn't add a name to it. Since Steve had been investigating him, she didn't want him to know that she was still in touch with her old friend. She was as guilty as Steve about hiding things, she supposed.

She turned off her computer. She was very good at keeping secrets when she needed to. It was something to remember when she thought about Steve keeping his secret from her.

In her heart, she knew she was more afraid of what could happen to him than that he'd kept his job with the FBI a secret. Loving a man, knowing that every time he left might be the last time she would see him, wasn't easy. It was hard with Paul too.

When she went downstairs, Paul and Walter were studying the thirty-foot blue spruce that was growing in the entrance hall. It grew in the same opening that the large, spiral staircase occupied. John had argued with his family to have a skylight put in above it so the spruce had enough light. They didn't like changes to the house.

"You know, Mom," Paul said. "I think this tree looks a little off color. Maybe a little yellow. Could it be anemic?"

"No. It's natural for evergreens to cycle through some color changes as they grow." She touched the needles of the tree closest to her as she walked down the stairs. A few came off in her hand.

It was a pleasure to see the tree growing each day. She and John had planted it when they first moved here.

"I told him the same thing," Walter said. "If you don't know anything about plant life, it's best to leave it alone."

Paul shrugged. "I'd hate to see you have to take it out, that's all. Ready?"

Paul had seen the tree every day of his life. Peggy

liked that he'd thought about its health. She agreed with him about not wanting to take the tree out. She was very careful with it, and regularly consulted an arborist who was a friend of hers. She might have him come by and take a look, just to be sure.

"I'm ready," she said. "Let's hope things go better today."

Walter snickered. "Or at least they're as *interesting.*"

Traffic was light from Queen's Road to the convention center. They made excellent time. Despite what had happened yesterday—or maybe because of it—the parking lot was full. People were lined up at the gate waiting to get inside.

"Looks like the murder helped attendance," Paul said. "I'll let you two off here and park the car. Don't get into any trouble while I'm gone."

Peggy poked him. "There were crowds here yesterday that had to be turned away. Maybe some of them are lookey-loos, but gardeners from across the world attend the flower show every year. Just because you don't like gardening, doesn't mean other people don't."

Her son laughed. "You are so predictable. Just mention something bad about flowers and you get all riled up."

She ignored him and got out of the car. Walter was already out and waiting for her. It was nine-forty-five; the gate would open at ten. Peggy hoped everyone was ready for the surge of traffic that would come through the doors.

"Good morning again, Peggy." Reggie saluted her. "Looks like a busy morning. I hope things go better today, I surely do."

"Thanks. I hope so too."

### *Daisy*

*Daisies have been known since at least 2,000 B.C. They were cultivated for their herbal and medicinal properties. These flowers have always been used by pharmacists and physicians from around the world, as the daisy has some hybrid in every culture. During medieval times in England, it was known as 'daes eage' which meant 'day's eye', a correlation to using the flowers as a cure for eye ailments. The plant has been used at one time or another to treat nearly all the parts of the human body.*

# **Chapter Nine**

The convention center was humming with activity as everyone did last minute prep for the visitors waiting outside. Thousands of colored chrysanthemums made up everything from rainbow bridges to tents and animals. Thousands of daisies had been used to create dream gardens and everyday items such as wheelbarrows, tractors, and fountains. The smell of roses, every shade imaginable, brought cottages, forests and carriages with flowered horses to life.

"Wow!" Walter stopped walking, staggered by the hours of work that had gone into creating these microcosms of life. "I had no idea it would be this way. What an accomplishment!"

Peggy smiled when she saw the amazed look on his sallow face. "I told you another murder wouldn't be better than seeing all of this."

Paul made it inside before the gates opened. Peggy let Walter wander the premises as he pleased. Rebecca Bandy, whose exhibit had been torn apart by the police, was still desperately trying to get it back in order.

"This was insane," Rebecca said to Peggy as the two of them were putting in clumps of violets, oxalis, and other plants to recreate her exhibit. "I wish someone would've told me. I could've been here earlier to get this cleaned up."

"The police wouldn't let anyone come in any earlier." Peggy tied pieces of moss to the sides of the cabin Rebecca had worked on. "I'm sorry this happened to you. Did you know Dr. Abutto?"

Rebecca Bandy was a tall, strong-looking woman with very short dark hair and a constantly angry expression on her plain face.

"I didn't know him at all." She used orange mums to decorate her attractive fence post. "I don't know why someone decided to kill him in *my* exhibit. Why didn't they kill him in his own exhibit?"

"I'm not sure." Peggy helped her lift a wagon wheel that had been knocked aside by the police. "Maybe this was closer for them. I think this may be a crime of happenstance rather than premeditated. There were thyme flowers where Dr. Abutto was buried. I think the killer was remorseful after the deed was done."

"Thyme flowers?" Rebecca considered the idea. "Do they know who killed him yet, or why?"

"Not as far as I know. It's hard to figure these things out most of the time."

Peggy finished helping Rebecca get set up before she walked down the concourse, checking in with the vendors and growers. Most of the people understood that the flower show had been disrupted under terrible circumstances. They asked about Dr. Abutto's family.

Others told her they planned to demand the money back that they'd paid for registration. There was no accounting for how people would react to adversity.

She finally reached The Potting Shed's exhibit on her return trip. Selena and Sam had set it up and they'd done a great job. Peggy was afraid other exhibitors might get upset if she had anything to do with her own exhibit. There were prizes for the best and most interesting features at the show. She wasn't judging them, but she would be handing them out.

"What do you think?" Sam asked when he saw her. "I think everything held up okay."

Sam wanted to promote the landscaping aspect of the business, of course. Peggy hadn't objected—the landscaping promoted the shop and vice-versa. It was hard to notice one without the other.

To make that happen, Sam had created a real waterfall with rocks and bright green moss. It had taken him days to put it all together. The back of the exhibit appeared to be the back of a house. It was meant to state, 'Your backyard could look like this!'

Selena had spent hours creating bluebirds out of mums that had been dyed blue. There were rows of dwarf asters in purple, blue, and pink that were accentuated by columbines and coreopsis. On one side, the tall flowers, including fox gloves, day lilies and campanulas that created a showy height which set off the rocks and the waterfall.

"It looks wonderful, breathtaking!" Peggy raved. "Who wouldn't want their backyard to look this way?"

"I wouldn't," Paul said. "Not unless Sam was going to take care of it. I don't even like to think about all the work that went into this."

Sam and Paul shook hands.

"You pay me and I'm part of the deal," Sam said. "Ask your mom. I'm not cheap, but I'm easy."

Selena giggled. "You can say that again."

"Anyway." Peggy shook her head. "I have to go check in with everyone else. The exhibit looks fantastic, you two. Lunch is on me. Let me know what you want and I'll send Paul out for it."

"I'm not here to run errands." Paul's trained eyes searched the crowd that had begun to throng through the convention center. "I'm supposed to be here watching out for you."

Sam frowned. "What happened?"

Peggy waved her hand as though it was unimportant. "Police protection. I'll explain later."

She left quickly before she got trapped into answering other questions. Paul stayed with her even though the crowd swelled so much that both of them were crushed as they strolled down the concourse.

The media was on hand again, from different cities across the region. Peggy did several interviews which included questions about the murder. She kept her answers circumspect, not wanting to hinder the investigation. She didn't want to spend all her time talking about the murder either.

"It looks as though murder is good for business," one

reporter from Atlanta quipped.

"I think this show would've done very well without the unfortunate circumstance. It's a time-honored event every year, with a devoted following."

"Would you like to show us Dr. Abutto's exhibit?" the reporter asked.

"I'm sure it's off limits. Thank you so much for coming today." Peggy shook the woman's hand and walked away. They'd have to figure it out by themselves.

Paul stayed at Peggy's side all morning as she made the rounds talking to all of the vendors at the show. Most were happy to be there. Their exhibits looked good and the crowd continued to grow.

Contrary to her earlier statement, Selena went out to get lunch for Peggy, Paul, and Sam. She came back with sub sandwiches and news that the parking lot was full and traffic was spilling into an alternate lot.

"There's Dabney Wilder." Peggy pointed out the head of the convention center. She knew he also was responsible for several other public venues in Charlotte. "I wonder if Al has had a chance to talk to him yet."

"We're not doing that, right, Mom?" Paul finished his sandwich and balled up the wrapper. "You're way too busy keeping the show running to be involved in the investigation, right?"

Sam and Selena both laughed. Over lunch, Peggy had told them all the details about the two visits from different Tanyas and her dinner at Bob's Chicken Coop last night.

"Peggy's never too busy to ask questions and otherwise get involved in anything she isn't supposed to be involved in." Sam chugged the last of his bottled lemonade.

"That's true," Selena said. "Badly put together, but true."

"It'll only take a minute." Peggy kept her eye on Dabney to keep from losing him in the crowd.

"You stay right here. I'll be right back." Peggy said.

"If you're going, I'm going." Paul got to his feet. "It's not like he's gonna know I'm on the job. I won't spook him, but if something goes down, I'll be there."

"Paul—"

"Let's do it." He helped her to her feet. "I've always wanted to see my mother, the botanical detective, in action."

"Oh, all right then." She touched up her lipstick and picked up her bag. "Don't say anything."

"I won't," he promised with a smile. "This is all on you."

They walked through the crowd that was hovering around The Potting Shed's exhibit. Sam had handed out hundreds of flyers already. Selena had made more while she was out getting lunch.

Dabney was with a man Peggy recognized, Tim Roseboro. Tim was a wealthy man who came from a rich and important background in the city. One of his forefathers had signed the Mecklenburg Declaration of Independence, a historic document that had preceded the national version. His father had been on the city council for many years.

The family was ensconced in a huge mansion on

Sharon Road, aptly named Rose Cottage, presumably for the beautiful, old rose garden that grew in front.

Peggy knew Tim from working with the committee to bring the flower show to Charlotte. He'd been deeply involved in the process.

"Dabney. Tim." She approached them with a smile on her face. "What a wonderful turnout, don't you think?"

"Especially after the terrible thing yesterday." Dabney shook his head, his wild blond hairdo flying everywhere. He was a famous Charlotte attorney who'd once run for DA. After the loss, he went over to the defense side, taking on the biggest and richest clients in the state. "I never expected to see this crowd today. It's amazing."

Tim also said hello to Peggy. "No one can buy that kind of publicity. You know everyone here is expecting to see something that relates to the murder."

"That's a little harsh, don't you think?" Peggy asked.

He shrugged his shoulders. He was a short, thin, studious-looking man, although rumor had it that he was nothing like that. He'd dropped out of several universities across the state. He wore thick, square, black-framed glasses that made his face look too pointed.

"I don't care. Whatever brings the people in. My mother is so happy to have the show here. She'll probably be here everyday. She called the governor yesterday when the show was canceled. She wants it to come to Charlotte every year from now on."

Elaine Roseboro was a formidable woman, from what Peggy had heard of her. Peggy guessed that she must be in her nineties now. She was small but had the ego of a queen. Peggy could imagine the demands she'd put on her son.

"I'd like that too," Peggy admitted, turning to Dabney. "Would you mind if I take a minute or two of your time? I have something I want to ask you."

Dabney shrugged and told Tim he'd see him later. "What is it?"

Peggy's green eyes were sharp as glass. "I heard you had dinner with Dr. Abutto at the Chicken Coop the night he was killed. You may have been the last person to speak with him before his death. Did he say anything unusual?"

*Chamomile*

*Chamomile has a long history of curing digestive problems and having a calming effect on the body. The flowering plant, part of the daisy family, is native to Europe and Asia. The ancient Egyptians used it for fevers and other ailments.*

# Chapter Ten

Dabney's blond eyebrows shot up. They looked remarkably like large, fuzzy caterpillars. "I'm sure I wasn't the last person to see him alive. That might be an exaggeration, don't you think?"

"Well, I know the security guard at the gate saw him before he came inside here. As far as we know, no one else was in the convention center. I was wondering what you two talked about? Did he seem upset at all?"

Dabney grinned quickly, uncomfortably. He straightened his tie. "Are you working for the police now, Peggy? Shouldn't you be asking questions of the vendors?"

"I've spoken to all the vendors," she assured him. "This is me being curious."

"It's annoying." He glanced at Paul. "Is this your bodyguard?"

"No. This is my son."

Paul shook his hand. "Nice to meet you."

"You look familiar," Dabney told him. "Have we met before?"

"People say I look a lot like my mother." Paul shrugged. "I think it's the hair."

"I don't know what you heard or who you heard it from, Peggy," Dabney said. "I had dinner with Abutto. It's not unusual for me to have a meal or coffee with someone who's here at the center. My wife is interested in orchids. I asked his opinion on getting some for her."

"I see." Peggy didn't lose eye contact with him.

Dabney laughed. "That's what this is all about, isn't it? I should've asked you about raising orchids. I'm sorry if I hurt your feelings. Everyone in Charlotte knows that you're the plant lady."

"I appreciate that." Peggy put her hand out to him. "Do you have my business card?"

"No. I'll be glad to take one."

Peggy promised to get a card to him and thanked him for his time. She and Paul went back into the crowd. They sat down again at the picnic table in the backyard Sam had created. Selena was passing out flyers.

"Well?" Sam asked. "Did he kill Abutto?"

"He was uncomfortable about something." Peggy glanced around to make sure no one was listening. "I think I threw him off. He thought I was asking about his meeting with Dr. Abutto because he was looking for information about orchids."

"That's a good thing." Sam finished off Selena's lemonade too. "You don't need him sending someone after you to look for the duffel bag too."

"He was nervous," Paul admitted. "I don't think Al has questioned him yet."

"I don't either," Peggy agreed.

"So what's next?" Sam asked. "Need me to jump in somewhere?"

"I'm not sure what to do next," Peggy said. "If something comes up, I'll let you know. Thanks for volunteering."

"I know the way it is. Either I volunteer or you draft me." Sam shrugged. "Same thing, either way. At least I keep some of my dignity by volunteering."

Paul laughed and finished his soda. "I can't believe you were so against me becoming a cop, Mom. You've got your own people on the job all the time."

Sam agreed, chuckling.

They were interrupted when Selena came over to get Sam to talk to a potential landscape customer.

Peggy's phone rang. She could hardly hear it in the noisy crowd.

It was Dorothy. "We have some samples we need you to look at. Anyone can keep that flower show going, Peggy. Are you our forensic botanist or not?"

"All right. These are extreme circumstances. I'll try to find someone to fill in for me."

Peggy had a working member of the flower show

committee paged. She knew Adam Morrow had to be around somewhere, even though he hadn't answered her calls or texts.

Adam had been her right hand man setting up the show. They didn't meet regularly, or even work together. She'd given him tasks and he'd taken care of them. He'd updated her when something was done or needed to be done.

He finally called her after hearing the message on the PA system. "Sorry, Peggy. I got a burst water pipe over here. The plumber has been here so I think we're good to go. My pond didn't look like much when it was empty and my koi didn't like it either. What can I do for you?"

Adam ran four florist shops in the Charlotte area. He was good at dealing with emergencies.

"I loved your setup," she told him. "I came by this morning but your assistant said you were out. I thought the wedding theme was awesome. You always come up with good ideas."

He laughed. "What are you buttering me up for?"

"I need to leave the show, hopefully for only a few hours." She told him about her obligation to the medical examiner. "Trust me, she's not someone you want to mess with."

"Like I believe you're afraid of anyone," he quipped. "Don't worry about it. I can walk around and listen to people complain while I hold their hands as good as you can."

"Thanks, Adam. I'll let you know when I get back."

Peggy told Selena and Sam she was going. Sam didn't

care. He was negotiating the promise of a new landscaping contract for a country club in the Ballantyne area.

Paul walked out with Peggy, texting as he went. When she asked what was so urgent, he told her he was letting Mai know that he'd be at the ME's office.

"She said we could do lunch. She hasn't eaten yet." Paul grinned. "It was only a sandwich. I could eat again."

"You're a pretty good husband. I know Mai appreciates you."

"Sometimes it's hard to tell, especially with the baby coming. There's a lot of tension."

He left her by the front gate, talking to Reggie's replacement, while he went to get the car.

The daytime guard was Pete. Reggie got off right after the opening of the flower show.

"Yeah," Pete said. "Good crowd. We had the Republicans here last month. What a bunch of angry people."

Peggy smiled at his stories about Republicans. "I guess flower growers are probably happier people."

"For the most part. There was this one guy when the exhibits were being set up. I thought about him when I heard about the dead guy, you know?"

Her bright red brows knit together. "Was the angry man with Dr. Abutto?"

"No. I don't remember seeing the guy from South Africa, God rest his soul. I'm talking about that lawyer you always see on TV. The one with the big, fluffy blond hair. I can't remember his name. Not a great commercial, huh?"

She knew who he was talking about. "Dabney Wilder. He helps run the convention center."

"Yeah. He always expects me to valet his car. I'd tell him I'm too busy, but you know where that would end up."

"Who was he with?"

"I don't know who the other guy was." Pete shrugged. "He was chewing him out royally right here in the parking lot. I thought I might have to call the police. Then they calmed down and walked inside together."

"What did he look like?"

"He was short and he wore weird glasses. It looked to me like the lawyer could pick him up and throw him on the ground like one of those wrestlers on TV."

Paul pulled the car up beside her. Peggy thanked Pete for his observations.

She got in the car and told Paul what the security guard had told her.

"I can't believe I leave you for a minute and you're chatting with the security guard about the murder." He smoothly entered traffic going out of the parking lot.

"We weren't talking about the murder. He was telling me about Dabney, and what sounded like Tim Roseboro, arguing in the parking lot."

"Does that have something to do with anything that's going on?"

Peggy smiled. "You never know."

Traffic seemed to be confined to the convention center area. Once they got out of that congestion, there were very few cars. They reached the medical examiner's office and morgue in only a few minutes. Mai was sitting on the front steps, waiting for Paul.

After they'd parked, Paul eagerly ran to his wife's side. Mai was of Vietnamese descent with huge, almond-shaped brown eyes and a pretty face. Most of the time, that young face was hidden behind a microscope or heavy, black-rimmed glasses. Today in the sunshine, her long black hair was down on her shoulders and her smile was sweet when she saw Paul. Her belly was getting rounded in her fourth month of pregnancy.

"Hey there!" He wasted no time kissing her. "What are you thinking about for lunch?"

"Hello, Peggy." Mai looked at her mother-in-law. "Would you like some lunch too?"

"No thanks. I've already eaten. You two go on. I don't think I need protecting for a while."

Mai put her arm around Paul. "I was thinking about walking down to where all the food trucks park. We could have our pick."

"Sounds good." He winked at his mother before he turned away. "You won't believe the morning I've had."

Peggy was glad they seemed so happy together. She knew a child on the way could be difficult. She also knew it only got harder from there, but she was thrilled by the idea of being a grandmother!

She went inside the building and greeted the security guard there. He ran her bag and everything from her pockets through a scanner as they talked about his wife and young son.

"He's having a hard time getting to sleep at night," the guard told Peggy. "We're worn out every day. The doctor doesn't seem to know what to do."

"Have you tried a little chamomile before bed? It might do a world of good."

"Is that okay for him to take? He's only three."

"Of course. I gave it to my son. It won't be forever. Sometimes children go through these things. You can buy it in any grocery store. Look it up on the Internet. Ask your doctor, if you're unsure."

Peggy wrote the word *chamomile* on the back of a piece of paper from her bag.

"Thanks a lot. I think we'll give this a try."

She picked up a white lab coat with her name on it and went to her desk. There were dozens of Post-its all over the surface of the desk and the lampshade. Before she could look at any of them, Dorothy found her.

"It's about time. Do we want to solve this homicide or not? I need my forensic botanist, not the plant lady for a while. Have you had lunch?"

### Geranium

*Geraniums are sometimes referred to as storkbills for their wild first cousins, pelargonium. They bloom throughout the world in temperate areas. What is known now as the true geranium is a product of years of extensive breeding to produce dozens of colors and various shaped flowers. Their scent made them a favorite during England's Victorian era.*

# Chapter Eleven

Peggy was glad she'd had lunch already. Dorothy took her back to the morgue where they looked at Dr. Abutto's body on the slab.

"Now I know all this stuff," Dorothy held up a pink flower, "is thyme. You told me that. What I'm wondering is what this other stuff is? Specifically, does it have anything to do with his death? We found it all over."

Peggy looked at the sample of the greenery in the plastic container marked with a question mark. "That's easy too. It looks like some geranium petals mixed with some mum petals. It wouldn't be surprising for you to have found this on him. These two flowers have been used a lot at the convention center."

"Great." Dorothy took a deep breath. "I know you said the thyme had some meaning to people who believe in that kind of thing."

"Yes. It was a way of conveying messages that was created in the Victorian age."

"What about the geranium and the mums?"

Peggy looked at Dorothy's anxious face. "Well, geraniums mean gentility and mums have different meanings according to their color. This one is spray painted so it's hard to say."

"But nothing threatening, huh?"

"No. Not really. Sorry."

Dorothy looked at the body before she covered it again. "I was hoping you might be able to provide some clues."

Peggy noticed another plastic container on the table. "What's this?"

"We thought it was probably pollen or some other botanical element. It's just white dust. It wasn't even inside of him or anything. I didn't think it looked important."

Dorothy handed her the container. Peggy shifted it back and forth in her gloved hands.

"I don't know exactly what it is, but I can tell you it's not botanical. Are you sure it's not some kind of drug?" She told the ME about the missing bag. "There's been some conjecture on whether or not he might've been smuggling drugs into the country with his orchids."

"I didn't know that." Dorothy looked at the white substance. "Why am I always the last to know? We'll have it tested. Thanks."

Peggy looked at her friend's covered corpse. "I've talked to Aris for years. We'd never met, but once we had when he got here for the show, I didn't notice that he was different at all from the kind, knowledgeable man I'd had dealings with. I find it hard to believe he'd smuggle drugs here. He was so against them."

Dorothy shrugged one thin shoulder. "You never know. Human nature changes. Maybe he didn't want to do it. Maybe it was something he felt he couldn't avoid."

"Maybe so."

"He has a daughter, right?" Dorothy looked at his file. "How old is she?"

"I think somewhere between eighteen and twenty. I wonder if they've told her about his death yet. I'd call her but I've never spoken with her. Aris was very private about his personal life."

"It's probably for the best anyway." Dorothy left the autopsy room. "Professionals know how to handle this kind of thing. They do it every day."

Peggy remembered what it had been like the night John had died. She'd been lucky. Al was the one who'd come to her front door and told her what had happened. She disagreed with Dorothy's assessment. It was better to hear bad news from someone who cared about you.

"I don't have anything else right now." Dorothy left Peggy at her desk. "I'm sorry I had to insist on you coming in right away. It was kind of a bust."

"That's okay. I had someone who could cover for me. Besides, the city and county pay me pretty well to be at your beck and call."

Dorothy looked like she was going to sneeze and laughed instead. "I get it! Beck. That's my name. Police humor. I love it. See you later."

That wasn't what Peggy had meant but she smiled as she checked all the notes on her desk before she trashed them. She called Paul. He was on his way back from the Goofy Gyros truck with Mai. He said he'd be ready to leave in a few minutes.

Peggy went backwards through her routine, grabbing her bag, hanging up her coat. She waved to the guard at the door and went outside to wait.

It was too beautiful a day to be inside. Even with the large glass ceiling on the convention center and being surrounded by every plant imaginable, it still wasn't the same. She sat on the steps, as Mai had done. She was about to call Steve and see what he was up to when her cell phone rang.

She didn't recognize the number and the name came up as unknown. With a little flutter in her stomach, she pressed the button to answer the call. "*Nightflyer*?"

"Good guess," was his reply.

His voice was scratchy, growling. She wasn't sure if it was on purpose and he was disguising his voice or if he sounded that way. She'd only met him once, briefly.

"Where are you?" She scanned the area as though he might be hiding behind one of the cars in the parking lot.

"I can't tell you that. Let's say I'm not in Charlotte. I only have a few minutes to talk. I'll throw away this phone when we're done."

"Okay. Do you have something important to the case?"

"I do. Think about one of the principle exports of

South Africa. After that, think about the only thing precious enough that could make your friend give up his life."

Peggy's eyes got wide as her mind raced. "Are you saying—"

"Think about it."

She knew he was about to hang up. She had to get in one last question. "You knew about Steve, didn't you? Did you know he thinks you might've been involved in John's death?"

The line went dead. She uttered a curse that had once earned her a spanking when she was eight-years-old the first time she'd repeated it after hearing her father say it.

"Was that news from Steve?" Paul asked as he walked up with Mai.

"No. It was Adam telling me about some problems at the show." She put away her phone. There was no way of knowing when she might be able to ask those questions again.

She hoped telling *Nightflyer* about Steve's investigation into him didn't compromise his work. She probably shouldn't have asked the question, but the knowledge that John's death wasn't what it had seemed was gnawing at her.

"Not surprising," Paul said. "I heard from Al and Captain Sedgwick. They both had plenty to say about you grilling Dabney Wilder. He got on the phone with them and the DA, not to mention the mayor, as soon as we left. I'm going to be writing parking tickets for the next ten years."

"That's crazy." Peggy hoped she could set things right for him, if it came down to it. "I asked the questions. You had to be there because you were protecting me."

"Yeah. I think I need someone to protect me."

Mai kissed him and smiled at Peggy. "I might as well go back to work if we're going to talk shop. This isn't as interesting as the dead body waiting for me inside. I'll see you later, sweetie."

They kissed again and Peggy could see that Paul only let her go with great reluctance. It was sweet and poignant. How wonderful it was to be young and in love!

"We're on our way back to the show, right?" Paul started walking toward the car.

"Yes. I'm afraid I wasn't much help to Dr. Beck. I couldn't identify what might be the most important aspect of the trace evidence they found on him."

Paul opened the car door for her. "Was this some weird, little known plant specimen? I thought you knew them all."

"This wasn't a plant at all. I'm not sure what it was. It looked like fine white dust. They're checking it out." She thought about what *Nightflyer* had said but didn't understand it enough to discuss it. She wished she knew how he always knew what was going on.

His words made her feel as though she was right about Aris. Maybe it appeared that he had been doing something wrong, but he might've been killed for trying to do the right thing.

They drove back to the convention center in heavier traffic. When Paul saw the huge crowd at the flower show, he made his mother wait to get out of the car until he could park and get out with her.

"You left me waiting there earlier. I don't see what the big fuss is now."

"I don't want to lose you in the crowd. Think how bad it would look on my record if I lost my own mother." He grinned and hugged her. "Cheer up. Al says if nothing strange happens today, you're on your own again tomorrow."

She kissed his cheek. "Like that would ever be a good thing!"

They started crossing the busy road together during a lull in traffic. Peggy heard the sound of a car moving very quickly. When she looked up, the car was already on them.

Before she could react, Paul yelled, "Mom! Look out!"

He wrapped his arms around her and threw both of their bodies out of the path of the fast-moving car. They rolled on the pavement as the car whizzed by without slowing down.

Several bystanders rushed to see if they were all right, complaining about traffic and wondering who was responsible. Two women helped Peggy to her feet.

Paul was still on the ground. Peggy grabbed his hand.

"Are you all right?" she asked her son. "Do you need an ambulance?"

With the help of another man, Peggy helped her son to his feet. He looked dazed but said he was fine.

"Are you okay?" he asked her as they both heard the sounds of sirens coming from the distance.

"Maybe a little bruised." She hugged him carefully. "You saved my life."

"Just doing my duty, ma'am." He grinned then rubbed the side of his face that had been scratched by the pavement. "I can tell tomorrow will be fun. I probably won't be able to walk. I think my bruises have bruises."

By the time the two Charlotte PD cars stopped, and the officers got out to check on the situation, Peggy and Paul were asking the people who'd helped them what they had seen.

"What's going on?" the first officer to arrive asked. "Is that you, Paul? Were you hurt?"

They explained the situation to the officers. Paul gave them the information they had.

"It was a black Mercedes. The license number started with MLB. I only saw one person in the car."

"I think I saw a sticker from Friendly Car Rentals, the place at the airport." One of the women who'd helped Peggy up added to the description.

"There was a black Mercedes with that sticker at The Potting Shed when the first Tanya came to visit me," Peggy whispered to her son. She gave him the partial plate she remembered.

Paul gave the information to one of the officers and then turned to the small group of witnesses. "I want to thank everyone for their cooperation. If we don't have your name and phone number already, please give it to us so we can get in touch with you if we need to."

The two responding officers chuckled. "Leave it to Paul to investigate his own hit and run."

"I don't think the driver was aiming for me." He looked at his mother. "I think *you* were the target."

### *Sunflower*

*It is believed that Native American tribes cultivated the sunflower as early as 2,000 BC. It is native to the US, taken back to Europe and spread across the world by explorers and botanists. It has been used for dozens of purposes, including food and medicinal uses. Cultivation included bigger seeds and larger crops. People around the world came to realize the usefulness of this plant quickly as the seeds were eaten and pressed for oil. They were also used to remove warts and treat strokes.*

# Chapter Twelve

Peggy heard her cell phone ring. It was on the street with her lipstick and sunglasses that had fallen out of her bag. She went to answer it, limping a little, and could see Steve's face on the screen, but the rest of the phone wasn't working. The screen was broken and apparently, the phone was damaged inside too.

"That's going to be a problem." She picked up all her belongings and stuffed them into her bag again. One of the straps on the bag was also broken.

"What's up?" Paul asked, looking at the broken strap. "It's just a pocketbook, Mom. You can get another."

"It was a one hundred and sixty five dollar handbag," she said tartly. "And you're right, I can get another. My cell phone is broken too. Steve tried to call."

Paul's cell phone started ringing. "Guess who?"

He tapped the name on the screen. "Hi, Steve. She's right here. We had a small problem, but we're okay—except for Mom's phone and pocketbook." He held out the phone to Peggy.

"I'm okay," she told Steve. "Paul thinks someone tried to run me down. I think it was the same car at The Potting Shed with the fake Tanya."

"Are you on your way to the hospital?" Steve asked in an anxious voice. "I'm on my way there now."

"Don't go to the hospital," she cautioned. "We're really fine. We're both a little bruised, but we're going on to the flower show."

"Peggy—you should have someone take a look at you."

"Al just pulled up, Steve. I have to go." She gave the phone back to Paul with a shake of her head.

It only took a moment before Al's phone rang too. Al managed to say the right words that allayed Steve's fears. When he was done talking, he hung up. "He's on his way here anyway. There wasn't anything I could say to prevent it."

Paul, Peggy, and the responding officers, explained everything again to Al. By this time, the witnesses had gone into the flower show. Al had the officers get traffic moving again as he, Paul, and Peggy moved out of the middle of the street.

"This was exactly what I was afraid of." Al shook his head. "Thank goodness you were here, son. You probably saved your mother's life."

Paul took the praise uncomfortably and changed the

subject. "So what now? The two women who approached Mom about the missing duffel bag want to get rid of her? That doesn't make any sense. If they'd kidnapped her to get the information, that would be different."

Al put his hands into his pockets. "I don't know. Peggy manages to stick her nose in so many places that it doesn't belong, it could be anyone."

"Including Dabney Wilder." Peggy told him what Pete the security guard had said about Dabney's fight with Tim in the parking lot.

"First of all," he reminded her, "you don't have positive ID on Tim Roseboro. Just because a description sounds like someone, doesn't make it so."

"They were together at the flower show too," Peggy added. "They looked—uncomfortable. I think something is going on between them."

"And second of all, you weren't supposed to discuss any of this with Dabney Wilder," Al continued. "He's a lawyer. He could sue all of us. Leave him alone. Come to think of it, leave Roseboro alone too. Take care of your flower show. It seems like that would be enough to keep you occupied."

They had reached the front door of the convention center by then. Peggy held the door for a few dozen people to leave. It was getting on in the day. Visitors that had arrived early were leaving.

"I'm taking care of the flower show. I was with Dr. Beck earlier and identified some plants that had nothing to do with Aris's death. I'm part of this investigation, Al, whether you like it or not. I'd rather not be run over, but if you can figure out who was driving that Mercedes that almost killed us, we might have another piece of the puzzle."

One of the officers that had responded to the hit and run came up and quietly gave Al some information.

"That's fine." Al shook his head. "That Mercedes was reported stolen three days ago. The rental company is probably in the clear. Good chance if someone rented it and didn't take it back that they used fake ID."

"Dead end," Paul said.

"I've been thinking since I talked to Dr. Beck." Peggy pushed her ideas forward anyway. "Has someone actually spoken with the real Tanya? I know she's supposed to be at her school in London. Has someone personally verified that?"

"What are you thinking?" Al frowned.

Before Peggy could answer, there were some shouts and chaos as dozens of flower show visitors ran for the front door to get out.

"What's going on in there?" Paul glanced inside the open door.

"I'll have to get back with you on that." Peggy walked in. "I'll have to figure out what's wrong."

"No rush!" Al grinned at her before he started walking away from the entrance.

Paul went inside with his mother. Visitors were running, as though being chased, down the concourse.

"What's wrong?" Peggy asked one of them. "What happened?"

"There's an animal loose in there," the man told her.

"Someone said it's a skunk."

"Oh dear."

Peggy knew exactly where to look. One of the growers from Minnesota had given her grief about several aspects of his exhibit. He grew plants and animals for the film industry and wanted to showcase both.

Her first issue was with the type of plant he wanted to exhibit. They were full-sized marijuana plants. He claimed to have a license from Minnesota to grow the plants. Peggy had to tell him that his license wasn't valid in North Carolina. He switched to eight-foot sunflowers, which were lovely.

The second disagreement they'd had was over the skunk he'd wanted to bring, claiming the animal as a living thing too, and that he should be entitled to show it.

Peggy had said no, of course, even though the skunk was de-scented. As soon as she heard skunk, she went to exhibit three hundred and fifty where Ken Benigni was talking to some enthusiastic gardeners.

"Ken? Could I have a word with you?" she asked.

"Sure." He told the gardeners he'd be right back. "What's up?"

Peggy smiled sweetly at him. He looked like a mountain man with a full, dark beard that covered most of his face, and long, unkempt black hair. His clothes were worn and dirty and his boots had holes. Still he was very successful at what he did. His plants and animals had been in many major motion pictures and TV shows.

"Did you bring your skunk with you after I asked you not to?"

He hung his head. "I can't leave Matilda at home. She's been with me since she was born. It was too hot for her to stay in the truck. You don't want her to get dehydrated, do you? Skunks dehydrate quickly."

"Where's Matilda right now?"

Ken looked around his exhibit. "She was right here. Let me check her box."

Of course, Matilda was gone. She'd gone for a stroll and had somehow managed to get in an elevator, unnoticed. She got off on the second floor.

Screams of 'skunk' and shouting came from upstairs. People ran down the stairs and pushed into the elevator to get away.

"She won't hurt a fly," Ken assured Peggy.

"She can't stay. You'll have to find somewhere for her to be during the remainder of the flower show. I'm sorry. Can you go get her now?"

Ken argued. Peggy was resolute, although she compromised on one small aspect.

She sent him to get Matilda. "I can't believe he brought the skunk," she said to Paul when Ken was gone.

"I can't believe you said he could keep the skunk at your house while he was here." Paul chuckled. "I don't know whose face I'd like to see more when the skunk gets there—Steve's or Shakespeare's."

"I'm glad you were here to handle that." Adam Morrow was standing behind them.

"Thank you for filling in for me." Peggy shook his hand.

Adam was an ambitious man who'd taken his father's single florist shop on Wendover Road and developed it into a chain. He wasn't the usual type of flower-loving florist. He knew a lot about plants, but he wasn't keen on working with them.

"Not a problem." He pulled a cell phone from the pocket of his sharply creased jeans. "Excuse me, Peggy. We're having a run on people who want to know what every flower means after you told the media that the thyme had significance on Dr. Abutto's grave."

Paul and Peggy went to see how Sam and Selena were doing at The Potting Shed exhibit. There was a large group of people listening to Sam describe how to create a backyard garden that would be friendly for birds and butterflies.

Selena was leaning against the fence watching him. "He's good. You should have him out in front of the shop everyday instead of flowers and flower pots."

"I would if he'd do it. Why do you think his workshops are always so well attended?"

"Yeah, I know. He's already sold a dozen people on setting up new landscape work. Definitely a garden wonder child. I wonder if he ever regrets giving up med school?"

"I guess you'd have to ask him," Peggy said. "It wasn't my idea for him to continue this work. But I wasn't going to say no once he said he wanted to stay."

"Well don't expect me to do that when I finish my degree. I'm going out on my own."

"Did you ever decide on a major?" Paul asked her.

"I've decided on several of them." She shrugged. "At

the rate I'm going, I'll be eighty before I'm done."

Peggy laughed. "I guess you and Sam will be running The Potting Shed then. I don't think I'll be around, except in spirit."

Steve reached them at that point in their conversation. He almost lifted Peggy off the floor with his hug and then kissed her long and hard on the lips.

"Are you sure you're okay?" He looked her over carefully. "You could have a concussion and not know it."

"I'm fine. *Really.* Thank you for coming back. I hope you were done at the airport."

He put his hand on Paul's shoulder. "You're okay too?"

"I'm fine," Paul muttered, his face turning red.

"We're both fine, thanks to my son's superior reflexes. I heard the car coming toward us. I didn't think to move."

Steve hugged them both. "I'm so glad he was with you."

Paul extricated himself from Steve's embrace and straightened his jacket. "It's what I'm trained to do. That's why I was there."

"I'm done at the airport," Steve answered Peggy's question as an afterthought. "We picked up a lot of prints and botanical evidence. Dr. Beck will probably want you to look at it. I won't know if we have anything that will help until forensics goes through it."

"I hope that goes better than what forensics had from Aris's body and the crime scene. What I looked at wasn't much."

"We definitely need a break in this case." Steve watched Sam sell two more landscaping contracts. "Anything interesting happen that didn't involve someone trying to kill you?"

Peggy told him about the skunk. "Are you going back to the office today?"

"I haven't had lunch yet." He looked at his watch. "I guess after that, I'll probably meet with Al and see what else we can come up with. I don't like the idea that someone is out there trying to think of ways to hurt you."

Paul posed his questions about why someone would want to kill Peggy. "Maybe it was a warning, but if so, what were they warning her about? We know the Mercedes was stolen, and she spotted it with one of her Tanya visits. We have to figure out why they went from trying to get the duffel to running her down."

"I agree. Can you stay with her? I'll come back and pick her up."

Paul nodded. "I wouldn't want to be anywhere else right now."

"Thank you." Steve kissed Peggy. "Be careful."

"In the meantime, could you drop something off at the house for me?"

"Sure. What is it?"

Peggy had Paul get on his cell phone with Ken Benigni. "Her name is Matilda. I'm sure you'll get along fine."

### *Juniper*

*This shrub grows from 4 - 6 feet, usually with a twisted trunk. The green/blue berries take more than 2 years to ripen. They have an aromatic scent that has been used to flavor gin and as seasoning for lamb and mutton dishes. The perfume industry has used them to give aftershaves a masculine scent for years. Juniper was one of the first shrubs to populate the British Isles after the Ice Age, about 12,000 years ago.*

# Chapter Thirteen

Steve wasn't happy about taking the caged skunk back to the house, even if it was de-scented.

"Just think of her as one of your veterinary patients. You've taken care of horses and cows. Why not skunks?"

Her husband had plenty of reasons 'why not'. He still took the skunk back with him, after Peggy promised it was only for a few days.

Ken was tearful as he watched Steve take Matilda out of the convention center but he was thankful for Peggy's help. "You won't mind if I come and see her, will you?"

"I don't know a thing about taking care of a skunk. You'll have to come and feed her, and whatever else is necessary, while she's my guest."

"I was right," Paul said after Steve and Ken were gone.

"That look on Steve's face was priceless. I wish I could've captured it on my phone."

"You were afraid he'd knock you down, right?" Sam slapped him on the back.

Paul shook his hand. "You mean because I know he's FBI now?"

"I've looked at him differently," Sam admitted. "I never thought of him carrying a gun under his hoodie."

"Hey! I carry a gun too. That doesn't impress me."

"I guess I'm more easily impressed." Sam looked away. "Maybe I should get into law enforcement too. That way every man Peggy knows would be carrying a gun."

"I don't think she needs that, guys." Selena smiled at her wise words. "I know I don't."

"I'm going to check on everything again," Peggy said to Sam. "Selena told me you've done great today. You still have three more days. Have you thought anymore about hiring someone to help you at the shop?"

"I have." He shrugged. "That's about it. I'm sure I'll be thinking about it a lot harder when I'm out trying to keep up with these new contracts."

Peggy and Paul started down the concourse again. Everything seemed to be running smoothly, although several vendors complained about the skunk. The crowds were thinning as the afternoon waned. By five, when they closed the doors, she expected most people to be gone.

She checked with the employee of the convention center stationed at the front door. The numbers were good for that day. Peggy hoped they'd be even better tomorrow.

With everything downstairs running well, Peggy and Paul went upstairs. Aris's crime scene-taped exhibit was a stark reminder of his death. Some visitors stopped and took pictures of the spot that was out of bounds for them.

"I suppose the crime scene people have looked at everything in the exhibit," she said to Paul.

"You know they did. They usually don't miss anything. Why? Is something bothering you?"

Peggy didn't want to tell him about the call she received from *Nightflyer*, but she needed someone to bounce ideas off of.

"Suppose Aris was smuggling drugs into the flower show. What kind of drugs would that be?"

"I'm not sure. From South Africa, it could be any of the usual drugs—cocaine, heroin—anything botanical too." Paul looked at the front of the exhibit with her.

"That area really isn't particularly known for drugs, is it?" She pursed her lips. "The only thing I think of with South Africa is diamonds."

"That's true. Diamonds are kind of yesterday, I think. I'm not an expert on international smuggling."

The wheels were turning in Peggy's head as they walked through the exhibits upstairs. If Paul wasn't with her tomorrow, Peggy decided she'd come in early and look closely through Aris's demolished exhibit. Maybe even if Paul with her. She could always distract him.

Everything was running smoothly upstairs too. They took the elevator back down and Paul went to the restroom. He told Peggy to wait where she was.

"If you're gone when I get out, tomorrow I'll have to cuff us together. Okay?"

Her green eyes narrowed on her son's dear face. "Do you really expect me to agree with that?"

"No. I expect you to wait for me."

"I'll be here."

Peggy leaned against the wall near the snack area. Machines that held chips and candy bars mingled with soda providers and juice box vendors. There were dozens of people seated at the plastic tables, enjoying their break from the flower show.

There was a maintenance room next to the vending area. The door was closed, but Peggy could hear voices through it.

"We have to find it," a familiar voice said.

She recognized it as Tim Roseboro's voice, even though it was muffled.

"Take it easy. We'll find it. It's gotta be here somewhere, right?"

That was *definitely* Dabney Wilder's voice.

It might be a long-shot, but could they be talking about the missing duffel bag?

Peggy moved a little further into the vending room. She wanted to hear if they had more to say, but she didn't want them to know she was listening.

Al might be right about her taking her life in her hands by confronting Dabney. He was a little on the sleazy side, even though he was a well-known attorney. Everyone knew if you had the money, he'd defend you.

Not that everyone didn't deserve a fair defense. There was something sleazy about Dabney—probably the reason no one voted for him when he'd run for DA.

Tim Roseboro was a puzzle. Why would *he* be involved with whatever Aris had been smuggling? And how did the three of them come to be part of what had happened?

There were too many questions and not enough answers.

Paul came out of the restroom and briefly looked around, a frown forming on his freckled face. His eyes lit up as soon as he saw his mother.

"Were you testing me?"

"No." Peggy held him back as Tim and Dabney came out of the maintenance room. The two other men were straightening their suits and ties, appearing incredibly nervous and guilty.

"Is that why you came in here?"

"I heard them talking through the door. They're looking for something. Maybe they're looking for Aris's duffel."

"Maybe," Paul joked. "Or maybe they're looking for a new place to buy their next sports car. Who knows?"

He started walking back toward The Potting Shed exhibit.

Peggy followed him. "Don't you find it a little odd that these two rich, well-connected men would be skulking around in a maintenance closet?

"I find everything rich, well-connected men do a little odd."

They passed a beautiful exhibit created by a grower from Florida. In the midst of all the spring and summer blooms, Jazzy's Junipers, had chosen to create a winter scene. It played well with their product, six and seven-foot junipers. They'd brought them potted to the flower show. From the looks of the crowd gathered around the log cabin and sleigh, the junipers were doing very well.

Peggy took two small sprigs of the dark green foliage that held a black berry or two. She put one in her pocket and one in her son's.

Paul pulled his berry out and examined it. "What's this?"

"Juniper. In the language of flowers, this plant means protection." She linked her arm through his. "I think we might need a little of that."

He put his arm around her shoulders. "I appreciate that, Mom. But really, I'd rather have my revolver."

"You were always stubborn."

"And who did I get that from?"

Peggy gazed at the side of his face as they walked. "Do you really think there's something to the FBI investigating your father's death as something other than a domestic disturbance homicide?"

"You know I've always felt that something wasn't right about Dad's death. When you and I argued about me going into the police academy, you accused me of wanting revenge."

"Yes. I did."

"It was really justice that I wanted for him. I want to know what happened and why he died, especially now that I know about the FBI connection." His jaw tightened as he spoke. "Don't you?"

Peggy agreed, theoretically. She was afraid of what she might have to sacrifice to find justice for John's death. That had always been her argument against Paul being on the job. She didn't plan to lose her son the same way she'd lost his father.

The same way she could lose Steve.

### *Spruce*

*Spruce trees are long-lived and grow in colder climates. One tree in western Sweden has been found to be more than 9,000 years old. The wood from spruce has been used to build homes and boats for generations. The resin was used to seal roofs and to keep ships seaworthy in the past. The fresh roots are a source of Vitamin C which Captain Cook used to keep his crew from developing scurvy. The essential oils have been used for various purposes too. Spruces weren't used for ornamental trees until the 1800s when their conical shape began to be admired.*

# Chapter Fourteen

Steve was waiting at The Potting Shed exhibit when Peggy and Paul reached it.

"You're back early." Peggy kissed his cheek. "It must've been a short meeting."

"Actually, the meeting was canceled until six tonight at the ME's office. Al and Dr. Beck would like their forensic botanist at the meeting." He put his arm around her.

"What kind of evidence did you find on the plane?" she asked impatiently.

"That's why we're having the meeting. So everyone is updated at the same time."

"Tease," she scolded.

"So the skunk is in the library at home. I thought Shakespeare was going to knock me down trying to get at it."

Peggy wasn't expecting that. "In the library?"

"She needed to be in a room with a sturdy door. The library seemed like the best place."

"You could've put her in a spare room." She sighed. "Never mind. We'll take care of it when we get home." She filled him in on her agreement with Ken about Matilda.

"I guess that means he'll be staying at the house too." Steve glanced at his watch.

"No. He's coming over each day to take care of her."

"Yeah. Right."

Sam laughed. "You know her *too* well."

"Or well enough," Paul added.

"If you're done ganging up on me, I think I'm going to go. With traffic, and grabbing a quick bite for dinner, we'll barely make the meeting at six." She glanced at Steve.

"That works for me," he said.

Walter Bellows appeared out of the crowd that was mostly making for the front entrance now. "I assume we're about ready to depart. What a fascinating show. I'm so glad I came. Did you see the escaped skunk earlier? Maybe not as exciting as a murder, but entertaining nonetheless."

Steve snorted. "I saw the skunk. She's living at our house now."

Walter was further amazed by this unexpected revelation and continued talking about it as Peggy said goodbye to Sam and Selena.

"I can handle taking a shift on watching your mother if you want to go home," Steve suggested to Paul.

"Okay. I'd like to have dinner with Mai. I haven't looked at my email recently either. Captain Sedgwick might want me to be at the meeting. Or he might want me to take the nightshift at the house."

"Thanks again for what you did today." Steve shook his hand.

"She's not just another case, you know," Paul reminded him. "Not that I wouldn't have done the same thing for anyone. You don't have to thank me."

"Sorry. How about I buy you a beer sometime, no women?"

"Sounds good," Paul said. "I've got some Mom stories that will make you laugh."

Peggy ignored them, starting toward the door with Walter chatting continuously about the flower show and the skunk. Steve was with them by the time they'd reached the guard shack. Pete was still on duty. He waved them through.

Steve's car was parked by the gate. He opened the front door for Peggy. Walter slid inside with a quick, "Thank you, my good man."

Peggy laughed and got in the back seat. "How do you rate parking up here in the No Parking Zone?"

"I'm with the FBI. We always get the best parking places."

"I won't tell Paul you said that since he had to park in the lot."

"So you say the skunk is staying at your house for the remainder of the week?" Walter asked.

Steve grudgingly started the car and went out into the long line of traffic waiting to exit the flower show. Bellows might be in the front seat on the way home, he decided, but he wasn't going out to dinner with them.

Shakespeare was happy to see them when they got back to the house. Steve said goodnight to Walter and let the dog out while Peggy went to check on Matilda.

The little skunk was very well-mannered. She peered back at Peggy through the cage bars with curious black eyes.

"I'm not sure if I'm supposed to do something for you," Peggy told her. "Ken will be here later. Don't worry. It looks like you have enough water. You should be fine."

The skunk sniffed Peggy's nose then lay down on the straw bedding in the cage. Peggy laughed. If only Shakespeare was as quiet and gentle as Matilda.

She and Steve met in the kitchen. Shakespeare was eating and Steve had taken off his jacket. He was rolling up his sleeves and seemed to be getting ready to cook something.

"I thought we were going out to eat?"

"Maybe we should stay here. We're close to the ME's office and I don't really want to share you with all the people you know who can't help stopping by our table when we're out. We have cheese and vegetables for omelets."

"That's fine with me."

Peggy sliced some sourdough bread they had left over from their last trip to the bakery. She poured some Muscadine wine for both of them. She'd been dying to try the new blackberry wine from their favorite local spot, Rocky River Vineyards.

"I'm glad the flower show went better today, even though you were almost killed in the street." Steve whipped the eggs with a little extra force than was necessary.

"It really wasn't that close." Her memory of that moment when the car plunged past them still made her heart beat faster.

"I think Dabney Wilder is involved." Steve put the egg into the omelet pan. It sizzled and immediately started to cook. "I've been looking into his background. He owns the plane that brought Dr. Abutto to Charlotte. I haven't found any reason for him to need extra cash. I don't like that this incident happened right after you talked to him."

"I thought we weren't talking about evidence before the meeting." She pointed the bread knife at him as she got out the butter.

"I thought you wanted to know what I was thinking."

She walked up behind him and put her arms around him, resting her head against his back. "I did. I do! Thanks for being so good-natured about Matilda."

"I can handle anything you throw at me."

"Good. I hope that's all it takes."

Steve turned around and started to kiss her when a loud rap at the kitchen door drew growls and barking from Shakespeare.

"You hold him," Peggy said. "I'll answer the door."

"I don't think so," Steve argued. "I'm not the one in protective surveillance. You hold the dog and I'll answer the door. If it's Bellows, I'm not inviting him in for dinner."

She laughed and went to sit down, calling Shakespeare to her. She put both arms around his chest and held him as he sat down, snuffling her ear and whacking his tail on the wood floor. "Okay. We're ready."

It was no mean feat to hold the hundred-and-forty pound dog in place when he was excited to see who was at the door.

Steve took his revolver out of the holster that had been under his jacket. He opened the door a crack and peered outside. "Yes?"

"Sorry to bother you. I've come to look after Matilda. This is Peggy Lee's place, right?"

"That's Ken," Peggy told Steve. "Let him in. He needs to take care of the skunk."

Reluctantly, Steve put away his gun and let Ken inside. It looked like he was doomed to share his wife during dinner that night, no matter how hard he tried not to.

Ken eyed Steve and the gun in his holster very carefully as he went inside. As soon as he saw Peggy, his gaze latched on to her.

"I'm so sorry. I was thinking about Matilda all afternoon. I hope she hasn't been any trouble. Could I see her now?"

Peggy offered to show him the way to the library while

Steve started working on an extra omelette.

"This is a great place you have." Ken's dark eyes moved over every detail as they walked through the house. "Have you lived here long?"

"Most of my life."

They walked past the blue spruce towering through the middle of the house.

He whistled in admiration as he looked up to the top of the tree. "Wow! Did you plant it? That's amazing."

Peggy opened the library door. She felt Shakespeare's interest as he sniffed at Ken's heels. Smelling the skunk, as the door opened, got his full attention. It took both hands to hold him back from entering the room.

Ken crouched down and rubbed Shakespeare's neck. "You're a big boy, aren't you? Having a dog here should make Matilda feel right at home. We have a St. Bernard back in Hibbing. The two of them are best friends."

Peggy let Shakespeare go. The dog rubbed noses with the skunk through the cage bars. He whined a little and jumped around. Matilda settled back down to sleep.

"I brought her some food. She eats dry food but I try to dress it up some with vegetables and plants. She loves rose petals." Ken smiled at Peggy as he took out a handful of pink rose petals from his pocket. "They were on the floor. I didn't think it would matter if I brought them to her."

Matilda gobbled up the rose petals and Ken stroked her fur.

"I'll be here for you every day, little girl," he promised. "It's only a few days. Better for you to be somewhere safe than picked up by the wildlife people."

Peggy agreed with that. She'd lied to animal control when they'd come to the flower show after Matilda's escape. She thought there was no point in making a big deal out of a problem that had already been solved.

"We were about to eat dinner," she said to Ken. "Why don't you join us?"

Peggy took Shakespeare back into the kitchen. Ken followed after he'd finished feeding Matilda. Steve was laying out three plates with bread, eggs, and strawberries on them.

They sat at the old wood table in the kitchen. Peggy had allowed Paul's initials to stay carved in the underside of the table, despite John's wishes to the contrary. There were times, after John had passed and Paul had moved out on his own, that she'd reached down to feel the carving. Somehow it had made her feel less alone.

"So this house is in your husband's family." Ken grinned at Steve.

"Not me," Steve denied as he poured himself more wine.

"My first husband," Peggy clarified after sharing the story about the house with their guest. "She's a grand old lady. I hope I never have to leave her."

Ken agreed. "If I had a place like this, I wouldn't leave either. I built my own place up in Minnesota. Last summer, I replaced the tar paper on the walls with vinyl siding. It looks real good."

"More wine?" Peggy asked him as Steve glanced significantly at his watch. It was five forty-five.

"Yeah. I don't mind if I do." Ken dared a peek at Steve's revolver. "You must be a cop."

"Yes," Steve agreed, not wanting to go into the details of his career.

"He's actually a federal agent," Peggy clarified.

"Oh." Ken looked at the revolver again and took another sip of wine. "I guess that's why they call this show international, huh? Federal agents onsite, and that customs guy who was there after that orchid man was murdered."

Peggy exchanged glances with Steve. "What customs guy?"

### *Marijuana*

*Cannabis Sativa, marijuana, has been cultivated for thousands of years as everything from food to paper, cloth and rope. It was used by the Chinese a thousand years ago to ease pain and for spiritual enlightenment. Marijuana is still a popular recreational drug for more than 25 million Americans, despite legal penalties.*

# Chapter Fifteen

"There were no customs officials scheduled to be at the convention center."

Steve got off the phone with his information officer as he and Peggy were driving to the meeting at the medical examiner's office. "We have video surveillance from that whole timeframe."

"Maybe Ken thought there was a customs official." Peggy shrugged. "I hated that we had to run him off that way. My father would've killed me for being so inhospitable."

"But why would Ken think he saw a customs official? They may have told Ken they were customs officials to make it all right for them to snoop through Dr. Abutto's exhibit."

Peggy didn't want to point out that Ken had been a

little difficult getting set up at the show. If anything, it would seem he'd be worried about ATF agents confiscating his marijuana plants.

"I don't know if I'd make too much of it," she said as they reached the office. "Ken is a little flamboyant. People tend to get imaginative when they know a murder has taken place."

Steve pulled the car into an open space. "You have a good grasp of the situation."

She frowned. "Is that like saying I have a smart mouth?"

"Not at all. If you say Ken is imaginative, I believe you. But I still think it's worthwhile mentioning at the meeting. It may have some bearing on the case."

They went inside together. Al and Dorothy were already there. A few federal agents and some Charlotte PD officers were on hand as well. The men and women threw uneasy glances at one another.

"Let's go into the conference room," Dorothy suggested.

Everyone followed her down the main hall. There was no security guard to get by. Peggy also was surprised that Paul wasn't there.

Everyone was seated, Charlotte officers on one side— federal agents on the other side of the long wood table. Dorothy took the chair at one end and Peggy sat in the other.

"Thanks to Dr. Lee for giving me a little nudge this afternoon," Dorothy began with a nod in Peggy's direction, "I had some dust that we found tested today. We learned that it was diamond dust."

There were a few murmurs from the Charlotte police side of the table. The FBI side looked smug.

"Our lab also verified some white powder we found on the plane that had transported Dr. Abutto from Capetown. It was diamond dust."

Peggy had come to recognize, and dislike, Steve's right hand man, Norris Rankin. She hoped he'd grow on her after a while.

Had Steve known about the diamond dust from the plane? From the look on his face, she'd say he knew and was surprised that Norris had blurted it out to one-up the police findings.

"I guess we can assume Dr. Abutto was smuggling diamonds with him when he came from his home," Al said. "Establishing that fact can make a big difference to our investigation. If he'd been trying to sell drugs of some kind, we'd be looking for other dealers."

"Knowing we're dealing with diamonds means we can look for people in this area who could facilitate that," Steve said. "I'm sure the police can be a big help in that endeavor."

"Do we know if the diamonds have been cut?" a young Charlotte officer Peggy didn't recognize asked, voice quivering a little.

"There wouldn't be any dust if the diamonds weren't cut." Norris cut him down.

"The dust was the only thing we found, besides a nine millimeter slug in his chest. He would've bled out very quickly but, as I've told a few of you, Dr. Abutto wasn't dead when he was buried in that pile of dirt." Dorothy passed around pictures of the corpse and the bullet that had killed him.

"Dr. Lee." Norris leaned forward at the table. "Any botanical information that was found on or around the body that would suggest a lead we should follow up on?"

Peggy sat forward. "The only botanical effects that were found with Dr. Abutto were from the exhibit, except for the large amount of thyme. We don't know yet where that came from."

"So, no help there." Norris studied the folder in front of him with a disappointed look on his face.

"We've had another breakthrough thanks to our friends at Scotland Yard." Steve made the announcement. "Lieutenant McDonald, would you like to fill us in?"

Peggy was very proud of Steve. He was obviously willing to share credit where it was due.

Al stood up, grabbing his folder and hitching up his pants. "I got a tip today and followed through on information regarding Tanya Abutto." He nodded to Peggy but didn't mention her. That was fine.

"Scotland Yard thought they had located Miss Abutto at a university in London. They reported back, after I'd questioned them about the validity of the girl's identity. The woman in question wasn't Miss Abutto. As of our last conversation, Scotland Yard has advised that they believe Miss Abutto has been kidnapped."

Peggy's mind raced with that information. This is exactly what *Nightflyer* had been talking about—this and the diamond dust as a product of South Africa.

She doodled in her notebook as various officers and agents made their reports.

This might prove that she'd been right about Aris not being the type of person to smuggle anything. When a person was pushed, such as threatening his daughter, anything was possible.

As her mind followed the evidence, it seemed to her that someone from this area— probably someone who was part of the flower show—had managed to force Aris to smuggle diamonds. He'd been killed, possibly to keep him quiet. That probably meant Tanya would be eliminated as well.

Was the girl somewhere in the Charlotte area too? Or had she been taken in London and kept there?

Peggy thought Tanya's life was the most important matter in front of them. Finding Aris's killer was important too, but there was nothing else they could do for him right now. It was possible Tanya could be saved.

"Dr. Lee," Dorothy addressed her. "Do you have anything else you'd like to add to the conversation?"

All eyes fixed on her. Peggy blinked. "I'd like to see us concentrate on finding Tanya. She may not have been killed, as her father was. Her time might be limited."

"Scotland Yard is handling that aspect of the investigation," Norris told her in a not-so friendly voice. "Let's stay on target here, Dr. Lee."

Peggy felt properly chastised. She wasn't giving up on the idea.

"Do we have any proof that she's still in England? She may have come here with her father. It would be easier to control him that way and possibly easier for the killer to get rid of her."

Everyone looked at their folders.

One of the agents spoke up. "We saw signs that Dr. Abutto wasn't alone on the private jet, Director Newsome. We don't know who was with him, but the passenger list does have a female on it."

"The chances are better that the female listed was a flight attendant." Norris shot down the other agent's idea too. "We need to concentrate on finding those diamonds. They'll lead us to the killer."

Peggy didn't say anything else. When the meeting was over and the handshaking and back-patting had commenced, the young agent who seemed to agree with her, quietly came to her side.

"I'm Millicent Sanford." She extended her hand. "Millie."

Peggy took her hand and smiled. "I'm Peggy."

"I think you're on the right track with the kidnapping of Tanya Abutto. There was nothing that verifies that it was Dr. Abutto's daughter on the plane with him, but now that we know she was kidnapped, there's nothing saying it wasn't her."

Millie glanced around the room primarily filled with men.

"I guess we need proof of that," Peggy said. "Do you have a recent picture of her? It's been a while since Aris shared anything about her with me. I think they'd grown apart when she went away to school."

Millie whispered, "I'll send you one in an email."

Peggy handed her a personal business card. "Thanks. Let's see what we can find out."

On the way home from the meeting, she asked Steve why Millie wasn't his second-in- command, instead of Norris. "She seems very knowledgeable."

Steve grimaced. "You mean she agreed with you about Tanya."

"Whatever. Norris isn't exactly a nice person, is he?"

"He's not supposed to be nice. He has a nice conviction record. That's what the FBI looks for in their people if they want to promote them."

Peggy studied the side of his face as they stopped at a red light on Fourth Street. "Does that mean you have a nice conviction record?"

"It's pretty good. Enough to warrant my promotion."

"The only difference is that Norris has a terrible way of talking to people. Didn't you think he was rude slapping me and Millie down that way?"

"I'm his boss. You're my wife, and part of this investigation. I can't take sides. I'm sure you know that. You'll have to overlook his personality defects."

She understood. "I think he's wrong anyway. Too bad I don't get points for having a nice conviction record."

Steve laughed and rubbed the back of her neck. "Are you trying to take my brand new job away from me?"

"Heavens, no. I don't want to work for any law enforcement group, not even the police. I'm good with being a contractor, talking about what I know."

He pulled the car into the driveway. "Is that Ken's truck? I thought he went back to his hotel."

"I don't know," she hedged. "It's definitely his vehicle. I'd know it by the giant skunk eating marijuana airbrushed on the side."

"I don't think that's airbrushing. Is he going to have to stay with the skunk?"

"Probably not. Maybe." She smiled at him. "It's a big house. We probably won't even notice him."

### *Red Rose*

*Red roses range in color from burgundy to bright red. They have names like Charlotte, Forever Young and Rouge Baiser. Red roses are the flowers of passion and love. They show respect and courage. The quantity of red roses given has meaning too. A single red rose shows love. A dozen shows gratitude. Bright red also means love, while dark crimson can mean mourning.*

# Chapter Sixteen

As soon as Ken saw Peggy get out of the car, he rushed out of his old truck to explain that he'd lost his spot at the campground where he'd been staying.

"I thought you were supposed to pay when you left," he explained. "That's the way they do it in Minnesota."

"So they took your campsite." Peggy looked at Steve with a question in her eyes.

"You can stay here until the flower show is over." Steve made the offer through clenched teeth as he opened the kitchen door. Not only did Shakespeare run out to greet them, so did Matilda.

"How in the world did you get out of that cage?" Ken asked after picking her up.

"Shakespeare probably helped her." Peggy put down her bag. "I'll get a room made upstairs for you. She can stay in there with you."

"I don't want to put you out," Ken said. "But thanks for the offer."

Steve went upstairs to their bedroom and closed the door behind him.

\* \* \*

Peggy got Ken and Matilda settled in for the night. She glanced at the dark street. A Charlotte police cruiser was in the shadows of the old oak again. She knew they must've decided to give Paul the night off.

She set the house alarms and turned off the downstairs lights. Shakespeare ran up the spiral staircase with her. She opened the bedroom door and there were candles everywhere.

"Steve!" she persuaded Shakespeare to stay in the hall and closed the door.

He handed her a single red rose. "I looked this up in the language of flowers. It means passionate love. This is how I feel about you, Peggy."

She took the rose from him and smelled it.

"I knew you'd do that." He grinned. "I ordered it specially. It's an heirloom perfume rose. Like it?"

"Love it." She put her arms around him and kissed him. "It's not our anniversary. What's the special occasion?"

"There isn't a special occasion. Or every day with you is a special occasion. I know we've had some issues lately. I want you to remember that you're always special to me."

"You're always special to me too, whether you're a veterinarian or a secret agent."

"Secret agent, huh?" He kissed her and drew her closer. "I guess I should've worn my tux."

Peggy smiled in a wicked way. "I like you better this way. There's less to take off."

\* \* \*

At two thirty-five am, Peggy's cell phone started ringing. She thought it was the alarm clock and tried to hit the snooze button. When it didn't stop, she groaned and opened one eye.

"I think that's your phone," Steve muttered.

"I think you're right."

Peggy answered the call, barely understanding that the man on the other end was working for the alarm company responsible for the convention center. Her name had been put on the roster for contacts in case of emergency during the flower show.

When she finally understood the message, she thanked the caller and shut off her phone. "The alarm went off at the convention center."

"Do you have to do something with that?" Steve asked in a sleepy voice.

"I'm supposed to go and make sure everything is okay." She was already tossing back the comforter and swinging her legs out of bed.

Steve sat up too.

"You don't have to get up. I'll throw on some

sweatpants and ride down there on my bike. I'm sure it's nothing. I'll be back in twenty minutes."

"That's not happening."

"The officer outside will follow me there," she told him. "There's no reason for you to lose sleep over it."

"Are *you* going?" He peered at her after turning on his bedside light. "Then I'm not staying here."

"Okay. Let's go."

They got dressed. Shakespeare thought it was time to get up. He wanted to go outside and then eat breakfast. He followed Steve and Peggy downstairs, excited that the night was over.

"Everything okay?" Ken stood at the top of the landing. "Need some help?"

"We're fine," Steve assured him. "The alarm went off at the convention center. Go back to sleep."

Peggy turned off the outside alarm and answered another call on her cell phone. This time it was Charlotte PD telling her that the alarm had gone off at the convention center. She told them that she was on her way and put on a light jacket.

Shakespeare was whining, not understanding what was going on.

"I don't want to feed him this early," Steve said. "It'll throw off his schedule for the day."

"Let him relieve himself and bring him with us." She yawned as she looked for her bag. "I guess we should take your SUV instead of the FBI car. He's usually good in a car, but who knows?"

Steve put the leash on the dog and grabbed his keys. "Better not take any chances."

Shakespeare made his outdoor constitutional fast. He was so excited when Steve called him into the backseat of the SUV that he jumped in with one leap. He sat on the seat, wagging his tail, as Steve put the doggy seatbelt around him.

"Anything wrong?" Walter called out from his front door after turning on his outside light.

"Everything's fine," Peggy said. "Go back to sleep."

Before Steve could get inside and start the engine, the blue flashing lights from the police car came on. The officer drove the vehicle into the end of the driveway.

"Here it comes," Steve said. "Do you want to say it again or should I?"

"Your turn."

"Everything is fine, officer." Steve rolled down his window.

"I'm supposed to escort you to the convention center. Captain Sedgwick says it could be a cover for something else going on. Follow me."

"I should've let you say it." Steve started the engine.

"You'd better get moving or he'll come back for us."

They followed the fast-moving police car through the nearly empty streets. There was a street cleaner out and a few cars at Krispy Kreme Donuts. The lighted 'hot donuts now' sign was on.

"I wish I had a hot donut now." Steve turned right to

follow the police car.

"Me too. And a hot cup of tea."

Shakespeare whined and wagged his tail.

"I think he does too." Peggy reached back a hand to stroke him. "Almost there. Let's not talk about food again. He'll think we're holding out on him."

Steve smiled. "As big as he is, he might eat us if we don't feed him."

They finally reached the convention center. There were several police cars in the parking lot with their lights flashing. Reggie was at the guard shack, talking to an officer. The alarm was still going off.

"I thought someone would've turned it off by now." Peggy pointed at a new green Jaguar in the parking lot. "That's Dabney's car right there. I wonder if he's inside?"

Steve parked the SUV near the gate, ignoring the frowns he received from the police officers waiting there. He took out his badge as he stepped out and showed it to them.

"Is Dabney inside trying to find the off switch?" Peggy asked, wanting to cover her ears to block out the annoying alarm. She felt sorry for the people who lived around there and had to be awake at that time of the morning.

"No one is inside, Peggy," Reggie said. "I've been here all night. Probably a bird or something tripped the alarm. It happens."

She swiveled to glance at Dabney's car again. "They put me on the alarm list, but I have no idea where the switch is to turn it off. No one gave me an alarm code either. If Dabney's not here, you should call him."

Standing beside Steve as Reggie looked up Dabney's number, Peggy was puzzled. Surely as manager of the center, he'd get the first call. If so, why wasn't he there?

"Maybe he didn't feel like coming." Steve shrugged. "If it happens all the time, he probably wants to leave it to you."

"That would be a mistake. I think it's odd that his car is here but he's not."

"Maybe he went home with someone else. People do that kind of thing. Police get missing person calls every day from small events like that."

"No answer." Reggie put down his phone. "Just like last time."

"Find someone on that list to turn off the alarm," an officer growled standing close to him.

"Yes sir."

Peggy couldn't explain it. It was like a sixth sense that told her something was wrong with Dabney. It sounded crazy so she didn't say anything as she sneaked over to look into his car.

The overhead lights in the parking lot were so tall that the glow they cast was difficult to make out fine details. She bent down and peeked into the passenger side front window.

Dabney was sitting in the driver's seat with his head on the steering wheel.

### *Poppy*

*The poppy family is large and vibrant, containing both wild and cultivated flowers. Not all poppies are the kind used for heroin. Non-heroin poppies are a favorite of perennial gardeners. The flowers attract bees, butterflies and hummingbirds, making them a delight in any garden. They can grow more than a foot tall and range from shades of red to blue.*

# Chapter Seventeen

"Steve!" she yelled. "It's Dabney. I think he's hurt."

Several police officers ran to the car with Steve.

"Stand back, ma'am," one of them said. "The door is locked. We're going to open it."

Peggy and Steve stood back from the door. The officer used a Slim Jim to get the door open.

Dabney slid out of the car. He would've fallen on the pavement but a second officer stepped in to catch him. Together, the two officers laid him in the parking lot. One of them felt his neck.

"No pulse."

Steve stepped forward and opened Dabney's suit coat. Even under the odd lighting, it was easy to see the bloodstain that had spread across his chest. "He's dead.

Someone call the morgue. We need crime scene and the medical examiner out here."

More police cars arrived along with crime scene techs that set up secondary spotlights to better see the car and Dabney.

"Does it look like he was shot too?" Peggy asked Steve when he had a moment to answer.

"I don't think so. It looks like a knife wound to me. Let's see what Dr. Beck has to say. I'm going to take Shakespeare home and come back, unless you're going home."

"I'm still supposed to go inside and look around. I wish someone on Reggie's list would come out and turn off the alarm."

An older brown Chevy, that had seen better days, chugged into the parking lot. The driver was challenged by police who finally let him through.

"I'm Dabney Wilder's assistant." The young man adjusted his glasses. His voice cracked as he asked what was going on. "There are a lot of police out here for an alarm."

Peggy smiled at Steve. "I'm not going home just yet."

She went to talk with Dabney's assistant. "I hope you're here to turn off the alarm." Peggy took the young man by the arm and started walking toward the convention center. "I can't get inside to check on things until you do."

"You must be Dr. Lee." He looked at his cell phone. "I'm David Mueller. This kind of thing happens sometimes. The alarm company assumes Mr. Wilder has already been to the scene and turned off the alarm. They call me if the police keep bugging them."

"I'm sorry to tell you this, David, but Mr. Wilder is dead."

"Dead?" He nervously took off his loose glasses and cleaned them on a cloth. "What happened?"

"Let's go inside and I'll explain. This alarm is making my head hurt."

The keypad for the alarm was to the right of the door, behind a large cement post. David didn't even have to look up the code. He turned on the light and punched it in. The noise stopped.

"Thank goodness." Peggy turned to him. He was average height and weight with light brown hair and hazel eyes mostly hidden behind his glasses. He looked as though he could be right out of college.

"What happened to Mr. Wilder?"

"We found him outside in his car. It looks like he's been murdered."

"Murdered? Him too? First that African man and now Mr. Wilder." His eyes were unfocused.

"I'm sorry. I know it must be a terrible shock for you."

He stared at her until it seemed he'd taken it all in. "I know it's an awful thing to say, and please don't tell anyone I said it, but I'm not surprised at all. Mr. Wilder was friends and enemies with some terrible people. I tried to stay out of their way as much as possible. I don't know how he lived that way. He had threats against him every day."

Peggy patted his arm. "That must've been a hard way

to work for you. I've heard stories about your boss. I knew him a little. Has there been anything recent that you think might have caused this?"

David seemed to search through his thoughts. "There was something unusual going on with the flower show. He got a lot of angry phone calls from some people. Last week, some criminal types stopped in at the office."

"Criminal types?"

"I know, right?" He nervously grinned. "But these weren't the kind in expensive suits like most of the others. These were badly dressed, smelly men. They wanted more money for something."

"Something like what?"

"I'm not sure. A lot of times, Mr. Wilder kept things from me. I'm not complaining—I didn't want to know about that side of his business. It seems to me that it had something to do with a plane."

Peggy barely had time to thank him and store away the information he'd given her before Norris Rankin joined them as they stood in the doorway.

"Dr. Lee?"

"Yes? Oh, hello Norris."

"Steve wanted me to come down and walk through the building with you. There's supposed to be an officer with us. I don't know where he's gone. It's a circus out there."

Not particularly wanting to be alone with Norris, Peggy wanted to wait for the officer.

"It might be better since technically, the police department has jurisdiction here."

"I'm not worried about jurisdiction." Norris scowled at David. "Is there someplace you should be, son?"

"You should probably go and talk to Lieutenant Al McDonald," Peggy said to David. "Tell him what you told me."

"Does that have anything to do with this case?" Norris put his hand on David's arm to detain him.

"Nothing at all to do with this case," she assured him. "Go on, David. Find Al McDonald."

"Thanks, Dr. Lee." David gazed at the FBI agent whose hand was still on his arm.

Norris let him go. "All right. Just remember who I report to, Dr. Lee. I don't want to cause any problems between you and Steve."

Once David was gone, Peggy started into the flower show. She was gritting her teeth in frustration as she picked up her clipboard that she'd kept at the welcome center in case she forgot her master copy of vendors and growers in her tablet.

*The pompous little--*

"You don't have to worry about causing problems between me and Steve, Agent Rankin. We can sort out our own disagreements without your help."

Peggy ignored him striding beside her as she began to examine each exhibit, making sure things were as they were supposed to be. Agent Rankin was an irritation—she could feel her temper rising.

"You've never worked this type of case before, have you?" Norris kept talking. "I could tell you were out of your league at the meeting."

She stopped and faced him. "Are you purposely trying to make me angry? I realize we don't know each other. I hope we're not getting off on the wrong foot."

Peggy had no plans to explain herself to him or relate her experience dealing with other cases like this one. She took several deep breaths and started off down the concourse again.

"I'm sorry you took my remarks the wrong way. I only meant that it's unusual for a husband and wife to work together this way. I don't want it to be a problem. I've known Steve a long time. He's a good friend."

Could he be any more annoying? Peggy thought about asking him to go away, but knew she had to keep going. They'd sent him in there with her for a reason.

Nothing seemed to be out of place. The exotic scents of the plants and flowers were pleasant. They were most potent at night, especially so since they were closed in. She focused on that instead of the irritating agent dogging her steps.

They passed a re-creation of a large field of red poppies, their black and white centers seeming to stare at them. It was a powerful exhibit from a grower from Mississippi who was hoping to influence buyers to purchase his seeds. Not only were the flowers beautiful, they were useful too.

"I don't understand why people grow flowers," Norris said. "I can see trees. They make sense. Flowers don't do anything."

Peggy thought about the red rose Steve had given her last night and smiled. She could ignore this man for a little longer. He had to see that he couldn't bother her. His relationship with Steve might be important. She didn't have to like him, only tolerate him.

"What's this?" He leaned over and smelled a plant. "This thing smells awful. Why would anyone plant it?"

"It's called skunk cabbage. It might smell bad, but it's very useful."

"Can you eat it?"

Peggy was tempted to tell him he could eat it. She knew it would burn his mouth and that might be a little revenge. She refrained. "No. It's not edible."

They were upstairs, across from Dr. Abutto's exhibit. The drooping crime scene tape still made it off limits.

Peggy really wanted to have a look at what was left here. It was hard during the day because she'd look suspicious standing on the wrong side of the tape. This might be a good time, while the convention center was empty, and no one was watching her, except for Agent Rankin.

She had to think of some way to get rid of him.

It came to her suddenly. He thought she wasn't capable of taking care of business. She could use that to gain some free time, even if it was only a few minutes.

"Oh darn." She frantically examined the list on her clipboard. "The sheet for the rest of the vendors must still be downstairs at the welcome center. It was silly of me to leave it behind. I know there has to be more than two pages. I guess I'll go downstairs and get it."

"Wait." He glanced at his watch. "This is already

taking more time than I thought it would. I'll go down and get it. It'll be faster. Sit down over there and I'll be right back."

Peggy sank down on a bench. "Oh, thank you. Just the idea of walking down and coming back again was giving me palpitations."

"Sure."

She watched him jog down the stairs. The elevator was switched off for the night and she had no idea how to turn it on. She'd thought it was a bad thing—until now. Norris would have to walk back upstairs too.

As soon as she couldn't see the top of his head, she ducked into Dr. Abutto's exhibit.

Everything was such a mess. Between the police searching it, and whoever killed him ripping it apart, it was hard to see where anything useful could be.

Most of the orchids had been tipped over. Some were smashed against the floor. A few were left. She touched one with a careful hand. They were so delicate and felt so fragile. She knew they were really strong and durable plants. It was humans who thought they weren't hardy, mostly because of their exotic beauty.

She peered closer, examining the clear rocks in the hormone enriched gel that Aris had used to grow his prize-winning orchids.

Was it possible?

She put a finger inside one of the broken glass beakers and brought a rock out with it. It looked like glass. She couldn't say it wasn't without testing. It could be glass. The thick gel stuck to it. She wiped it off, but still wasn't completely sure.

Surely Aris wouldn't have hidden the diamonds with the orchids? What about the duffel bag that everyone was looking for?

All it would've taken was someone looking inside the beakers that had been smashed, or the whole beakers that still held the living orchids. Her father had always said the best place to hide things was in plain sight.

She heard footsteps on the stairs and pocketed the stone before going back to sit down and wait for Norris.

### Lily of the Valley

*Convallaria majalis is the scientific name for lily of the valley. It is a perennial found across the Northern Hemisphere. The lily blooms in late spring and has bell-shaped white flowers and small orange/red berries. The flowers have a sweet smell, but all parts of the plant are deadly poisonous. There are several legends involving this plant from fairies being found around it, to the flowers being created by a nobleman's blood, spilled while he battled a dragon.*

# Chapter Eighteen

"I couldn't find any kind of list down there." Agent Rankin was a little out of breath when he reached her. "Are you sure you don't have it with the rest of the papers?"

"I don't think so. I mean, I looked." She rifled through the papers on her clipboard again and then glanced back at his face. "Oops! I'm sorry. They were right here all the time. I didn't even see them."

He took a deep breath. "That's okay. Let's get moving, huh?"

The rest of the exhibit check was fine. Maybe a bird had managed to get inside and set off the alarm. Peggy doubted that Dabney's killer had wanted anyone to find him so quickly.

Peggy walked slower than usual, resting now and again at various exhibits and pointing out things that she knew

Norris didn't care to hear. He didn't realize it, but she'd found his Achilles' heel.

"We're almost to the door, Dr. Lee." His tone was impatient by the time they'd reached The Potting Shed exhibit. "Can you make it, or do you need me to get a wheelchair or something?"

She huffed and puffed. "I think I'll be fine. I can see the door from here. If you need to go ahead, don't mind me. I'll be right out behind you."

He looked at the door longingly. "Are you sure? I don't think anyone else is in here. You should be fine."

"I'll be all right. You go ahead now. These old legs don't want to move as fast as they did when I was your age."

He muttered something under his breath about working with incompetent people. "All right then. I'm going outside. I'll talk to you later."

"I'm sorry. What did you say? My hearing isn't as good as it used to be either."

Norris apologized loudly before he left her there.

Peggy laughed, but not for long. Steve came in as his second-in-command passed him in the doorway.

"What's taking so long? You could've walked this in ten minutes. Why does Norris think you need a wheelchair?"

"I don't know." She smiled and kissed him. "But I think I might've found something we've been looking for." She took the diamond out of her pocket.

"Is that what I think it is?"

"Only one way to find out. That gel Aris had the orchids growing in has left a dense film on it. It will have to be cleaned before it can be appraised."

"Where did you find it?" Steve held the stone up to the light.

"Let's find Al so I only have to say it once. I'll meet you upstairs."

\* \* \*

Peggy volunteered to get all of the diamonds out of the beakers. She wanted to save as many orchids as she could. She knew no one else would care about that aspect as soon as they'd found out that the stones in the beakers were the diamonds they were looking for.

An armored truck, driven by police officers, delivered all of the diamonds with the orchids to her house. She invited Walter to help her with the task while a security guard stood nearby. It was millions of dollars in cut diamonds. The insurance company for the convention center hadn't been crazy about taking the stones to her house. She had prevailed, with Al's help.

She also had to rely on Adam Morrow to keep the flower show running for most of the day while she and Walter worked on the diamonds.

Both the FBI and Charlotte PD were anxious to get their hands on the stones that had undoubtedly cost Dr. Abutto his life.

"What about the other dead one?" Walter asked as he cleaned the thick fluid from the diamonds with a special solution. "The one you found in the parking lot. Why was he killed?"

"I'm not sure." Peggy lifted another orchid from a beaker filled with diamonds and moved it to another beaker with a careful hand. "We still don't know why Aris was killed, not exactly. The police are theorizing that whoever made him smuggle the diamonds here killed him when they couldn't find them."

"What about the missing daughter?"

"Another mystery. The FBI thinks Aris was trying to make sure Tanya was safe before he gave the killers the diamonds."

"That didn't work out so well, did it? What do you think happened?"

"I'm not sure. I know my friend is dead and his daughter is still missing. I understand why he would've smuggled the diamonds to save her life. I don't understand why the person who had him do it killed him before he got the diamonds."

"Maybe something will come up that will solve the case. In the meantime, I would like to say what an honor it has been assisting you."

Peggy didn't tell him that ordinarily she would've had help from Sam and Selena. She was glad he'd enjoyed the experience. It had taken a large part of the day to transfer all the orchids. Now she'd have to keep an eye on them for several days to make sure they were all right. She didn't know what would happen to them now that Aris was gone. She might have to adopt them herself.

When she'd finished with the diamonds, Peggy laid them out to dry. She called Al. He who told her to leave them where they were. The security company would keep an eye on them for the police.

Walter wanted to go back to the flower show with Peggy, but he had other commitments. She locked the sliding glass door in the basement when he was gone, and went upstairs to change.

After slipping into a peach-colored Chanel suit, Peggy did her hair and makeup. While she got ready, she gazed at the red rose Steve had given her in a vase on the bedside table.

She realized that everything really was all right between her and Steve. It had taken a little time to get used to the idea that she'd married another man in law enforcement. She knew he was as good a man as John.

Steve made her happy. Shield or no shield, she loved him and knew that he loved her. They were going to have a wonderful life together.

With a smile on her face, Peggy checked her email. There was another message from *Nightflyer*. It was cryptic, as always.

*"Watch your back. I fear there may be some difficult decisions coming your way. Check out Internet news. Charlotte Observer newspaper won't air the story until tomorrow. Wonder who the leak is?"*

She wasn't sure what he was talking about until she went to her favorite online news source and there it was. *Botanist finds diamonds with orchids.*

Peggy read the details quickly. They were very accurate. It seemed to her that whoever leaked this to news sources had to be with the FBI or Charlotte PD. No one else would know those details.

Immediately her mind went to Norris Rankin. She shook her head. She couldn't blame bad things that happened on the man because she didn't like him.

She called Al and texted Steve to show them what she'd found. Al agreed that they needed someone to pick up the diamonds right away.

"How soon is that? I'm on my way to the flower show to hand out some awards."

"Let me get back with you. I know they're gonna want to send more security people to transport those. The State Department might send someone for them. It might take a few hours to set it up."

"Al, I love you. You know I do. But I can't wait around that long. I've already put too many of my responsibilities off on Adam. Please try to do better than that."

"Look, Peggy, I can't promise anything at this point. I've got two unsolved homicides tied in with these diamonds. The Chief is breathing down my neck. You have one security guard already there. Lock your doors and set your alarm. I'm sure the diamonds will be fine."

Steve texted back pretty much the same thing. *The State Department is coming for those. In the meantime, I'll send Norris over to keep an eye on them. Love you.*

Peggy balked at that idea. Norris may have been the one to tip off the media. She didn't like the idea that her house could become part of the theft and people might look for the diamonds here. They hadn't listed her address in the press release, but how hard would it be to find her since they'd put her name out there?

No wonder *Nightflyer* had alerted her.

She heard Paul come in the house as she was trying to

decide what to do. Norris wasn't there yet. The security guard was downstairs, but he was only one man. She wasn't convinced the diamonds would be safe.

"Mom?" Paul yelled up the stairs, much the same way he did when he was twelve. "I'm here to escort you to the flower show again. Are you ready?"

Peggy grabbed her handbag and went downstairs. Shakespeare was outside in the backyard. "I'm going down to let Shakespeare in. I'll be ready as soon as I get back up here."

"Take your time." Paul was eating an apple. "Have you got any peanut butter? Mai showed me how to dunk apples into peanut butter. It's really good."

"Help yourself." She closed the door to the basement as she went downstairs.

Before she called Shakespeare in, she looked at the diamonds again. They still weren't sparkling like cut diamonds should. Someone else might have to do a better job cleaning them. She was sure the gel hadn't really harmed them.

That was when the idea hit her.

Her handbag wasn't big enough to hold all the diamonds. She found a garden bag with the logo from last year's International Flower Show in Atlanta on it. She put all the diamonds into the bag and covered them with a flowered scarf. They weren't that heavy.

Was it safer for her to take the diamonds with her to the flower show?

She wasn't really sure, but it seemed like the last place a thief would look for them. She certainly didn't want to see them stolen again after Aris had given his life for them. Besides, they might need them to bargain for Tanya's life.

Maybe it was a little unconventional, but it felt right. She could leave the garden bag at The Potting Shed exhibit. Sam and Selena would keep an eye on them.

With everything decided, at least in *her* mind, Peggy texted Steve.

*I have the diamonds. Send the State Department to the flower show.*

### Dahlia

*The dahlia is the national flower of Mexico. They were grown by the Aztecs and brought to the new world by Spanish conquistadors in the early 1600s. Hybridization began in the 1800s. Dahlias are easy plants to grow and will bloom from mid-summer through fall.*

# Chapter Nineteen

*What?* Steve texted back. *Peggy, what are you doing?*

She ignored the text as she and Paul left the house. The alarm was set. Shakespeare was inside, chewing on his toy.

Ken had left Matilda the skunk in her cage hours ago to head back to the flower show. Peggy called him and told him he'd have to wait to feed the skunk until that evening when she and Steve were home. Ken knew nothing about the diamonds.

Paul didn't know she had the diamonds with her—which put him in a good mood.

He chuckled as he drove to the convention center. "I can't believe you're housing a skunk. All those years, we never had a pet at all. Now you have a dog the size of a pony and a skunk in the upstairs bedroom."

"Matilda isn't a permanent guest. When Ken leaves at

the end of the week, she'll leave with him." She smiled at him. "Matilda has been a much better guest than some of your college friends."

He winced. "It was only a small trashcan fire. Even Dad understood that college kids get a little wild sometimes."

"Like I said."

There was a big crowd for the flower show again. Peggy knew they'd received extra publicity because of Dabney's death. It was grotesque, but she acknowledged the truth of it.

"Want me to help you with that bag?" Paul asked after they'd parked near the gate. He'd learned something from Steve.

"I've got it. Thanks. It's only a few things Sam needed today."

Pete greeted them as they walked by. "Let's try to keep everyone alive today, huh? I thought flowers were safe and beautiful."

"They are," Peggy agreed. "It's the people who aren't so safe. See you later."

She went immediately to The Potting Shed exhibit. There was another large group of people talking to Sam about landscaping.

"He did a mini-workshop on setting up a pond." Selena pointed to the tiny pond in a washtub. "They ate it up. Now there are going to be thousands of washtub ponds around Charlotte. It's going to become the not-so-cool thing to do."

Peggy shrugged. "Whatever brings in business. At least he didn't plant a garden in a toilet. I hate seeing those alongside the road."

She took the garden bag and put it with Sam's gear under the table where he was standing.

"Hey, Peggy!" He introduced her to some prospective customers. "Most people know her as the plant lady. She also works as a forensic botanist for the city."

Everyone was suitably impressed by that information. They had dozens of questions to ask about Dr. Abutto's death, as well as Dabney's murder.

"I'm sorry. I have to run. We're handing out some awards for the outstanding exhibits here this week at the conference area, near the stairs. I'd love it if you'd sign a contract for Sam to do your landscaping and then join us. Thank you for stopping by."

Peggy shook a few hands and whispered to Sam, "There are diamonds in the garden bag under the table."

The expression on his handsome face was comical. "Say again."

"You heard me. Don't make a big deal out of it. I'll be back in a while."

Sam watched her leave with a deep frown settling over his healthy, tan face.

"You look like somebody stole your last bag of mulch," Selena remarked.

"Or something like that. Why does she *always* do these things to me?"

Peggy found Adam Morrow in the rapidly filling

conference room.

"Thank goodness you're here." He took her hand and smiled. "I'm worried about how these vendors are going to take it when they don't get a prize from the judges."

"They do this every year in Atlanta. I've never seen anyone act like less of a lady or gentleman about it. There's no reason why it should be any different here."

"You weren't out talking to those dahlia growers this morning. I was afraid they weren't going to let me leave their exhibit without promising that they were going to win something."

"I'm so sorry I've had to put so much on you, Adam. Believe me, I had no idea all of these terrible events would happen."

"That's okay. I'm happy to help out." He frowned and leaned a little closer to her. "I read this morning about the diamonds. Wow! What a score."

"Hardly worthwhile. Aris and Dabney are both dead. We're still not sure where Tanya Abutto is. What good are millions of diamonds if even one person dies?"

"Peggy, you're one in a million. I might be willing to sacrifice a few people for a couple of million dollars."

She didn't respond and hoped he was joking. She knew he was having financial difficulties and might have to close one or two of his stores. People said rash things they didn't mean when they were desperate.

"I think it's time. Thanks again for your help, Adam."

He bowed slightly. "My pleasure, as always."

Peggy ran her hand lightly across her hair and adjusted

her peach-colored jacket. She went up on stage and addressed the crowd, taking a moment to honor Aris and Dabney.

She gave out four awards. Adam was right. There were definitely some hostile looks from the losers. It was only a chunk of plastic, she wanted to say to them. How much difference did it make in the long run?

She'd made the decision not to include The Potting Shed in any of the award categories, even though the rules hadn't forbidden her from doing so. She didn't like the idea of there being even a hint of impropriety.

Peggy thanked the panel of judges and the audience gave them a round of applause. The winners stood on the platform with their awards and had their pictures taken by media people and bloggers for the International Flower Show. She stepped aside and let them have their moment.

Several disgruntled growers and vendors waited impatiently for her to finish the ceremony before complaining about their loss. She tried to soothe their ruffled feathers and mouthed platitudes until she could get away.

Already tired after her day had begun with the alarm going off at the convention center, she stopped at the snack area for a cup of hot water. She always brought her own tea bags. She needed a double shot of Earl Grey to get through the rest of the day.

Her cell phone rang. It was an unknown number. Thinking it might be *Nightflyer* again, she answered.

"Peggy Lee?"

"Yes." The voice sounded muffled, but not like *Nightflyer* at all. "Who is this?"

"The man who told everyone you have the diamonds. I have Tanya Abutto. I think a little horse trading may be what's needed right now."

Peggy sat down on a bench near the stairs. Her heart fluttered uncomfortably. She wasn't the person that should talk to a kidnapper. She wished she could put him on hold or have him call back so she could locate Steve or Al to handle this.

"Still there?"

"Yes." She swallowed hard on the sudden rush of fear. "I'm here, but I'm not who you need to talk to. Let me find someone who can negotiate with you."

"I think you're exactly who I need to talk to. I didn't mention negotiation. Here's the deal. You give me the diamonds and I give you the girl. Sound good?"

"I can't make that deal," she sputtered. "I don't have the diamonds. I found them, but the FBI has them. Actually, I think it's the State Department that has them. I'm sorry but I don't have their phone number."

"Listen carefully. No tricks. I want the diamonds. You want your friend's daughter? Take the diamonds to the main branch of the library on Seventh Street at four today. Come alone. I'll call you when I see you. Any police or FBI, the girl dies. Got it?"

Before Peggy could agree, or at least argue that she couldn't possibly do this, the phone went dead.

She stared at the rapidly cooling cup of hot water in her hand.

What was she going to do?

**Fern**

*Ferns have been around for more than 300 million years. The American Fern Society was established in 1893 and has more than 900 members which share their love for the plant. Spring foragers have been eating the new, tightly-curled head of the plant for at least that long. Some are delicious with a little butter. Others are toxic and should be avoided. Be sure you know your fiddleheads before you eat them.*

# Chapter Twenty

Peggy sat on the bench for a long time, watching as people walked by. Most of them seemed to be having a good time. They were exclaiming over the giant ferns in the last exhibit they saw or looking at pictures on their camera phones of amazing bulb gardens that they wanted to plant in their yards. The show was always good about giving gardeners new ideas.

Two women from Charlotte were talking about signing contracts with Sam for landscape service because they wanted to see him with his shirt off. The humor in that finally lifted her out of the terrible black hole the phone call had dropped her into.

It was wrong for the kidnapper to try and get her to bring him the diamonds, but that was what had happened. She had to deal with it.

Standing, she gazed across the crowded concourse and

saw Steve's face as he came toward her. She couldn't help
Tanya by herself, no matter what the kidnapper said. Steve
would help her decide what to do. Together, they would
save Aris's daughter.

"You look like you saw a ghost." He teased her as he
put his arm around her. "Are you okay?"

"Much better now that you're here." She turned her
head into his neck and whispered, "I got a call from
Tanya's kidnapper. He wants to trade the diamonds for
her."

Steve's arms tightened around her. "Don't worry.
We'll figure it out."

The cup of water was too cold to use for tea. Peggy
saw a neglected heart-leaf philodendron that looked as
though it hadn't been cared for in ages. Despite all the
thriving plants around it, the poor thing appeared near
death.

She poured the cup of water on the plant and loosened
the soil around the roots a little. She pinched off some of
the shriveled brown leaves and took out the trash that
people had left in its pot.

Steve waited patiently as she set the plant to rights.
He'd seen her do this a hundred times at doctor's offices
and other professional buildings. Her gentle caring always
made him smile.

"I need more hot water." She saw him smiling at her.
"I was trying to help the poor little thing. The water wasn't
hot anymore."

"That's okay. Let's get some hot water and call Al. He
has to know what's going on."

"If we make a mistake with this, the kidnapper could kill Tanya."

"I know. Let us deal with it."

"I think the kidnapper knows me, personally, I mean. He sounded like it."

"I don't know. Maybe. Or he saw the information about you on the Internet."

"He said he was the one who leaked the information about the diamonds to the media." Peggy got another cup of hot water and they walked quickly back to The Potting Shed exhibit. Steve had called Al as they'd walked through the crowd. He also called Norris, who was still on his way to their house.

"I figured it was better to let him go there," Steve explained. "It looks more like the diamonds could be in the house instead of in your bag, or wherever you put them."

By that time, they were standing close to Sam who caught their conversation.

"She put them down here on the floor by my feet," he told Steve. "I haven't moved since. I think I've lost ten good years of my life waiting for someone to come by and try to steal them. Please take them now."

Steve and Peggy walked around and into the back of the exhibit. Sam was standing very still at the front, behind the table filled with information flyers.

"The garden bag, right?" Steve asked her.

"Of course."

"You can move now, Sam. It's fine."

After Steve's permission, Sam let out a long sigh then ran out of the exhibit toward the restrooms.

Selena laughed. "He looks so big and tough, but I swear I could take him."

"What do we do now?" Peggy asked.

"We wait for Al." Steve put his arm around her shoulders. "We'll come up with a plan."

Al arrived a few minutes later with a host of blue-uniformed officers and Police Chief Rodney Mickleson. Norris came a few minutes later with Millie Sanford and several FBI agents. They created a ring around the exhibit that clearly discouraged foot traffic.

"This better not take very long," Selena said. "Sam will surely die when he sees it."

Al, Chief Mickelson, and Steve huddled together at the back of the exhibit where the fake house ended behind the garden Sam had created.

Peggy waited impatiently, tapping her foot on the concrete floor. How long was it going to take for them to decide what to do? What if the kidnapper saw them meeting and decided to blow the whole thing off? She was worried about Tanya. *That poor girl.* Did she even know about her father's death?

Finally, Steve and Al walked toward her. Chief Mickelson was on his cell phone.

"What's going on?" Peggy asked.

"We've decided to go ahead with the drop," Al told her.

"Against the better judgment of the FBI," Steve added.

Peggy glanced uneasily between the two men. "What's the problem?"

Al heaved a big sigh. "Chief Mickelson thinks you should do the drop, Peggy. We figure the kidnapper knows you or he wouldn't have contacted you. Anything else might get the girl killed."

"Doing it might get Peggy killed." Steve stared at Al, anger in his gaze. "Just because this nutcase calls her doesn't mean she should be out there. We could replace her with Agent Sanford who knows how to handle herself in this type of situation."

"The kidnapper is obviously familiar with Peggy—we don't know how familiar." Al looked back at the female FBI agent. "Agent Sanford is probably a very good agent, but she doesn't look like Peggy."

"I don't think she should do it." Steve stood his ground.

"I don't see how I *can't* do it." Peggy put her hand on his arm. "I know it's dangerous, but Al is right. I don't want to be responsible if something goes wrong."

Steve grabbed her hand and they walked away from the exhibit toward the welcome center. "You aren't trained for this. Anything can happen in these situations. Doing it this way puts the kidnapper in control. Do you understand that?"

She nodded. "Certainly. But if I can help, I want to. I'll be fine. You'll see."

He wrapped his arms around her. "I guess I don't have any choice. Too many people have died already for these diamonds. Let's make sure you're not one of them, okay?"

"Okay." She kissed him. "Thanks for worrying about me."

Al, Steve, and Peggy left the convention center to go somewhere quiet so they could plan the operation. Peggy called Adam and asked for his help again. He gave it, reluctantly. She felt sure he wouldn't be so quick to volunteer if the flower show came to Charlotte again next year.

They didn't have much time to get ready. It was already three-thirty. The library wasn't far, but traffic could be unreliable.

Steve had requisitioned a surveillance van. It was big and black, waiting in the parking lot for them. Peggy went in first. Norris was already inside, sitting in front of some equipment.

She rolled her eyes. Hopefully, he wouldn't be responsible for her well-being.

"We'll have the diamonds in this case." Al showed her. "It has a tracking device that we can follow from the van. If he takes the case, don't worry about it. Don't worry about the girl either. Let us take care of that part."

"It would be good for you to wear a vest too." Steve held one up. It was black and not at all something that could be worn with a peach suit.

Peggy examined it as Steve helped her take off her jacket. She put on the vest and replaced the jacket over her top. The big black space on her chest was a dead giveaway.

She reached in her bag and pulled out a spring green scarf that she tied around her neck, letting the flowing ends of it hide the vest.

"It doesn't matter how it looks," Steve told her. "It will protect you. The most important thing—if there is any gunfire—lay down. Don't get up. Don't even lift your head. We'll be right there if it happens, but things can go wrong very quickly."

"And we have a listening device in case the kidnapper gets up close and personal." Al installed the earpiece and let her take care of the rest. "If you see anything, or you're afraid, say something. We'll hear you."

Norris lounged back in his chair. "Don't you think that's a tall order for her? I mean, she's already terrified. She's gonna blow it the minute she gets out there. I agree with Steve. We should put Millie in and take our chances."

"You're not taking any chances," Peggy reminded him. "You're going to be sitting inside this van where you don't have to worry about anything happening to you. You handle your part. I can handle mine."

They were big, brave words at a time when she wasn't particularly feeling big and brave. She knew Steve was right and that a hundred things could happen that would mess up the whole thing up.

What choice did she have? She owed this to her old friend. She couldn't save him, but maybe she could save his daughter.

### *Ficus Benjamina*

*Commonly grown in offices and apartment buildings because it tolerates low light and poor care. The plant is also known as a weeping fig. It grows wild in the forests of India where it is known as Ben-ja. It is also known for losing its leaves after they turn yellow, creating an unattractive specimen. They are considered throw away plants as most indoor gardeners would rather than replace them than take care of them.*

# Chapter Twenty-one

Peggy walked serenely into the Charlotte Mecklenburg Public Library on Seventh Street at exactly four p.m.

At least she hoped she looked serene. It was all she could do to keep her teeth from chattering. Her heart was pounding in her chest and her legs felt wobbly.

*Pull yourself together*, she commanded. *You can do this.*

The library wasn't crowded. It was near the end of the school day. Most people were involved with their children, getting on and off buses and doing their homework, at that hour.

She was glad to see that the library was almost empty. There was a homeless man with all of his belongings gathered around him as he slept in one of the chairs by a window. Two librarians were chatting at the desk. Another woman was there browsing the Internet. One man was looking at the books on the sale cart.

Peggy pulled in a deep breath and slowly focused on the people around her. None of them looked familiar. Of course, they were only guessing that the kidnapper was someone she knew. They might find the man was a compete stranger. That could throw a wrench into their plans. They hadn't said it, but she thought they were counting on her identifying the kidnapper before things could get ugly.

She took a seat away from the homeless man, next to a dusty ficus, and put the case that held the diamonds on the floor. She carefully dusted the little plant's leaves.

Nothing happened.

Peggy waited with her hands trembling, hoping nothing was wrong. Her cell phone rang, making her jump. Both librarians' heads swiveled toward her. One of them made a gesture that was probably *turn off your cell phone*. She was too nervous to be sure.

"Where are your cop friends?"

She glanced around. She didn't see anyone else talking on a cell phone.

"I didn't tell them. I got the diamonds together and came over. Where are you?"

"Never mind that. Come outside and start walking down Seventh Street."

Peggy did as he said. She knew the only thing down that way was a parking deck.

"Don't let him get you into the parking deck," Steve

said in her ear. "Make up some excuse. Tell him you're scared of the dark. Anything."

She didn't reply. Her cell phone was still on. She wasn't sure if the kidnapper would be able to hear her answer Steve.

"Okay," the man on the phone said. "I can see you now. Continue walking."

Peggy walked slowly past the library. She was almost to the large parking deck, trying to figure out what she was going to say if he asked her to go inside.

"Stop there. See that city trashcan next to you?"

"This one?" She pointed, wondering where he was.

"That's right. Drop the case into the trashcan and walk away."

"Which way?"

"Any way. I don't care. Walk back up to the library."

"Where's Tanya?" Peggy demanded.

"Don't push him," Steve warned in her ear. "We've got him when he gets the case. Walk away."

Peggy put the case into the trashcan. It was a tight fit. She hoped someone hadn't seen her putting it in there and got to it before the kidnapper.

"I'll call you later and tell you where you can pick up the girl," the kidnapper said.

"I don't think that's good enough." Peggy didn't care what Steve said. She'd read about too many kidnappings that had ended badly because they couldn't find the victim after the ransom was paid. What if the locater device in the case stopped working? They would have no idea where Tanya was.

"Look, I could kill her right now."

"I'm still standing here next to the diamonds," she argued. "I could take them and leave. I want better reassurance about Tanya."

"Peggy—" Steve's whispered warning sent a shiver down her spine.

"What are you doing?" Al said, grabbing the microphone from Steve. "Get out of there. Let us do our job."

"Okay, okay. I get your point. Walk back to the library and I'll let her out there."

"All right," she agreed. "But if I see you down here at the trashcan before I see her, I'll call the police."

The man on the phone swore. "Just do what I say. The girl will be there."

Peggy started walking back toward the library. The man on the cell phone hung up. She kept glancing over her shoulder as she got near the corners of Seventh and Tryon Streets. She didn't see any movement.

"Come over to the van," Al said in the earpiece. "Your part is done."

She stopped and waited, not feeling safe doing what Al had asked. If the man was still watching her, it could be enough to make him change his mind. She stood on the corner and kept watch, praying that he would keep his word and free Tanya.

"Peggy," Steve said in her ear. "Come inside."

She didn't answer. A moment later, a fast-moving black SUV turned the corner where she stood. A door opened and Tanya tumbled out on the pavement. The SUV moved even faster, racing down Seventh Street to reach the diamonds.

Peggy helped Tanya to her feet. The girl was crying and scared. Together they removed the plastic ties that had bound her hands and the red blindfold that had probably kept her alive since she couldn't see the kidnapper.

The driver of the FBI van moved even faster. Two police cars sped out of the parking deck, blocking the SUV from moving. The driver, wearing a red ski mask, only had time to retrieve the case from the trashcan before they had him.

When the sirens and lights started on the police cars, everyone in the area began to take notice. A dozen agents and officers were all over the kidnapper, cuffing his hands and dragging him into the FBI van as though he was an animal they'd scooped off the street.

Peggy wrapped her arms around Tanya's trembling body. "I'm your father's friend, Peggy Lee. Let's get you out of here before the media catches on."

Paul drove up on cue, opening the back door for his mother and the rescued girl. He was back in the driver's seat a moment later, right as a Channel 9 News van pulled up.

"Where is my father?" Tanya was sobbing so hard she could hardly catch her breath. "I heard him talking, the kidnapper. He said my father is dead. Is he dead, Peggy?"

Peggy nodded. There was no point in giving the girl

false hope. At least she could hear it from someone she knew.

Tanya collapsed, her arms tight around Peggy as she cried into her shoulder.

"Hospital, right?" Paul murmured.

"Yes." Peggy held Tanya all the way to the hospital. When the girl began to protest being taken to the medical facility, Peggy calmed her down. "We have to be sure you're okay. This is for the best right now. Let's get through this and we can talk about your father."

Tanya finally agreed, on the condition that Peggy stayed with her. Peggy did that, not leaving the girl's side as the doctors and nurses examined her and found her a room to spend the night.

Finally, one of the doctors beckoned to her. Tanya had fallen asleep clutching Peggy's hand.

"We've given her a sedative. She's dehydrated, but otherwise she seems to be in good shape. We think it would be a good idea for her to spend the night here and get some sleep. It's not going to be easy for her tomorrow, or for the foreseeable future."

"All right. I'll stay with her. Thank you, doctor."

Peggy waited there, with Paul outside the room, until she saw Steve at the doorway. She carefully moved out of Tanya's tight embrace and ran to him.

She threw her arms around him. "I never want to do anything like that again."

"And I don't think you ever should." He kissed her and held her close. "You did a good job. We've got the kidnapper in custody and the girl is safe. We didn't lose the diamonds. It was a win-win all around."

"Thank goodness." She wiped the tears from her eyes. "Who was it?"

"We were right about him knowing you. It was Tim Roseboro."

"Tim Roseboro?" Her green eyes flew open wide. "Why would he do such a thing? His family has always had plenty of money."

Steve shrugged. "Not according to him. He said the family finances have been going downhill since the stock market crash in 2007. He's tried everything but he's in hock up to his eyebrows. The family is about to lose that big old house on Sharon Road."

She sat down on one of the green plastic chairs in the hall. "That's incredible. Did he kill Aris and Dabney?"

"We don't know yet. He had plenty to say, until we got to the station. He started yelling for a lawyer right away. We probably won't know anything else until tomorrow. I think he'll make a statement. This type always does."

"I'm glad that part is over with. I hope he admits to killing Aris so Tanya has some closure. It's hard when you don't know what happened."

Steve agreed with her. "I suppose you're staying here with her and leaving me with the skunk and the mountain man tonight."

"I can't leave her alone. I'm the only one she knows, poor thing. She must be very disoriented. She knows her father is dead."

"At least she can start the grieving process," Steve said. "Paul is going to stay out here. We don't know for sure that this is over. Do you need anything from the house?"

"No. It's only for the night. I'll be fine."

"Okay." He kissed her quickly. "I love you. Call me later."

When he was gone, Peggy sat in the hall with Paul while Tanya was sleeping. The girl awakened for a while at around seven p.m. She refused anything to eat and went right back to sleep.

"We don't know what she's been through," Paul reminded her. "It's gonna take some time for her to recover. Really, sleep is the best thing now."

Peggy laughed at him. "When did you get so wise?"

"I got it from my parents. They were both wise people, even if I didn't think so when I was a kid."

Tanya called out and Peggy hugged her son before she went back into the hospital room.

No one slept much that night. Tanya woke up several times, realizing over and over that her father had been murdered. Peggy comforted her as best she could. Even though John had been dead for years, she remembered doing the same thing the night she'd found out he was gone.

Paul was right. Only time could take away the edge of that kind of grief. It would never truly go away.

### Magnolia

*Magnolia tree fossils have been dated back to 50 million years ago. The tree was destroyed by the Ice Age in Europe but survived in Asia and the Americas. It is a primitive flowering plant, it is fertilized by beetles instead of bees. The magnolia is the state flower for both Mississippi and Louisiana.*

# Chapter Twenty-two

In the morning, Steve brought Peggy a change of clothes. She used the shower in Tanya's room and drank several cups of tea as she tried to wake up.

Tanya seemed calmer. Her grandmother was flying in from South Africa. Peggy felt better knowing the girl would have a family member there with her.

"Thank you for staying with me," Tanya said before Peggy had to leave to go to the flower show. "My father always considered you one of his greatest friends. I can see why."

Peggy hugged her, brushing tears from the corners of her eyes. The doctors wanted to run a few more tests. She left with Steve and Paul when they came to get Tanya.

Paul yawned on the elevator as they went downstairs. "I'm hungry and tired. I'm going home. I haven't heard if someone is taking over for me today."

Steve shrugged. "I haven't heard either. Maybe we should go to see Al before you leave for the flower show."

Peggy agreed. She still had about an hour before she was supposed to be at the convention center. She said goodbye to her son and Steve drove them downtown.

Police headquarters was filled with reporters and dozens of plain-clothes vice squad officers who'd made a big drug collar during the night. Steve and Peggy managed to slip by the media and went to the second floor to meet with Al.

"Are you okay?" Steve asked as Peggy yawned for the tenth time in as many minutes. "You know, it won't be the end of the world if you let that guy take your place again. You look like you could use some sleep."

"How bad do I look?" Steve had brought her clothes and a few toiletries, but no makeup. She only had the lipstick in her bag.

"Not that bad. Just tired. Probably no one else would even notice."

The elevator doors parted. The first person Peggy saw was Elaine Roseboro.

The older, diminutive matriarch of the Roseboro family looked furious. She was well-dressed, as always. Her steel gray hair and makeup were perfect. Her lips were pushed tightly together. Peggy could tell she'd been crying.

"Excuse me." Steve navigated him and Peggy through the group of lawyers that were there with Elaine, probably trying to salvage as much as they could of their family name.

Peggy didn't know Elaine well. They'd met a few times at Rose Cottage for one charity event or another. Still, she couldn't simply walk past, after seeing the grief, anger, and disbelief written on her face.

"I'm so sorry that this has happened to you." Peggy grasped the other woman's hand. She felt like a giant hovering over her even though she was only medium height.

"I remember you." Elaine raised her chin and looked down her nose. "You're the one responsible for bringing the flower show to Charlotte."

Peggy wasn't sure what to expect from that opening. She braced herself for a vitriolic response in case Elaine blamed her for what had happened to her son.

"I enjoyed it." Elaine carefully inclined her head. "I apologize for my ass of a son who used it to further his own stupidity. I hope you can convince the committee to bring the flower show back again sometime."

Peggy smiled and realized that she'd been holding her breath. That wasn't what she'd expected. There was no further time to talk to Tim's mother. Al opened his office door and pulled Peggy and Steve inside.

"What a mess!" Al took a seat behind his cluttered desk. "We've got Roseboro on kidnapping charges, although he claims Dabney Wilder dreamed up the whole scheme. He's talking to the DA now, trying to reach some kind of plea agreement if he testifies to everything that happened."

Peggy sat down in a chair in front of the desk. "What *did* happen?"

"Roseboro says he needed money. He says Wilder set

up the kidnapping and the plane. They told Dr. Abutto if he smuggled the diamonds into the flower show, he'd get his daughter back."

"And then he killed Abutto when he didn't deliver the diamonds?" Steve asked.

Al shrugged. He looked tired too. "I don't know. Roseboro says he had nothing to do with killing Abutto or Wilder. He had the girl and wanted the diamonds. He sent the fake Tanyas to try and get the duffel because he thought they were in there."

Peggy glanced at the closed door. "Do you think that's true?"

"I can't say yet. We questioned him last night. The FBI questioned him this morning. He's willing to admit to threatening Abutto and being part of the kidnapping, but not the murders. I guess we'll see what kind of deal he works out with the DA."

"So it's okay if I go on to the flower show without a guard dog, right?" Peggy smiled at him.

"I'm not comfortable with the idea," Al admitted. "Captain Sedgwick is shorthanded. Unless the FBI wants to send one of its agents with you, I guess you're going alone."

"Let me see what I can do." Steve frowned at Peggy. "I know it can't be Norris. Someone got on his bad side yesterday."

Peggy smiled and kept her thoughts to herself.

Steve stepped back into the hall to see if Agent Sanford was there.

"You're gonna drive him crazy with this, aren't you?" Al shook his head. "I'm glad I don't have to work cases with Mary. I'd never hear the end of it."

"If you think Tim killed Aris and Dabney, why worry about me at all?"

"I don't know. I don't like it when things aren't wrapped up. I like cases to be like pretty presents, complete with wrapping paper and a bow. I'm not feeling that kind of confidence right now. Why would Roseboro admit to kidnapping but shy away from murder?"

She shrugged. "Maybe he doesn't want to go that far. Maybe kidnapping is bad enough. Murder would be worse."

Al shuffled a few papers on his desk. "In my experience, when a man like Roseboro admits to something, they admit to everything. I might be crazy. I know I'm getting old. This thing doesn't feel done to me, though. Which could mean you're still in danger."

Steve came back in the office with Agent Sanford. "Millie will go with you to the flower show. We'll talk later. Norris and I are heading in to meet with Roseboro."

Peggy got to her feet and gave him a quick kiss on the cheek. "I'll check in with you later."

"Be careful. And don't alienate Sanford, huh? I have to work with these people."

Agent Sanford volunteered to drive them to the convention center, with a quick stop for breakfast biscuits on the way. She was bright and easy to talk to. Peggy wondered again why Steve hadn't make her his second-in-command instead of Norris.

"Do you think this Roseboro person murdered those two men?" Millie asked her.

"I can't even believe he kidnapped someone." Peggy wiped her mouth after finishing her biscuit. "He never seemed the type, you know? I believe him when he says Dabney Wilder set the whole thing up. I could even see Dabney as a killer."

"People do strange and stupid things sometimes," Millie said. "Especially when there's a lot of money on the line. I guess it's the desperation factor."

"I'm not trained in these things like you are," Peggy admitted. "But my late husband used to say that it takes someone intense and physical to stab someone to death. The gunshot? Maybe. That isn't so personal."

Millie flipped her bright red hair and finished her coffee. "I guess wrapping it all up with one person is too much good luck to ask for, huh?"

Peggy laughed. "It would've been nice. I'm not sure where we'll go from here if Tim didn't kill Aris and Dabney."

"Me either."

They got back in the car and headed to the convention center in very light traffic. That changed when they got near the complex. There were lines of cars waiting to get into the parking lots.

Millie waited patiently until there was a chance to park near the gate. She put a cardboard FBI BUSINESS sign on the dash and they left the car there.

"What's up for today?" she asked Peggy.

"It's pretty much a carbon copy of yesterday, in a good way, I hope. It should be filled with complaints from vendors and growers, an award program this afternoon, and the various electricity and water issues that have come up every day."

"Sounds like fun. No wonder you do forensic botany work."

"I only get calls once in a while for forensic botany work. I run a small garden shop in downtown Charlotte that keeps me busy. The police hire me on a per case basis and I do some lecturing at Queen's University too."

"The garden shop sounds nice. I have some pots on the terrace at my apartment. It's not much, but I grew enough tomatoes last summer that I didn't have to buy any. Not bad, huh?"

"Sounds great. We help a lot of people with terrace and balcony gardens. My partner does small ponds for small spaces."

"The hunky Viking?" Millie laughed as she slowed her rapid stride going into the building. "I noticed him right away."

"He's setting up our display." Peggy pointed to Sam. "I'll introduce you."

"Seriously? Is he available as a live-in gardener? Forget the pool boy. He's gorgeous."

"That's Sam. He's got a green thumb and a silver tongue."

"I wouldn't mind giving *that* combination a try."

Peggy tried to decide if she should tell Millie that Sam

was gay. Really, it was none of her business. Sam seemed to be adept at keeping the women he did landscape work for happy. Why should she interfere?

She introduced Millie and Sam. Millie's dark eyes wandered over Sam's tight, white Potting Shed T-shirt.

"I'll leave you two to sort it out. I'm going to walk up the concourse and gather today's problems."

"I should go with you." Millie protested but her eyes never left Sam's handsome face. "It may not be safe."

"I'll be here when you get back," Sam said. "I don't want anything to happen to Peggy."

Millie reluctantly gave up looking at him to join Peggy. "Someone should sculpt him. I'd like to have that statue in my garden, know what I mean?"

"Believe me, I hear it all the time."

"I bet you do. There are probably women out there who only hire him to watch him work." Millie grinned. "I would."

Peggy smiled. "I'm sure that's true."

There were several complaints about the night-time cleaning crew bothering displays. One exhibit lost power. Peggy got on her phone and called the number she'd been given in case that happened.

Another exhibit, the one with the huge pink magnolia trees set in pots, had lost water. Peggy assured them that she'd take care of it. The owner, a man from Texas whose huge hat made him look as though he was going to fall over, thanked her and asked her out to dinner.

Peggy handled that request as tactfully as she could.

She didn't want to create any more bad feelings about the flower show for anyone. As it was, two murders later, it seemed unlikely it would happen in Charlotte again.

"I think he likes you." Millie glanced around as they left that exhibit. "He obviously doesn't know Steve is your husband. I don't think he'd be as likely to try and mess around with you."

Peggy blushed. "You know, that's one thing that has surprised me about Steve— garnering such goodwill with his superiors that they promoted him to being director in Charlotte. He seemed so ordinary to me when I first met him."

"It's those ordinary ones that get you. Steve's good at what he does. He kind of slides right in while no one is looking and gets the job done. Believe me, he was promoted because he's done good work."

Even having seen Steve in action, Peggy still found it hard to have that image of him. "It floored me when I found out the truth."

"Really?" Millie wrinkled her nose. "I guess I see him differently because we've worked together for a while. He's good at not showing his real face. I'm sure it's different being married to him."

Peggy wasn't so sure about that. She was still waiting to wake up and find all the pieces in the puzzle that had become her husband.

Adam Morrow came running up to them, out of breath and white-faced.

"Peggy, something awful has happened. Can you come with me?"

### *Saw Palmetto*

*The saw palmetto is part of a large family of plants. There are more than 2,000 varieties throughout the world. There are five species of palm native to South Carolina where the saw palmetto is on the state flag and is considered the state tree. The date palm is considered the original species since it dates back 6,000 years ago where it was grown for food in Mesopotamia.*

# Chapter Twenty-three

"Of course." Peggy started moving quickly in the direction he'd come from. Millie was right beside her, a hand on the gun under her short jacket.

"Who's this?" Adam asked.

"This is Millie. What's the problem?"

"You'll see when we get there."

There were huge signs on the door and outside the building asking visitors not to bring in pets. There had already been a few violations of that ban.

A woman with bright blond hair was screaming at a small dog that was digging at the base of a palmetto tree planted in the South Carolina Master Gardener's exhibit. The dog wasn't leashed. It seemed the woman had brought it into the building inside her handbag.

"Someone get him out of there," the woman yelled. "He's gonna get hurt."

Peggy thought it seemed like the palmetto the dog was aggressively attacking was more likely to get hurt than the dog. Then she saw why the dog was barking and trying to get through the palmetto. Matilda the skunk was back at the show.

"Where's Ken Benigni?" Peggy demanded.

"Save my dog," the woman yelled. "That skunk probably has rabies. Doesn't anyone have a gun handy?"

The chaos got bigger as vendors and growers started coming closer to the fray. Peggy glanced at her watch. They were only moments from opening the doors to visitors. She had to do something fast.

"I'm going in there. Adam, page Ken for me. And someone find a security guard to escort this lady out." Peggy wasn't sure how the woman got inside. She was obviously a visitor and shouldn't have been there yet.

She took off her shoes and walked over the soft, green moss that had been carefully layered on a path that led past the palmetto and a model of a boy sitting at a fishing hole.

The whole scene had a lovely, serene quality to it—before the dog and skunk had arrived. South Carolina was showcasing some beautiful aspects of different gardens in the state, including Brookgreen Garden in Myrtle Beach. There was a smaller version of one of the horses from that statuary garden.

Peggy wasn't sure about the Pekingese, but she felt she had a relationship with the skunk. She went to grab Matilda and get her away from the dog. Hopefully, the dog would return to its owner when the skunk was gone. Problem solved.

What she didn't reckon with was that the little skunk was terrified by the loud, yappy dog. When she reached down to pick her up, Matilda sunk her teeth into Peggy's arm.

There was a loud groan from the crowd that had continued to assemble. Even the security guards were standing there, watching what was happening.

The bite hurt. Peggy drew back quickly and looked at it. It was small but bloody. She hoped Matilda really had all of her shots, as Ken had promised.

Not one to let go of a problem, she reached down again and this time, grabbed the skunk from behind and managed to lift her out of the situation without getting bitten again.

Everyone applauded. The Pekingese kept yapping, but now at Peggy's feet.

"There she is." Ken came running toward them. "Oh my God! Did she hurt you? I'm so sorry, Peggy. She knows better."

"Why did you bring her back again?" Peggy held a tissue on her arm to stop the bleeding.

"I couldn't leave her at your house this morning. She hadn't eaten and she looked so sad." Ken flung his arms into the air and made a face that asked how she could even consider it.

"I hope she's had her shots."

"Absolutely. Like I told you, I have children who come to my petting zoo in Minnesota all the time. That bite might hurt, but there's no disease in it."

A security guard finally stepped in to assist and picked up the Pekingese, giving the dog back to its owner. He then walked the woman out of the convention center.

Millie, Ken, and Adam accompanied Peggy to the first aid station. Millie did a credible job making a field bandage for the wound.

"You should probably get that looked at," the agent advised. "Have you had a tetanus shot recently?"

"I think I'm fine with that." Peggy flexed her arm in the bandage. "Thanks."

"You're welcome. I hope Steve doesn't yell at me for not keeping you safe from the skunk. I could've shot it."

Ken rolled his eyes. "Thank goodness you didn't. She means the world to me. That's why I couldn't leave her today."

"She's going to have to leave," Adam said. "The skunk has caused enough trouble. Get her out of here or I'll have to call animal control."

"Please, don't do that. I'll take her out to my truck. It's not that hot in the morning. I can close down for a while at lunch and take her back to Peggy's house."

"I can't leave to open the door and turn off the alarm," Peggy told him. "We have another award presentation today at noon."

"I'll take care of the presentation," Adam said in a long-suffering tone. "My assistant can take over my exhibit for a while."

"Thanks." Peggy got up and picked up her bag. "I promise this will be the last time today."

"All right." Adam smiled at her. "I'm glad to help out. You know I am. I don't want to miss any sales opportunities, that's all. I should've brought more help with me, like you did. I didn't expect to be so busy."

"If you need some help, I can send Selena down to watch your spot," Peggy offered. "I appreciate all you've done."

Adam said he thought he'd be fine. With the emergency over, Peggy and Millie finished checking with all the vendors and went back to The Potting Shed exhibit to sit and watch the crowd come in.

"I had no idea gardening was so popular," Millie said as people began streaming in through the door. "I knew I liked it, but I always thought I'm probably the only one."

"Not at all, thank goodness. Gardening has always been popular."

Large groups of visitors continued to pour in until noon. Peggy hated leaving the flower show again, especially when she noticed that Adam's name was on the list to receive a special award for a floral display that he'd created.

That was where Paul came into the picture. Yawning and holding a large cup of coffee, he walked in as Peggy was about to leave.

"You're my lifesaver," she exclaimed when she saw him.

"Not sure what we're talking about, but I guess I'll take the credit." He shook hands with Millie and thanked her for doing what he considered to be his job.

"Not a problem, Officer Lee. I had a great time with

your mother this morning."

"You must like gardening and plants."

Millie smiled. "I do, as a matter of fact. We also had an adventure." She told him about the skunk biting Peggy.

Fierce green eyes fastened on the white bandage on Peggy's arm. "Are you okay, Mom? Did you go to the hospital or something?"

"Of course not. The skunk has had her rabies shots and whatever else she was supposed to have. It hurts a little, but I'll be fine."

Millie shrugged. "Your mom is tough, Lee. I'm thinking we should recruit her."

"Anyway." Peggy ham-handedly changed the conversation. "Paul, could you take Ken and Matilda back to the house for me? The skunk can't stay here. I'd like to be here to give Adam his award. He's done so much for me. I hate for him to have to accept the award from himself. It doesn't have the same affect."

"Sure," Paul said, "if Agent Sanford doesn't mind hanging around a little longer. I'm supposed to be your bodyguard again. One of us has to stay with you."

Millie looked at her watch. "I'm fine with that. I don't have to report in until two. Go on, Lee. Take the skunk home."

Paul laughed and Peggy pointed to where he could find Ken and Matilda.

"Thanks for staying longer, Millie." Peggy went to find Adam before the award ceremony started.

"I've had a great time. I'd be glad to stay all day. By

the way, what are those pink lilies over there that smell so good? I'd like some of those."

"Those are Stargazer lilies. They smell heavenly, don't they? They'll perfume an entire yard. Or in your case, a whole terrace."

Millie breathed deeply of the wonderful aroma. "I won't always only have a terrace. Someday, I might have a big yard like yours."

"I'm sure that's possible."

Peggy found Adam right before he was ready to go onstage with the list of award winners and trophies. She explained that she could take over after all.

He seemed relieved to hand everything to her. "I wasn't looking forward to giving myself an award. I know how that would look."

"You don't have to do that. I loved your display. I can't imagine you not winning an award for it."

"Thanks, Peggy. That means a lot coming from you. I know we're not in the same field, but you have a knack for knowing what works."

"I appreciate that, Adam."

"Like you knew what to do with those diamonds you found." He shook his head. "I wouldn't have known what to think. You did the right thing. I heard Dr. Abutto's daughter was found alive."

"Yes, bless her heart. What an ordeal. I hate that she had to go through, it only to find that her father had been killed."

"I know. It was tragic." He glanced around and

lowered his voice. "Have the police found his killer?"

"I don't know." Peggy looked at the rapidly-filling audience. "I think it's time to get started."

There were five florists from three states that won awards for their work. Each of their winning displays had been put on tables so they could be featured with their creators in photos.

Adam's brilliant design had been created with orange blossoms and tiny white lights. There was even a small fountain at the center of the work.

When she called his name, Adam came over to her, took the award, and shook her hand, as the other floral designers had done.

"I'd like to add that Adam Morrow is more than simply a wonderful designer," Peggy said before she let him go back to his spot near his creation. "He's also been instrumental in helping the flower show come here to Charlotte this year, and keeping it running for the past few days. I couldn't have done it without him."

There was a brisk round of applause, followed by media photos. Even the local cable channel had been there to broadcast the whole thing.

Peggy hoped that would help Adam's business. He certainly deserved a break.

Millie was waiting for her when she got down from the stage. "I got a call from Steve. Bad news, I'm afraid."

### *Stargazer lily*

*The stargazer lily was developed in 1978 by a plant breeder, Leslie Woodruff. His hybrid was a cross between an Asiatic lily and an Oriental lily. There are no exact details of the mixture between the two plants. Woodruff was looking for the bright colors and strong growth habits of the Oriental lily and the fragrance and elegantly-shaped flowers of the Asiatic lily. The plant was named 'stargazer' because the flowers open toward the sky.*

# Chapter Twenty-four

"What's wrong?" Peggy asked.

"It looks like Tim Roseboro is clear on both homicides. The police checked his alibis this morning. Both of them are good. We're back to square one, as far as the murders are concerned."

"At least he can't deny that he kidnapped Tanya."

"No, we've got him on that. He gave the DA some evidence on his involvement in the plot to smuggle the diamonds into the country. Dabney Wilder was definitely involved, maybe masterminded the whole thing. His assistant, David Mueller, was involved too. They picked him up."

"He was such a nice young man," Peggy lamented. "What now?"

"We go back over the evidence we've collected and try to come up with another suspect. I imagine that will mean you going back to the medical examiner's office for further instruction. I'm supposed to report to Steve for my next assignment."

"So you'll be leaving Charlotte?"

"No. Steve, Norris and I are assigned here for now. We'll cover this part of the state and mostly be home every night. I'm off this case, but I'm headed to Gastonia to investigate some mail fraud."

"It was very nice spending time with you." Peggy and Millie had reached The Potting Shed exhibit again. "I don't know if the FBI is like the police or not. Do you get together sometimes—dinner, cocktails—that kind of thing?"

"Yes, we do. I hope that's an invitation to your place. I've seen the outside. I'd love to see the inside."

"Consider it an invitation then."

Paul was back and told them that Matilda was safe at home again. "I understand that you have a meeting, Agent Sanford. I'll see you later."

She nodded. "Officer Lee. I hope to see you at dinner very soon."

Peggy didn't have to tell Paul the news Millie had given her.

"Yeah. It's a shame Tim Roseboro didn't kill Dabney and Dr. Abutto. I have a feeling he made a good deal with the DA, even though kidnapping is a federal offense."

"Is it possible Dabney or his assistant killed Aris?"

"They were together at a charity function when the ME says Dr. Abutto died."

"I'm sure Tim is going to prison for a long time anyway," Peggy agreed. "I'm not sure what I'm supposed to do now. I guess Al still thinks I could be in danger or you wouldn't be here. Millie said I should check with Dorothy about looking back at the evidence."

"Why don't you give her a call?" Paul suggested. "I could do with some lunch. I'll buy, if someone else can run for it."

Selena had been standing nearby. "Not me. I'm busy keeping Sam in flyers. I'm glad this thing is over tomorrow. I've worked harder here than I usually do at the shop."

"I have to stay with Mom," Paul told her. "Sam is selling landscaping. I think that makes you the lunch gofer."

"Whatever. I'm everyone's go-fer."

Peggy called Dorothy. "It looks like I'm going to have to leave after lunch. Adam is going to love this."

Selena ended up going out for sub sandwiches again. Sam had a lull in foot traffic that allowed him to eat with the others.

"You're not going to believe the contracts I've picked up," he told Peggy as they sat at the picnic table. "We have to bring the flower show here every year, or make one of our own. We never get contracts when we go to Atlanta."

"And I don't get to go," Selena complained. "I thought that was a bad thing, until now. I'll be glad to stay home and take care of the shop next year."

"That's great news, Sam," Peggy agreed. "I hope you've chosen someone to help you out."

"He should be ready to go when I start back next week," Sam said. "You remember Jasper? He helped us with the pond at the shop? His pond business didn't work out so well. I think he'll be great."

"Is he still hot?" Selena asked.

"I guess so. He's got a girlfriend though." Sam smiled at her.

"Why can't we ever have someone work at the shop who's hot but not gay or otherwise involved?" Selena looked at Peggy.

"The next person we hire will be your choice," Peggy promised with a laugh. "That way it can be the man of your dreams."

They all laughed with her. Selena went to get more copies made of Sam's flyers.

"I guess I have to go and give Adam the bad news." Peggy sighed. "I feel like I should be paying him a salary."

"Except that no one's paying you either," Sam reminded her. "Don't worry about it. Adam can handle it. He's a good guy."

Peggy hoped that was true. It seemed to hold up when she went to give Adam the news.

"I'm not surprised," he said. "I'm also not prepared. My assistant had to go and get her sick daughter from school. I can handle the show responsibilities, if you can still share your second helper with me."

"That will be fine." Peggy took her keys out of her

bag. "I'd better leave you with these in case I can't make it back for closing. Thanks, Adam."

"You got it, Peggy."

Selena wasn't as happy to be rented out, as she called it. "I don't know anything about floral displays. How am I supposed to fake that?"

"The same way you do at The Potting Shed," Sam joked.

She growled at him.

Peggy took her arm. "Don't worry about it. You know about flowers, even if it is about growing them instead of arranging them. There are plenty of displays at Adam's exhibit. Mostly I imagine you'll be giving out flyers."

"Great," Selena remarked. "Who's going to have flyers printed for me and Sam if I'm at the florist exhibit?"

"Let's work that out," Peggy said. "I'm sure everyone can handle this. Don't forget, we're trying to catch at least one killer. I'd like for Paul to be able to care of other crime instead of babysitting me too."

Selena pouted. "Sorry. I forgot that worse things are happening than me being taken for granted. I'll watch the flower shop. You go get the bad guys."

Peggy hugged her before she and Paul left the flower show. She checked in at the welcome center for a moment while Paul got the car. More than ten thousand people had already visited. She didn't know what the numbers were for Atlanta, but those sounded good to her.

They arrived at the ME's office about twenty minutes later. Peggy saw Steve and Al's vehicles parked outside. It looked like it would be a bigger meeting than she had anticipated.

She really wasn't much of a meeting person. Norris had been right about that. She liked working at a project and getting results. Sitting around, talking about it, wasn't her cup of tea. But she was willing to do what it took to help find Aris's killer. She'd like to be able to tell Tanya and her grandmother that a killer was in custody.

To make matters worse, Norris and Steve, Al and Dorothy, were all waiting for her in the conference room. Mai was there too. She gave Peggy a bottle of water and a pad of paper.

"Are you staying for the meeting?" Peggy asked her.

"Yes. I hope they make it quick. Dr. Beck has me re-doing the autopsy on Abutto again. I'd like to get on with it."

Peggy understood her feelings.

Steve smiled and nodded at her. Peggy avoided making eye contact with Norris. She wanted to get past the unfortunate start to their relationship at some point, maybe not now. Al smiled at her, too, before she sat down.

"I guess we all know why we're here." Dorothy began the meeting—it was her conference room. "To bring everyone up to speed, my assistant ME will brief us on her findings after the Wilder autopsy."

Mai's findings included tox screen results, blood work and photos that made Peggy glad she'd had lunch a lot earlier. Most of it was information Peggy either didn't understand or didn't think she could use.

"We were all thinking that Mr. Wilder had been killed

with a knife," Mai concluded. "By examining the wound, I found that this wasn't a blade at all. It was short, rounded, and thicker than a blade would've been. We've been looking for what that weapon could have been, but we still aren't sure about it."

Peggy looked at the picture on the screen. The size and shape of the wound that had killed Dabney was unmistakable, at least to her.

Mai completed her analysis and Peggy added her discovery to the silence around the conference table.

"I believe the murder weapon was a pair of garden snips," she said. "I've got a pair in my bag, probably not as large as the ones that created this wound, but you should be able to get the idea."

### Night blooming cereus

*Night-blooming cereus is also known as moonlight cactus, part of a group of about 20 species in the family Cactaceae. The plants are native to tropical and subtropical America. They are widely grown for their unusually large, fragrant, night-blooming white flowers. More often than not, these plants are grown indoors. Many are climbing plants but others creep along the ground. They have projecting lobes which help them cling to trees and other objects.*

# Chapter Twenty-five

Everyone moved into the autopsy room. A few minutes later, Mai wheeled Dabney's body into the room with them.

It wasn't a pleasant experience for Peggy, but she knew it was important. She took the small, pink-handled garden snips out of her handbag.

She swallowed hard as Mai pulled back the sheet covering Dabney and addressed the group.

"As you can see, these are much smaller. There are several different sizes that gardeners use. This looks to me like it was done with a larger pair of snips." She held the garden snips above the wide, slightly curved wound in Dabney's side.

He was so white. It wasn't as though Peggy hadn't seen a dead man. The harsh florescent lighting made the scene too bright, washing out any color, even from his hair.

It was amazing how a person's personality affected

their features, even when they were asleep. Death took everything away, she thought, until a person was nothing but an empty shell.

Everyone stepped in close to look at the wound and the smaller snips. Peggy loved it when Steve moved to her side and inconspicuously took her hand in his.

The warmth of his touch and the small smile he gave her when they'd moved back from the table, made her feel less maudlin. It only lasted a moment. Steve went to speak with Al in a corner of the room.

"I think Dr. Lee is on to something," Dorothy said. "I think we should run some tests on this idea."

"Even if you prove that the murder weapon was garden snips, there must be thousands of them at the garden show," Norris said. "I doubt if we can get a court order to have them all checked for blood."

"Even if you could, that pair of snips could be long gone," Al added.

"But knowing what weapon was used is important," Steve said. "Dr. Beck, if you could expedite those tests, we'd appreciate it."

"Of course, Steve. We'll get working on it right away."

"What about Dr. Abutto?" Peggy asked, seeing her ambition of presenting the killer's name to Tanya and her grandmother slipping away.

"We don't have anything on that right now," Al explained. "Let's continue to re-examine all the evidence, with an emphasis on proving the theory of the garden tool killing Wilder."

Steve, Norris, and Al were done with the meeting. That left Dorothy, Mai, and Peggy standing in the autopsy room.

"Now what?" Mai asked.

"We send someone to the store to get large garden snips." Dorothy tucked her hands into the pockets of her white lab coat. "I'm open to any other outstanding ideas. Congrats on that one, Peggy. I think you're right on the money."

"Where is all the trace evidence that you found on Dabney?" Peggy asked with a sudden burst of intuition.

"Everything is over here." Mai walked to the side table. "Or in the refrigerator. There wasn't much. What are you looking for?"

"Was there anything *in* the wound?"

Dorothy's eyes widened behind her glasses. "I see where you're going, Peggy. If the person who killed Wilder had recently used the garden snips for some botanical purpose, there could be trace elements in the wound."

"Yes. If we can identify the elements, it might be easier to narrow down whose garden snips killed Dabney."

Mai's fine eyebrows knit together as she opened the plastic container that held tiny pieces of evidence she'd found on the body.

"I didn't notice anything unusual in the wound. Could it be something clear?"

"Let's take another look." Dorothy put on her safety glasses and gloves. She pulled a drop-down, lighted magnifying glass over Dabney's body then drew back the sheet again to expose the wound.

The medical examiner pored over the body with Mai standing beside her, trying to spot anything she might have missed.

"I see a little piece of something." Dorothy picked up a pair of long-handled tweezers and stuck them into the wound.

Peggy winced and swallowed hard but forced herself not to look away.

"What is that?" Mai asked as Dorothy's steady hand came back with a foreign particle held in the tweezers.

"I'm not sure. But I'm not the forensic botanist around here. Put on some gloves, Peggy. Let's take a look at this thing."

Peggy put on a mask and gloves before she took the tweezers from Dorothy. Mai sprayed the small piece of foreign evidence with a preserving solution.

The three women moved to the microscope.

What Dorothy had found in the wound was so tiny that Peggy wasn't sure she could identify it. It was the color of blood with no particular shape. She hoped it hadn't degraded past what could be used after being inside Dabney.

"What is it?" Mai asked.

Peggy adjusted the microscope after putting the specimen on a glass slide. "I'm not sure yet. It doesn't look like much of anything."

"Yet you recognize it because you're the best, right?" Dorothy encouraged her. "It has to be something. It's not part of the normal human body."

"I'm not sure." Peggy wondered how many times she was going to have to say it. She turned up the magnification of the lens she was looking through.

Amazed, she saw something she recognized.

"It's a thyme flower. It's probably one of the pink thyme flowers from Aris's grave."

"Quick!" Dorothy sent Mai to retrieve the samples of the pink flowers.

When Mai brought the other flowers back with her and Peggy had compared them, she knew they were the same.

"So Wilder may have been killed by the same person who killed Abutto." Dorothy created special containers for the two flowers. "Or at least he was killed by someone who had cut the same flowers."

Peggy looked up from the microscope. "That's been part of the puzzle the whole time. There was pink flowering thyme all over the dirt where Aris was buried, but there was no thyme at all in the rest of the flower show."

Dorothy tapped her fingers on the table. "Maybe this brings us a step closer. I guess the question is—who has the thyme?"

Mai looked at her watch. "I do."

Peggy and Dorothy laughed.

Mai smirked when she got the joke, and then took Dabney's body back to the cooler.

"Stay in touch," Dorothy said to Peggy. "Let me know if you find what you're looking for. And don't confront the person if you find him or her. We're the research backbone of the police department, not the part with the guns."

"I'll call if I need help," Peggy promised. "Let me know if you find anything new about Aris."

Paul was waiting for her. On the drive back to the flower show, she told him about Dabney's death wound and what they had found.

"You know, I like working with you," he said. "I get information right away. Normally, it could be days before I hear something about what the ME found."

"I like working with you too. I don't think Captain Sedgwick would like to pay you to follow me around all the time."

He laughed. "You're probably right."

Peggy dropped her bag off at The Potting Shed exhibit. She went immediately to find Adam and let him know that she was back.

He was relieved to see her. "Your assistant has been doing a good job for me. I don't know how you can handle all the whining from the growers and vendors. That man from Dallas actually asked me to get him something to eat. I told him to get it himself."

"They can be a problem," she agreed. She would've handled the man from Dallas with the exquisite cactus collection a little differently. A person had to eat, didn't he?

They walked back to Adam's exhibit so Peggy could grab Selena and thank her for her help. She really tried to make her feel appreciated. She didn't know what she'd do without her.

"Wow!" Adam's eyes got big when he saw the crowd at his display. "It must be the award. I'm *really* glad you're back now, Peggy. The keys to the convention center are in my blue jacket over there. Would you mind getting them so I can take as many orders as possible?"

"Sure. No problem. Thanks again." Peggy beckoned to Selena who was in the middle of a conversation with a woman whose hat had to be decorated with every kind of fruit in the world.

She went to get the keys while she waited for Selena. They were in the left hand pocket of the jacket. There was dirt or something in there with them. She dug around until she had the keys.

Something else came out of the pocket with them. The fine dust glittered on her hand.

Peggy glanced up quickly. Adam was totally involved in talking with two men she recognized from a large chain of florists.

*He hadn't seen her.*

Heart racing, she pulled an envelope from her bag and deposited the diamond dust she'd accidentally taken out of the pocket. She sealed it and marked where she'd found it and what time it was. For good measure, she used her phone to take a picture of the jacket.

Adam was still engaged, thank goodness.

Paul, who'd been waiting for her on a nearby bench, walked to her side. "What's going on, Mom? Did you find some evidence for the case?"

"Not here," she whispered.

"What?" he asked.

"I'm so glad you're back." Selena joined them. "This place was as busy as The Potting Shed exhibit has been without Sam to talk to all the people. I'm starving. Do you have anything to eat?"

Peggy gave her some dollar bills for the vending machines and asked her to meet them at The Potting Shed exhibit. "Thanks again for helping Adam."

"Sure." Selena's eyes narrowed. "Is something up that I should know about? You look a little guilty."

"Not here," Peggy told her too. "At the exhibit."

"So, what's going on?" Paul asked as they walked away from Adam's space.

"There was diamond dust in his pocket," Peggy whispered, still too nervous to say it out loud. "I put my hand in there to get the keys and they were covered in diamond dust."

Paul glanced back at Adam. "Is there any way he could've had diamond dust in his jacket pocket without being involved with Dr. Abutto's murder?"

"I don't know." She searched her brain. There had to be some explanation, besides the obvious. "Maybe he found the duffel bag we've been looking for. He might not even know what it is."

"That's some thin evidence. I don't know." Paul surveyed the crowd. "Unless there's something else to corroborate . . . "

Peggy was conflicted. Adam was a good friend she'd known for many years. It was hard to imagine that he'd killed Aris or Dabney.

"Maybe we should take a look at his garden snips, if he has any," Paul suggested.

"I don't think I can do that," Peggy demurred, ripped apart for the moment, by the idea that this could have happened.

"Why? We can legally collect evidence. I'm a police officer. It seems to me that we're at a good place to figure out if Adam is the killer."

Peggy didn't know how to explain to her son that it wasn't that they couldn't do it legally—it was that she couldn't find it in her to go after Adam this way. He was always willing to lend a helping hand. He'd given her and Paul a special discount on their wedding flowers. How could she even think that he might've killed Aris?

"I'm not comfortable with the situation." She sat down when they reached Sam and the exhibit. "I'd feel better if Al or Captain Sedgwick handled it. I-I don't think I can."

Sam sat down at the picnic table with them. "Out of flyers again. When is Selena coming back? What's up with the two of you?"

Peggy told him what had happened. "I don't want to think about Adam hurting anyone. Why would he do such a thing?"

Sam shook his head. "How much did you say those diamonds are worth?"

***Hollyhock***

*This plant was once known as holy mallow, so named because the first flowers came from the Holy Land, although their original home was in China. The tall, stately flowers have been planted across the world since the Middle Ages.*

# Chapter Twenty-six

"He has had some financial problems," Peggy agreed. "But so has every other small business in Charlotte. That doesn't make him a killer."

"It's circumstantial," Paul agreed. "He could even have the duffel and it would be circumstantial."

"We need more evidence," Peggy said firmly. "We can't *suppose* he could be the killer."

"What kind of evidence?" Sam asked.

"I don't know." Peggy worried her lip with her teeth. "Probably his garden snips."

Paul agreed. "That would do it. Where do we find those?"

"Probably close by where he's working," Sam answered.

"I could get Adam to loan me his garden snips," Peggy suggested. "I guess this could prove him innocent as well as guilty. I'd rather think about it that way."

Sam shrugged. "We can always steal them while he's not looking."

"Bad idea," Paul disagreed. "I'll pretend I didn't hear that. Don't forget, if what you find isn't done in the right way, he could've killed ten people and it won't be admissible in court."

Selena got there with pockets full of candy bars and chips. She glared at Sam when she saw him looking at her snacks. "What? I'm hungry. There's only junk food in those machines. It's not like they had an orange machine. Want some?"

"No, thanks," Sam said.

"I'll take the sour cream and onion chips." Paul took a bag. "I like to eat when I'm stressed."

While he ripped open the bag of chips, Sam and Peggy brainstormed about how they could get Adam's garden snips.

"What's the big deal?" Selena crunched some cheese curls. "He keeps them under the table in a bag. You can just grab them."

"I guess she's good for something besides making copies," Sam said. "Oh, yeah. That's right. Selena, will you go make more flyers?"

"I've already made hundreds today," she complained. "You're not doing anything. You make them."

"I can't." He grinned. "I have to go with Peggy to get

the snips."

"It would make more sense for *me* to go." She poked him in the chest. "I can say I accidentally left something there and grab the snips."

No one could argue with that plan, except for Paul.

"You have to ask him for the snips. Otherwise we have to have a search warrant. I'm sorry. That's the law."

"That's stupid." Selena picked up the folder with the copy of the landscaping information and trudged to the copying machine.

"I think it's unlikely that he'll give me the snips if he killed Dabney with them," Peggy said.

"You'd be surprised. I've seen people do some pretty stupid stuff." Paul smiled. "Most people think if they wash a murder weapon, the blood is gone. They don't know about what the medical examiner can do these days."

"It can't hurt to try," Sam agreed. "The worst that will happen is that he'll get suspicious. Make it a good reason to borrow them."

Peggy was trying to think of a good reason to borrow Adam's snips when her cell phone rang. She looked at the caller's name. "It's Adam."

"Hi, Adam." Peggy fixed her gaze on Paul's face for moral support. "What can I do for you?"

"I hate to have to bother you." He chuckled. "Well, I really don't. I think you owe me. Anyway, I need some stuff from my van and there's no one here but me. Would you mind getting it? I'd ask to borrow your assistant again, but I want to handle these customers myself."

Peggy agreed to help him. She said she would get his keys from him with a list of what he needed from his van.

When she got off the phone with him, Paul picked up his cell phone.

"This has gone far enough. Let's do this the right way. I'm sorry, Mom. If we're careful about searching the van, Adam won't ever know. If we do it with a search warrant, anything we find can be used as evidence. We're gonna have to do this my way."

Paul called Captain Sedgwick to update him on what had happened. The captain called Al to include him in the event. It was Steve who brought the search warrant about twenty minutes later.

"What are you doing here?" Peggy glanced carefully toward Adam's exhibit. It was a long way down the concourse from The Potting Shed, but she was nervous and feeling guilty. She thought she couldn't be too careful.

"Hello to you too." He smiled and kissed her. "Why didn't you let me know something else was up? You're not trying to take all the credit for the collar, are you?"

"I'm not even sure what that means. It's not that I'm unhappy to see you. I didn't expect you."

"This investigation is still a joint effort," he explained. "Al and some of his officers are waiting outside. We thought it would look less conspicuous for your husband to come and see you."

"I suppose that makes sense. I'll go and get the keys and Adam's list. Maybe you should stay here."

"That's fine. Take Paul with you."

Peggy walked with Paul to Adam's exhibit. He was extremely busy, taking orders and answering questions. He broke away from a customer when he saw her.

"What took you so long? I really needed that stuff a little while ago."

For a moment, Peggy was afraid he might not need anything from the van now. All of the plans would be for nothing.

Adam put down the clipped hollyhocks he was holding and took out his keys. He handed her a hastily scrawled list of items. "Thanks, Peggy. I'm finally on a roll."

She told him she'd hurry back. She and Paul went outside with Steve. The FBI van was in place by the gate again. Al and three detectives from homicide were waiting. Dorothy pulled up in the medical examiner's van as they reached the parking lot.

"I hope we know what the van looks like." Dorothy sounded a little annoyed to be dragged out of the lab while she was working.

Peggy pointed out the white van. "It's the white one with the flowers that says Morrow's Florist."

"Oh." Dorothy picked up her kit and walked in that general direction.

Everyone followed her. Al asked Peggy to remind everyone what they were looking for. "Peggy, you take care of the list Morrow asked you to get for him. We don't want to make him suspicious. We'll check over the van. You and Paul go back inside."

Peggy told everyone about the pink flowers. They were very small and could be easy to miss. "Even if he vacuumed the van, a few of them might be in the cracks around the edges."

Dorothy took a large pair of new garden snips out of her bag. "This is the approximate size of the cutting tool we're looking for. This head matches the wound sustained by Dabney Wilder. I'll be looking for blood residue, even though we don't think either man was killed here. Morrow could've changed clothes in here or touched something."

The agents and officers got ready to search as quickly as possible. They opened all the doors to the van. There were hundreds of items, large and small, inside. This was going to take some time.

Peggy went about her business collecting floral wire, a small pair of wire cutters, waxed string, and other items on Adam's list. She tried not to feel guilty that the FBI and the Charlotte police were searching his van. If she was lucky, he wasn't guilty and he'd never know this had happened.

When she had everything together, Peggy told Steve goodbye and wished him luck. She and Paul walked back to the convention center with a quick salute from Reggie.

"It's okay, Mom." Paul could see she was nervous. "I'm sorry it had to go this way, but if he has nothing to hide, he'll be fine."

"I know. But it would be like you doing this to one of your college friends. I hope he hasn't done anything wrong."

"We both know something is up with that diamond dust in his pocket," Paul reminded her. "Let's hope he only found Dr. Abutto's duffel bag."

"I guess we should go right down there." Peggy smiled at him. "I hope he doesn't need anything else out of his van anytime soon. They brought a small army to search one van, didn't they?"

"Better too many, in this case. They can get the job done sooner."

They passed Sam. He was standing by the table. "Have you seen Selena? I don't think it should take this long to make copies."

"She's probably at the vending machines again," Peggy said. "We'll swing by there and send her back."

Paul and Peggy walked quickly down the crowded concourse to reach Adam's exhibit. He wasn't there. There was a sign on his display table that said, *back in five minutes.*

"He probably went to the restroom," Peggy said. "The vending area is over there too. Maybe we can find Selena at the same time."

Paul smiled at his mother's practicality. "Once you decide what needs to be done, there's no stopping you, is there? You'll chase a man down to the restroom, if you have to."

"That wasn't what I had in mind," she explained. "I was thinking he'd see us go by as he was coming out and we could give him these things. I wouldn't go into the men's room to get him."

"Right." He nodded with a knowing smile.

"Stop it!"

"Okay. Just teasing anyway."

Paul followed Peggy to the vending area. There was still no sign of Selena. He checked in the men's room for

Adam.

"He's not in there."

Peggy could see the exhibit from where she stood. Adam wasn't back there either.

"I can't believe he'd leave his exhibit alone like that. I wonder where he is?"

Paul looked at his phone. "Al says nothing yet. He says stall Adam if we have to."

"I hope Adam isn't standing outside watching them search his van." Peggy fretted. "He may know what's going on already."

"Maybe. Don't panic yet."

"He can't go anywhere without his keys. He must be here somewhere."

Peggy's cell phone rang. It was Selena.

"Where are you?" she asked her assistant.

"I'm having trouble with the copy machine. Can you come, Peggy? It's really bad."

Selena sounded close to tears.

"I'll be right there. I'm sure it's nothing." Peggy turned off her phone. "Selena is really upset about the copy machine. I guess I'll have to check in there. I don't see any way she could've broken it. Probably only a paper jam."

Paul laughed. "She's a trip."

The office for the convention center was located in the back of the building in a cramped little room with no windows. There was a copy machine and a fax machine that anyone with an exhibit could use. There was also a telephone and a computer.

Peggy and Paul were talking about all the crazy things Selena had done since she'd started working at The Potting Shed. They walked into the darkened public office together. The door slammed closed behind them and the lights turned on.

The lock in the heavy metal door slid into place with a loud click. Peggy heard muffled crying and turned around.

Adam was behind them. He was holding a gun that shook in his trembling hand.

"I'm sorry Peggy. I didn't know what else to do."

*Cherry*

> *The cherry tree is in the same genus as prunes and plums, but the fruit is much smaller. The geographical range of a cherry tree is throughout most of Asia and Europe, northern Africa and most of North America. Originally from Asia, the cherry tree also includes cultivars that will grow in arctic regions. Most breeds, however, thrive best in zones four through eight.*

# Chapter Twenty-seven

"Adam?" Peggy decided it might be best to play dumb. She knew Paul had a gun under his jacket. She didn't want to cause a shoot out in this small room that could end with someone being hurt or worse.

"You know, when I heard Dabney and Tim Roseboro talking about smuggling diamonds into the country, I thought I'd hit the mother lode." Adam laughed but his voice was trembling too. "All I wanted was to get in on the act. Tim had that big house he was trying to save. Dabney was doing it for the hell of it. I really needed the money. You know I do."

"Adam, please put the gun down." Peggy walked toward him. "I know you didn't mean to hurt anyone. You're not like that."

"I'm not like that." He started crying. "I'm so desperate. I'm going to lose everything I worked so hard for, everything my father worked for. I have to go out every day and act like life is fine, but it's not. I thought maybe the diamonds were my best shot at changing things around again."

"You don't have to tell me this." Peggy was scared of what would happen when the story was told.

"I do. I have to explain." He wiped his eyes with his hand. "Why did you have to get involved? You shouldn't have sent your assistant to steal my garden snips. I realized then that you knew the truth. It was the jacket pocket and the keys, wasn't it? Peggy Lee wouldn't be at a flower show with no snips."

Selena shrugged. "I was only trying to help."

"It's okay," Peggy told her. "Everything is okay."

She knew Paul was standing behind her, trying carefully to remove his gun from its holster. But what then? The room was so tiny. Anything could happen.

"No. It's not." Adam steadied his gun. "I knew when I opened the duffel bag and it was empty. I knew something bad was going to happen. I begged Dr. Abutto to tell me where he'd hidden the diamonds. I went crazy when he wouldn't tell me, and I shot him."

"And buried him with thyme," Peggy added. "Not many people today know that thyme is a funeral plant."

"That's right. I was trying to do something for him. When I realized he was dead, I panicked. I still needed those diamonds. That's why I went to Dabney, hoping he would help me. I offered to help him look for the diamonds. We knew they were here somewhere. He laughed at me. One minute I was standing there with my snips in my hand, and the next, I'd stabbed him with them."

"You weren't yourself," Peggy assured him. "The DA will take that into consideration."

"We both know how this ends," Adam argued. "I can't go on any further. I don't want Sally to know what happened, at least not while I'm alive."

Sally was Adam's wife. Peggy could feel Paul tensing behind her. She didn't know what to do. Even if Adam meant to kill himself, what were the chances that he wouldn't hurt Paul or Selena?

"It doesn't have to end this way." Peggy walked right up to him and put her arms around him. His whole body was trembling fitfully. He was sobbing. She knew he was out of control.

"Get out of the way, Mom," Paul whispered. "Move away."

She didn't like the idea of her son shooting her old friend anymore than the idea of Adam shooting Paul. It couldn't happen this way. There had to be another ending.

"Give me the gun, Adam." She put her hand on the gun and tried to ease it out of his hand. His cold fingers were locked on it.

"No, Peggy. I have to take care of it. It's what my father would've done."

"Peggy—" Selena whimpered.

"Let me help you." Peggy was determined that Adam didn't have to die. He'd done terrible things, but he was in a terrible place. He needed help.

"No!" Adam pushed her away. His hand holding the gun moved downward as though he might decide to kill her before he shot himself.

A shot rang out in the tiny room.

Adam's tearstained face was a mask of surprise first—then relief—as he crumpled to the floor, dragging Peggy down with him.

Paul put his gun away and rushed toward his mother as he called 911 for emergency assistance. He gave them his badge number and location then dropped to his knees.

"Are you okay, Mom?"

"I'm fine. Was that you?"

His mouth tightened and his green eyes clouded as he unlocked the door. "My gun. Yes. I'll call Al now."

Selena launched herself at Peggy, crying and trying to explain what had happened. Peggy held the girl tightly as Al and his detectives rushed the doorway. Steve and his agents were right behind them.

Peggy could hear the sound of sirens coming toward the convention center. Her heart broke at the loss of another friend.

# Epilogue

Peggy and Steve hosted a cookout in the backyard. The weather was glorious with so many trees and flowers in bloom. Their guests strolled the grounds, exclaiming over the scents and riotous color. Pink cherry blossoms were everywhere, creating a carpet on the new green grass.

They'd invited agents Sanford and Rankin, along with Sam and Selena. Al convinced Mary to come along, even though the possibility for the shop talk she abhorred strongly existed. Ken Benigni was leaving for home right after lunch. It seemed right to extend an invitation to Walter next door. Paul and Mai also joined them.

"The corn is almost ready," Steve said, working the grill. "I've already got the potatoes warming and the veggie burgers are finished."

"I'm starving, so whenever you're ready." Peggy put out a pitcher of lemonade and some glasses.

The old oak trees shaded the group as they ate lunch. Peggy sat at the opposite end of the table from Agent Rankin. She was still hoping he'd grow on her. There hadn't been enough time for that to occur yet.

Tanya and her grandmother had left for home earlier that day. Peggy had the satisfaction of being able to tell them that justice had been done. The three of them had cried over their loss. Peggy knew it wasn't much comfort to say that the man who'd murdered their loved one died, but it was the best she could do. In the future, they'd at least feel a sense of right over the wrong that had been done to them.

"I still don't understand why Morrow felt that he had

to kill Dr. Abutto." Millie Sanford dragged up the first part of talking over the case they had all worked on.

"We're guessing he lost control of the situation," Al said despite a warning frown from his wife. "He wanted the diamonds. He might've thought he could threaten Abutto into giving them to him. A lot of times, threats get out of hand."

"It was remorse that made Adam throw all of the thyme he had into the grave with Aris," Peggy said. "At least that's what I believe. He didn't do anything for Dabney."

"I think we were fortunate the whole thing came together so well." Steve put his arm around Peggy's shoulders. "And I'm glad to say there won't be many cases like this where I need to work with a forensic botanist."

They all laughed. The warm spring breeze rustled the new leaves in the oaks above them. Shakespeare was too busy chasing squirrels to even notice that they were eating.

"On that note," Paul said with a grin. "I have some good news and some better news. I heard today that when my desk duty is up, I'm going to be promoted."

Everyone applauded and congratulated him. Their applause startled a pair of nesting bluebirds in the cherry tree. The birds scolded them angrily.

"Isn't there something else you wanted to say?" Mai raised an inquiring brow at her husband.

"Oh yeah." Paul took her hand. "We found out the baby is a little girl! Now we can stop calling her 'the baby' and call her Paulette!"

"Paulette!" Mai hit him lightly with a napkin. "That's

awful."

Peggy was so thrilled. She was going to have a granddaughter. The circle of life was coming around. She hugged Mai and Paul with tears in her eyes. Everyone else had to get in line behind her to congratulate the happy couple.

The lemonade was almost gone. She hadn't thought to bring the second pitcher out. She ran back inside to get it. She grabbed her new cell phone at the same time to take some pictures.

Steve had set her phone so she could pick up emails from her laptop. She glanced at it and saw she'd had an email from *Nightflyer*.

*Dear Peggy,*

*I hate to send this your way after you've barely had time to recover from your ordeal. A friend of mine is investigating an old murder in Charlotte and might call on you for your help. I sent him to you because he has part of the puzzle you'd like to solve about John's death. I'll speak with you when I can.*

*Nightflyer*

"Need any help?" Steve popped his head inside the kitchen door.

"No. I've got this. Thanks."

Peggy put away her cell phone and picked up the pitcher of lemonade.

**The Peggy Lee Garden Mysteries**

By Joyce and Jim Lavene

www.peggyleegardenmysteries.com

Pretty Poison - 2005

Fruit of the Poisoned Tree - 2006

Poisoned Petals - 2007

Perfect Poison - 2008

A Corpse for Yew -2009

Buried By Buttercups - an e-novella - 2012

A Thyme to Die - 2013

# Peggy Lee's Garden Journal

It's spring again! Time for seeds and new plants!

### *What's new for this year?*

In the sun, there is the new Everlast Series of dianthus. The plant is called Everlast because it will bloom all season, even going through some cold weather in the fall and spring. These are double dianthus so the blooms are big too. They come in white, burgundy, lavender and orchid colors. These are also perennials.

### *I love one time planting, don't you?*

Have you tried growing abelias yet? The new Raspberry Profusion is a very small abelia with mounds of fragrant raspberry colored blooms that will bloom from spring to fall. These even have reddish bracts for more color after the flowers drop. They are great in containers and are heat and drought tolerant.

New roses this year include an old-time, deeply fragrant rose called *Wollerton Old Hall* from English grower David Austin. This rose has delicate pink blooms which last for months. It can be trained to climb, or to grow as a shrub.

**In the Language of Flowers:** Looking for the perfect flowers to give your loved one? Try white clover which entices a special person to "think of me". There is also purple lilac for new lovers. Mix with pink carnations to say, "I will never forget you!" Be sure to include a small note explaining the 'language' so your loved one knows you took the time to make it perfect.

### Summer Squash Recipe: Squash Blossoms!

Squash blossoms are a tasty treat. I've never met anyone who didn't enjoy them, especially fried. Try this recipe for delicious fried squash blossoms and see if you don't agree!

You'll need about 20 squash blossoms for this recipe. Be sure to wash them gently before using.

Combine 3/4 cup cornstarch with 1 teaspoon baking powder and 1/2 cup flour along with ½ cup of water and 1 egg. Add salt and pepper to taste. Mix well. Should be like thick pancake batter. Chill for about ten minutes.

Separate the blossoms without breaking them. Remove the pistil in the center. Combine ½ cup ricotta cheese with 1/3 cup mayonnaise, I teaspoon of onion and 1 tablespoon of plain breadcrumbs. Mix this until smooth. Add about a tablespoon of this mixture to each blossom. Twist the top of the flower tight.

Heat about ½ cup of vegetable oil in a frying pan. Carefully dip each blossom into the batter, coating both sides. Place each battered blossom in the hot oil and fry until golden crisp. Remove and drain oil on paper towels. Add salt and pepper to taste. Serves 2-4 people.

### Garden tip for the growing season:

Pinch off the top of scarlet runner beans when they have reached the top of their supports otherwise the plant will become top heavy!

Enjoy the Spring!

*Peggy*

# About the Authors

Joyce and Jim Lavene write bestselling mystery together. They have written and published more than 60 novels for Harlequin, Berkley and Gallery Books along with hundreds of non-fiction articles for national and regional publications.

Pseudonyms include J.J. Cook, Ellie Grant, Joye Ames and Elyssa Henry

They live in rural North Carolina with their family, their cats, Quincy, Stan Lee and their rescue dog, Rudi. They enjoy photography, watercolor, gardening and long drives

Visit them at www.joyceandjimlavene.com

www.Facebook.com/JoyceandJimLavene

Twitter: https://twitter.com/AuthorJLavene

Amazon Author Central Page:

http://amazon.com/author/jlavene

58671665R00197

Made in the USA
Lexington, KY
19 December 2016